when summer ends

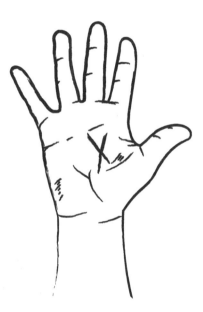

a novel by
Reyn Murphy

1

IT DOESN'T MATTER how quiet I try to be, I hear my breath over the shaking pine needles and feel my heart beating against the ground. The grass is cool on my stomach but I'm still sweating in the summer's heat and my arms are starting to itch. I don't move, though, cause I can see all around me and the gun feels light in my hand. My finger brushes the trigger. There's nothing to shoot, though. It's just pine trees that run along the cinder block wall and one orange tree with rotting fruit on the ground.

Then there's Daisy, who sticks out like a patch of snow in the mud, curled up in the hole she digs when it gets hot. She sits up just long enough to lick herself, then settles down in the same position.

"What the fuck, kid?" a voice booms.

I look back to the house and Brad's filling up the doorway, one hand on his waist and the other behind his head so you can see the muscles on every part of his arms. His shirt lifts up and shows his stomach sagging over his cowboy belt buckle. His eyes are dumb and angry.

"You left the door open."

"Oh," I say and wait cause I know that's supposed to mean something more.

"All the goddamn cold air's getting out."

"Ok," I say. But he doesn't close the door, doesn't move. He's standing there staring at me with his mouth half-open and I wonder why he pretends to care about the cold air.

"What the hell are you doing with that thing, kid?" he points to the gun, flicking his finger like he's shooting at me. I know he wishes he could, but I'd be ready.

"Nothing," I say.

My body feels like a bolt of lightning ready to strike. I imagine turning and shooting. Seeing him fight to stay up, grasping at the door before collapsing back, slamming it shut as he smacks the ground.

"You know that's not a toy, right?"

"I know," I say, even though that's the opposite of what he told Mom when he gave it to me. And keeps saying whenever she gets mad and takes it away.

"What's going on?" Mom's voice comes out from the house. I sit up and set the gun on the ground.

"Kid just left the door open, is all," Brad turns inside to say. His voice is softer. He pulls up on the waist of his jeans.

"What are you doing with that thing?" Mom's head pokes out from his shoulder like a deformed, two-headed alien. It's gross how they seem so different but are somehow the same.

When I'm in trouble she talks fast and sharp. The words go through me and I can't even say a thing, just hold my breath until it's over.

"He wasn't doing anything," Brad says.

He's covering his ass cause Mom didn't want me to have the gun in the first place. He's always doing that with her, then turning it around so I'm in trouble. I want to puke when he rubs her shoulders.

"What were you doing?" she asks, her eyes narrowing.

"Nothing," I say, and it's the truth. Lying down in the backyard isn't anything. She shouldn't be mad at me for that, but I can never tell what's gonna make her mad and what she'll let slide.

"Why do you have that thing out then?" she says, shooting daggers at the gun. When she's like this she's scarier than Brad. "You weren't aiming it at the dog, were you?"

"He's not that dumb, hun." Brad messes up her hair and she shakes him off. "Right, kid?"

Brad's always calling me kid. I hate it. I called him an asshole once and got grounded for a week. All I could do was watch Brad sit on the couch like a worthless lump, drinking the whole time and watching sports or people talking about sports. He'd yell at me to grab him a beer, or just yell at me, any time I left my room. So, I tried not to. I thought I was going to lose my mind, but then it got easier. I could go places in my head, like Grandpa and Grandma's, which is now just Grandpa's. Dad would be there on the rocks. And I'd just be lying down with him, like I wasn't in my room. It was better then and there with him.

When I told Dad that Mom and Brad locked me up in the room, he said not to worry. He said Brad wouldn't be around long, but that was two years ago and Brad's still here calling me kid. I didn't tell Dad about being with him at Grandpa's. I don't know why.

"Would you ever shoot the dog?" Mom asks.

"No," I say.

I wouldn't ever shoot Daisy. She's my favorite part of the family. I can't say that, though, cause Mom would get mad. But that's just another reason to like Daisy more. She never takes things the wrong way.

"Then you shouldn't be aiming it around her. Should you?"

"I wasn't even shooting it," I say. My cheeks burn. I sit back against the tree.

"Then where were you aiming it?"

"Nowhere."

"You can't aim a gun nowhere, kid," Brad says.

"Why did you even give him that thing?"

"I'll talk to the kid, make sure he knows what he's doing," he says.

They always talk about me like I'm not right here. Like I can't hear everything. When they stop looking directly at me, I stop existing.

"I don't have time for this right now. I'm gonna be late for work," Mom says and goes back into the house.

"Go grab some cans," Brad says as he turns to me. He puts his hands into his back pockets so I can see the veins that run up his wrists and disappear into his shirt, like his alien self bulging at the seams of his human skin.

Inside, the air-conditioning is blowing so hard it gives me goose-bumps. Its rattling shakes the whole house from all the way back in Mom's room. Still, from the way the floor squeaks, I can tell she's back there too. The coffee table is covered in beer cans leaving dark rings on the wood. Mom used to get mad about that, but she stopped caring. Some of the cans stick when I lift them, even though it's cool in the house. I bring the cans out and Brad has me set them on the ground against the wall on the other side of the yard. He can pump the gun up enough that it almost shoots like a real gun.

"Make sure you're paying attention, kid. You have to get the butt of the gun…"

"I know," I say. He told me this before.

"Just listen for once. I saw the way you were holding that thing."

"I wasn't gonna shoot Daisy."

"Fuck, kid, I believe you."

"And I already know how to shoot the gun. You don't have to show me again."

"Goddammit, fine."

He shoots, hits, and walks back inside with the gun while Daisy scrambles awake. Her tail is wagging like a helicopter as she picks the can off the ground and drops it at my feet. I kick it and it crumples in on one side. I would have hit the can too if he would've let me shoot. Then he'd have seen that I already know what I'm doing. I leave the rest of his cans by the wall and go back in the house. Daisy follows me inside.

"I'm gonna go to Derek's," I say.

Mom's putting on her good-luck earrings, the ones that used to be Grandma's, that she wears when she has to go to work. I don't think they do anything cause she always comes home complaining to me or Brad, who's back on the couch with a new can of beer on the table.

"You're going to Derek's?" she says. Her voice is dulled. She's dis-tracted and confused, probably trying to remember what day it is.

"Yeah," I say.

It doesn't matter what day it is now that it's summer. I don't have any homework and I didn't do anything wrong, so Mom and Brad can't stop me from leaving and they don't try. They don't say anything until I'm out the door. Then I hear her voice sharpen and cut into him. I can't make out the words, but her tone makes my throat tighten until I realize she's yelling at Brad and not me.

I hop over our wall into the Thompsons' backyard and walk through the hole in their bush. I used to be able to walk through standing up but now I'm tall enough that I have to duck. No one's back here, or ever here, as I pass under the other bush that lines the wall. At the corner, I hop up and drop down into Derek's backyard where Mom and Brad's voices completely disappear. The only sound is the ripple of the pool.

I slide open the kitchen door.

"To what do we owe this pleasure?" Derek's dad, Peter, folds his newspaper and smiles. He takes off one pair of glasses and puts on another. He even makes that look cool.

Derek's the only person I know who calls their parents by their first names, not Mom and Dad but Amy and Peter. He's done it as long as I can remember and it's always made it feel a little more comfortable here, even though it is weird. Peter doesn't mind that I hop the walls and come in the back door like this. Actually, he says he likes it, but that's still hard to believe.

"Is Derek here?" I ask.

"He's up in his room," he says and picks up his paper. "You want anything?"

"No, thanks."

"Well, you know to help yourself."

"Ok."

Peter and Amy always offer me food and drinks, which can be cool. But sometimes I feel guilty, like they're just saying it cause they have to. When he's drinking a beer, I don't worry as much cause I know his offer doesn't apply to those. Even though he let Derek try one once. Derek said it was the grossest thing he'd ever tasted. I've never tried any, but it made me curious. Brad offered me some of his one time, but I'd never drink from anything his mouth had touched.

The carpet on their stairs is bouncy so I run up two at a time. Derek is in the middle of a game and doesn't say anything when I come in. He wears glasses just like his dad and has the same curly blond hair, but he doesn't look cool. His cheeks are chubby and when he focuses they puff out like he's sucking on a bike pump.

He's got a TV with a N64 and GameCube. Mom says that just having a TV in my room would turn my brain into mush, but nothing's happened to Derek. She just doesn't want to buy one.

"Let's play two-player," I say.

"I'm in the middle of this."

Watching someone else play a video game is lame, so I grab his Game Gear. All he has so far is Sonic and I already beat it, but it's better than waiting around doing nothing. The rings chime like a toy alarm when I turn it on and Derek spins around.

"Did I say you could use that?" he says with a face like an angry squirrel.

"You're not using it."

"It's mine, though."

He twitches his shoulders and puffs out his chest. He gets worked up like this a lot. It's all for show.

"So what?"

"So if I say you can't play it, then you can't."

"You never said I couldn't."

"Stupid."

"You still playin' that game?" I say, while watching his death on replay—sniped from behind.

"Shit! Why'd you even come here?" His words flop out as if pudding had a voice and he slumps back in his chair.

"Let's play two-player."

"Let's go do something else. I'm bored."

"What do you wanna do?" I can't imagine how anyone could ever be bored with all the cool stuff Derek has.

"Let's go ride bikes."

"Lame."

"We can go to Jack in the Box."

"I can't." This sucks to say, especially because he should know. But he doesn't think about it, if he thinks at all.

"I'll buy."

Derek gets an allowance for doing chores, so he always has money—even if he hardly does anything. I have to do chores too, but I don't get paid. Mom and Brad don't think I should get money for helping out the family, but then I have to beg for it just to go eat. Derek pays for my food most of the time, but I hate it. It's not the same as buying my own. Sometimes I won't even get anything when he offers, but I'm hungry now.

"We should get Sven on the way," I say.

"If we have to."

If Derek's an ass to me, he's even worse to Sven. He thinks he's cooler cause Sven's super-shy and kinda dorky. But if he is actually cooler, it's only barely.

"I gotta get my bike. I'll be out front in five minutes."

"You should bring the gun!"

"Ok," I say before I remember Mom and Brad won't let me take it. But now that I said it, I have to. "Maybe ten minutes."

My fingers start to tingle and my mouth gets dry thinking about how mad Mom will get if she finds out. I run down the stairs, through the living room and into the kitchen. Peter is still reading the paper, wearing his first pair of glasses. He sets the paper down when I get to the door.

"Taking off already?"

"I'm getting my bike. We're goin' to Jack in the Box."

"J n the B, huh? What're you going to get?"

It sounds cool when he calls it "J n the B." It doesn't sound the same when I try to say it.

"I think… a Sourdough Jack," which is my favorite but normally I get the Jr. Bacon Cheeseburger since it costs way less.

"Good call," he says. He sounds excited and his eyes get big in his glasses. "Tell you what. You bring me back a Sourdough Jack and I'll pay for your food."

I wish Derek was more like his dad. I wish Mom was too.

"Derek said he'd buy my food."

"The man's got deep pockets."

"I'll get him to buy me two and I'll bring the second back for you."

His laugh fills up their whole two-story house.

"If you think it'll work," he says once he's stopped, and then the house goes back to normal.

I go out and hop the walls back into the Thompsons', then our yard, where Daisy is waiting in the corner. I lower down slowly so she has time to scoot back. Her long white fur sticks to my hand when I pet her. She follows me to the door but I can't let her inside cause she'd give me away. It's just Brad in the house, which is good cause Mom would know if I was taking the gun. She has a sixth sense for when someone messes up.

Brad's beer can collection has grown but I don't see him on the couch. I pause and try to listen while Daisy whimpers at the back door. When I hear the fridge close, I sneak down the hallway. Brad's steps thud, the couch poofs, and the hiss and pop of the can echoes through the house.

I get chills when I enter their bedroom. It's the coldest cause that's where the air conditioner is. Still, my face is hot. The gun's propped between the bed and Brad's dresser, which has books on top, but I doubt he can read them. I grab the gun, sling it over my shoulder, and look into the big mirror next to their bed. The reflection looks like me but the gun makes me look different—cooler. My feet feel light as I creak back down the hallway, sneak out the door and onto my bike without Brad knowing I was ever back. Peeling out the driveway, pedaling hard, racing around the corners feels like being in Dad's car when the top's down.

Derek's waiting outside with his new bike. He thinks it will make him faster than me, but I have time to air off the curbs and still beat him to Sven's. My heart's thumping, my lungs sting, and I'm starting to sweat. It feels good until we get to Sven's house, which creeps me out with its weird smell, overgrown bushes, and stuff piled up into the windows.

"Go knock," I tell Derek.

"No, you," he says and his cheeks are puffing out again.

"Fine. Chicken."

I set the bike on the ground and walk to the door. It's scary quiet, even though I know Sven's probably in there alone. He says his parents have to travel for work. They'll leave him and his brother for days, which would be cool if the house didn't feel like it was straight out of a horror movie. His brother spends all his time at friends' houses. I would do the same. Sven mostly just hangs out in his room reading comics unless we drag him out.

I knock and wait and knock louder, but the quiet at his house feels like a rat gnawing at my insides and I walk back to my bike. Finally, when I get there, the door opens. Sven stands in the doorway without any lights behind him, looking like a skinny, hunched ghost.

"Hey, Steve," I say.

His real name is Steve but I think of him as Sven cause he told Ashley that was his name. It was an accident, obviously, but he was too embarrassed to say anything after. She was the first girl he'd ever asked out. She was nice though. Unfortunately for him, that's how we found out. We were hanging by my locker when she said, "Hi, Sven." Derek and I started laughing too hard to correct her. Eventually, she figured out his real name—which she should've known cause they were in the same math class all year—but when she first said, "Hi, Steve" he was even more embarrassed. I know it makes him sad, so I don't call him Sven to his face, but it's hard not to think of him that way.

"What's up, Sven?" Derek says.

"Hey guys." Even when it's just us, Sven talks to the ground.

"We're goin' to Jack. You comin'?" I say. He's quiet, like he's trying to think of a good excuse. "Come on."

"Ok."

Sven's tall enough to ride his dad's big bike, but I'm faster than him too. I get to J n the B way ahead of them, skid out, and wait by myself. It wouldn't be a big deal but, as we get to the parking lot, I can see that Tommy Pescadero is hanging out with his friends behind the building. Derek and Sven ride way out of the way then pile their bikes on top of mine and we go inside. Derek won't stop staring out the window. We can only kinda see Tommy Pescadero and his friends, but we can really hear their music. It sounds like a war zone. Like a song from the Tony Hawk game Sven's brother played, but faster and heavier.

"Two Sourdough Jacks," I order when it's our turn in line.

"I'm not buying you two!" Derek says.

"Come on, I'm hungry."

"How come you're buying his food?" Sven asks.

"It's my money. I'm not buying you two," Derek says, ignoring him.

"One of them is for your dad."

"Did he give you money?"

"No."

"Then, too bad."

"I just want one, Derek."

"I'm not buying you anything, Sven."

"Your dad'll pay you back," I say.

"Why don't you use your own money? Oh, that's right."

My hands clinch and my arms feel like they're catching fire.

"Nevermind, don't buy me anything."

"I'm just joking—Christ, I'll buy you both."

The cashier doesn't say anything to me as Derek orders, but she gives me a look like she's embarrassed for me—some dumb thirteen-year-old that doesn't have any money. When she calls out our order, I have Derek get it. I'm barely hungry anymore.

We pick a booth just on the other side of our bikes, with a clear view of Tommy Pescadero and his friends. Derek stares out the window while he eats, keeping an eye on our bikes, but Tommy Pescadero could take them even though there are three of us. It doesn't matter that we have a bb gun. Luckily, he's busy talking to a girl.

Sven's staring at her. We're all staring outside. I realize too late and try to turn away cause people can tell when they're being watched and that's not something I want Tommy Pescadero to feel.

"She's dumb. But look at those tits," Derek says, like he's asking for trouble.

Derek talks like this all the time, at least when we're alone, but he's never kissed a girl. Neither has Sven but that's cause he's shy, especially since the Ashley thing. I'm the only one that's gotten anywhere. I kissed Sheena at Katy's birthday party and felt her boobs after school behind the gym while Katy stood around the corner to make sure no one was coming. But then she told everyone after and now Sheena won't talk to me, which is stupid and painful but she won't do anything without Katy's approval, and for some reason Katy doesn't like me. I try not to think about it.

"She's not dumb," I say.

"How do you know?"

Derek should know. The girl Tommy Pescadero is talking to, Christina, was his babysitter. I only met her once but it was obvious she wasn't an idiot. I was staying with him for a week and she hung out with us when his parents went out one night. Derek told me he was gonna kiss her. That was just more of his talk. I told him he had no chance cause she's two grades older, but he said he'd take her by surprise. He said if she wanted to kiss him, she'd let him. And if she didn't, then at least he'd have gotten somewhere. If I thought there was any chance he'd do it, I would've told him how stupid he sounded. Maybe I did, but he never tried. Instead, we played video games together all night. She was good and she even got Derek's sister Tiffany to play.

"Why do girls like Tommy Pescadero?" Sven says.

"They're idiots," Derek says.

"I don't think she's an idiot," I say.

"Of course you don't think so, you're an idiot too."

I shrug my shoulders, trying not to let it bother me, but it makes my stomach feel uneven.

When we go outside and grab our bikes Tommy Pescadero looks over and points at us, motioning us over. I freeze at first and my heart sticks in my throat, but then we walk toward him like we're walking on water. Each step is less stable. When we get to Tommy, I think I'm gonna be sick. Derek and Sven turn away, looking at me out of the corner of their eyes, and freeze. There's no time to get away. Tommy Pescadero is standing right in front of me. He would be tall even if he weren't wearing boots.

"You fellas were staring," he says. He doesn't yell. There's no edge in his voice, but it's just as scary as anytime Mom's ever been mad. It's also kinda cool cause I never imagined he'd ever say anything to me.

"We were just looking over," I say, my voice squeaking out of my closing throat.

"Oh yeah?"

"Christina used to babysit Derek. And me too one night."

It would be helpful if Derek said something but he won't. I don't have any hope of Sven doing anything, so instead I'm waiting, watching Tommy Pescadero and it feels like I'm drowning. No one has ever been so terrifying when they smile.

"Hey Christina, you know these kids?"

She's our only hope and she's looking at us like we're aliens that just beamed down in front of her. Tommy Pescadero is going to kill us, starting with me.

"Oh yeah," she says after about a year. I can breathe again and she smiles. "Hi, Derek."

"What about this one?" Tommy Pescadero asks her. He's talking about me, which makes my stomach bubble.

"We raced Rainbow Road on Mario Kart," I blurt out, cause I have to make sure she remembers me. "I showed you the shortcut."

All their friends laugh. Tommy Pescadero laughs. She laughs too. I think I melt.

"How could I forget?" she says, her words like a song.

"Whatcha got there?" Tommy Pescadero asks me.

"Sourdough Jack," I say and squeeze the bag a little tighter, hoping he doesn't notice the crinkle.

"No, kid. What's in the case?"

"Oh, it's a bb gun."

"What're you doin' with it?"

"We were gonna shoot stuff."

"No shit. Let me see it. I used to have one just like that when I was your age."

"I don't know," I say, but I don't know why I said it.

He steps forward holding his hand open, close enough that he could reach over and take it.

"I know. It's just…"

"Tell you what, how about we make a trade?" He leans forward and the sun disappears.

"Like what?" My face is hot. I should have just given him the gun, but it's too late. I have to hope his trade isn't a punch in the face for the gun. I try not to blink or squirm. I try to breathe and not think about what'll happen next, but my mind races through all the possibilities—dunking my head in the toilet, tying me to the flagpole, all the things I've seen in Mom's movies, like I'm watching them with my body spliced in. It hurts already.

"You want a beer?"

"Yes," I blurt out. If Tommy Pescadero, Peter, and Sven's brother like beer, I'm sure I will. It's definitely better than a punch in the face.

"I'll give you one. Which, you gotta admit, is pretty generous, man."

"Cool," I say and hand him the gun.

He pumps it up as much as Brad then turns and points it at his friends. They laugh, even though they should be scared. He's laughing too. He fires the gun at the dumpster. It rings hard and loud, even over the music. He stops laughing and starts pumping again. I feel shaky. My body has all the energy to sprint for a mile but I can't move. I look to Derek and Sven but they're both looking at the ground. When I turn back, Tommy's smiling again, the gun pointed at me. I throw my hands up, hoping he won't shoot but there's a pop and an explosion of pain that starts in my palm and claws its way down my arm.

"Fuck," I think I hear Tommy say, but it's all a blur. The only clear thing is the pain.

I look at my hand and there's a small dark hole in the palm, like a part of me just got sucked into itself. A star imploding. Then, black blood slowly trickles out and with it comes more pain. I stare at my hand, but my eyes won't focus. I scream.

"Shit, man. Why'd you raise your hands?" Tommy yells. "I was gonna shoot over you."

"Jesus, Tom," Christina says, as she walks over from the car. "Are you alright? Let me see your hand."

I hold my hand open and she turns it over, touching lightly on the other side of the hole, where it's still regular. Like nothing happened, but then drops of blood hit the ground and sprinkle my shoes. "It's still in there," she says in sing-song, even as she grimaces.

"Toss me a beer," Tommy says to a friend in the car. He catches the can with one hand still holding the gun. "Hold this. The cold will help. Drink it, too. That'll help more."

"Tommy, come on," Christina says.

The music is loud and the drums make my heart go fast. The guitar is screaming. The drive-thru speaker squawks behind me. Tommy Pescadero is still smiling. I try to think past the pain. Tommy Pescadero just handed me a beer. I turn to Derek and Sven, but they're quiet. Everyone is quiet, like it's Grandma's funeral after Mom and Dad stopped yelling at each other. Sven looks like my grandpa, slouched with his hand on his back. My eyes are burning. But I didn't cry then and I know I can't cry now. Not in front of Tommy Pescadero. So I open the can, wet and shimmering in the sun, and take a sip. It's not great or gross, just weird. I wonder why everyone likes it. But the second sip is better, and I do start to feel good. The pain gets pushed back by the cool in my hand.

"Do you want some, Derek?"

"No."

"I think beer's gross, too," a girl says. She's not as pretty as Christina but she has a nice smile and she's giving it to Derek. "You should try vodka. That's what I drink."

She hands him a plastic cup. He takes a drink and spits it out like I do with the pool water at his house. They all laugh. Derek's face squeezes tight. I take another sip from the can and hand it to Sven. He doesn't say anything, just takes a drink without making any sort of face. I can feel my heartbeat in my palm. I open and close my hand and it beats faster.

"So, what's up with that Sourdough Jack?" Tommy asks.

"I don't know. Do you want it?"

"Yeah."

I hand Tommy the bag and he smiles again. Sven's smiling too. I know the pain is there, but it feels like it's on the other side of something. And I can experience it without worrying. It's nice not to feel. Or worry.

I hear a door open and close; everyone is staring back to the building but I don't turn until I hear the voice.

"What are you kids doing out here?" the J n the B manager yells. "I told you not to hang out here with your shit music. And is that—are those beers?"

"Fuck you," Tommy Pescadero yells back and flips him off, hand high with a terrifying smile.

"Cute, kid. See how that works when the cops get here."

"Well, time to go," Tommy says.

The manager turns to go inside and everyone else scrambles. I drop the last of the beer on the ground and Sven and Derek and I run to our bikes. The music multiplies and fades. Car tires squeal. I grab the handlebar to lift my bike up and the pain comes back through my whole body like it's electric. Still, I can't help but smile almost the whole way back to Derek's—that is, until I realize Tommy Pescadero still has my gun. If I don't get it back, Mom is gonna kill me.

2

"WHY SHOULD *WE* go?" Derek says, and when he's like this he won't budge. "You're the one that fucking lost it."

When I grip the handlebar the pain is piercing, like the screaming from Tommy Pescadero's music. We've passed Sven's house, getting close to Derek's, and the sun's coming right into my eyes between the telephone lines. It's hotter now that we're not moving. I wish I had a beer. I wish I had my gun.

"You don't have to come, if you're afraid," I say.

"I'm not afraid, I just don't care. It would be a waste of my time."

"Steve?"

"I don't know," Sven says and he won't stop squeezing his brakes but he's smiling, kinda.

"Your brother knows Tommy, right? Does he know where he lives?"

"I don't know," Sven says, like always.

"Let's go back to the house," Derek says.

"I have to get the gun back before my mom knows it's gone."

"Or what?"

Derek doesn't understand. He couldn't. His dad is the coolest person on the planet. And his mom is the nicest. There's nothing he could do that would make them want to kill him. He climbs back onto his bike.

"I think my sister might know where he lives," he says and starts pedaling.

I can't tell if he's lying cause he just wants to go home or if she actually does. I don't know why his sister would know that, but I also don't know what she's like anymore. She used to hang out with us, until she went to high school. Then things changed. She started hanging out with cheerleaders and going to parties. Now she'll barely even say a word to us even though we're gonna start going to school with her next year. It sucks, but you almost get used to good things going away.

"Shit, what about Christina?" I ask. "She babysat you. Your mom must have her number."

"That was so long ago."

"Her number wouldn't change, though."

"You wanna talk to my mom?"

"I wanna do more than just talk to her."

"Me too," Sven adds softly.

"Shut the fuck up," Derek yells. It bothers him that people talk about his mom like that cause she's hot, but we wouldn't talk about her so much if it didn't bother him. Mom taught me that, and she's actually right. "Go ahead and tell her that you took the bb gun from your house when you weren't supposed to and now you need to get it back. Tell her that you were drinking beer with your new crush and you got so distracted you forgot about it."

"I don't have a crush on Christina, I just don't think she's dumb."

"I was talking about Tommy."

Sven chuckles.

"Does Tiffany really know where he lives?"

"That's what I said, isn't it?"

"Fine, we'll ask her."

We start riding again. I take my hand off the handlebars and it feels like floating, the wind whipping the sting in my hand away. I coast until we get to Derek's. His house is white and blue with a brand-new basketball hoop that's the full ten feet tall. It used to be the nicest house on the block, but now the whole street looks like that. It makes my house look like a shack, but at least it's not Sven's.

We go inside through the garage, into the house where the smell makes me hungry again.

Derek's mom, Amy, turns in the kitchen when we enter, her long blonde hair flutters and brushes her face as she smiles. She's tall, skinny, and perfect—and not just for a mom. It's like a music video. The last of the sun is coming through the window making the edges of her clothes see-through. Sven's pretending not to notice but I can tell he does by the way he's smiling.

"Hey boys, you better be hungry." When she says this, I start hearing Mom's voice in my head, yelling at me about the gun. It doesn't stop.

"Let's go upstairs," Derek says and grabs a soda from the fridge.

"Nope, nope. Dinner is almost ready. If you want, you can watch TV with your father."

"Am…"

"Don't start with me. You can sit with your father or you can help."

"I can help," I say.

"That's sweet, but you go sit."

"Kiss-ass," Derek mutters.

We go to the living room, to the sofa Peter says is so comfortable it's swallowed people whole. He's in his chair watching baseball. He claims it's the embodiment of summer, even though it starts and ends during school. Brad watches it too, but mostly he just drinks and yells at the TV. Peter doesn't yell, he just watches quietly and drinks a little too. But now he starts staring right at me. Does he know that I had a beer? Does he know about the gun? Is he mad? His eyes narrow so much in his glasses I can hardly see them.

"It's a good thing dinner's almost ready," he says finally. He smiles and his eyes light up, but I'm still too nervous to say anything.

"I can't believe you gave that burger away," Derek says.

My heart drops. I gave his Sourdough Jack to Tommy. We should have bought another one before we left. I didn't think about it in the chaos after the manager called the police, but Derek wouldn't have let me anyway.

Peter laughs and it surrounds me on all sides.

"Don't worry. It would have spoiled my appetite anyway."

"You were going to eat Jack in the Box?" Amy yells from the kitchen.

"I had entertained the idea," he yells back.

It even sounds nice when they fight. Like even if they're mad, they're not thinking about killing each other. He really doesn't seem upset that I forgot his burger. Maybe there's nothing that bothers him. Mom would be screaming and Brad would be cursing over her. Dad would've left. He did. I don't blame him.

"I'm sorry," I say.

"It's not a problem, buddy."

"You did him a favor by not bringing it back," Amy says from the doorway.

"Now, Honey, you love J n the B just as much as I do."

"I hate that you have a nickname for it."

"Sourdough Jack. Three tacos for a dollar. A dollar! It's earned that respect."

"You can go there now if you'd like. I'm sure the kids wouldn't mind eating your share."

"Hmm," he says and scratches his chin while he smiles at her, "that's a tough call."

"Well, dinner's ready if that makes it easier."

"Let me help you."

He gets out of his chair, walks over, and gives her a kiss on the cheek. They're so perfect it hurts my eyes. Derek says it makes him want to barf.

"Derek, get your sister," his mom tells him.

"Sure, Amy." Derek walks to the bottom of the stairs. "Tiff, dinner's ready," he yells up.

"Don't be lazy. Go up and knock on her door," his dad says.

That's as bad as Derek has to deal with, but he still sulks when he walks up. He comes down and Tiffany follows a little later, looking like a clone of their mom, just a little shorter. She used to dress like her too, but that changed when she got to high school, as well.

She sits next to Sven at the dinner table cause she knows he won't even try to talk to her, and she'll go back to her room before anyone else is done. My chest tightens at the thought of asking her for Tommy Pescadero's address. Even if she has it, I don't know if she'll give it to me.

Amy made chicken cutlets and smashed potatoes that are delicious. She also set out a salad that I won't eat but it *looks* cool, all green and orange and red. Derek, Sven, and I race to see who can finish first. It's Tiffany, but only cause she barely ate. Derek's second but I'm not far behind and there's enough for all of us to have more. I can't remember the last time my mom cooked. She'll bring food home from work, which is alright, but she comes home so late that I can only eat it the next day and chicken strips aren't the same when you have to microwave them.

"Don't get too full, boys. There's dessert," Amy says.

There's always dessert at their house. They have a cupboard just for sweets and it has everything. But tonight it's fresh apple pie and ice cream and even Sven pigs out. We finish and race up to Derek's room. I'm first, so I get a controller. Sven's second, but Derek gets the other controller since it's his room.

"I thought you were going to ask my sister for Tommy's address?"

"I will," I say. But the lump in my stomach disagrees.

"Didn't you need to get the gun back *right away*?" He does that thing with his voice where it climbs up his nose. I hate it.

"I'm gonna."

"Then go do it, pussy. Give Sven the controller."

I hand the controller over and walk out and, even though I'm worried about what Tiffany will or won't say, it's nice just to be away from Derek.

On the other side of the stairs, Tiffany's door is closed. The Stay Out sign stares at me. But I can't. I need to get my gun back or my mom will actually kill me. Her voice is still yelling in my head and, as much as ignoring getting made fun of works to get someone to do it less, it still sucks to hear Derek call me a pussy. Or to feel like one. The closer I get to the door the more it feels like my feet are in quicksand and my stomach is slowly sinking into it. I press on the band-aid Derek found me that covers the hole in my hand. I feel the bb like a button on a remote that releases the pain. It pushes me forward and makes my head all fuzzy. I knock on the door.

"What?" Tiffany says, like she doesn't want anything to do with anyone. Or maybe she already knows it's me.

I press on the bb harder.

"I—can I come in?"

"Fine."

Her room is completely different from the last time I was here, but I can't remember when that was. It's all posters of shirtless guys, sweating or wet. Except for the corner, just on the other side of her dresser, where there's a carving of a bird. It feels like a million years ago when she would tell us what birds were around just by hearing their chirps.

"What do you want?" she says, and starts putting her headphones back on.

"Do you—?" I try to breathe, focus. "Do you know where Tommy Pescadero lives?"

"Why?"

"He took something. Or, he has something of mine."

"He has something or he took something?"

"He has it. We were hanging out and I forgot it."

"You?" She pulls her headphones down in disbelief. "You were hanging out with Tommy Pescadero?"

I press the bb again, and my heart jumps but when it comes back down, I feel easy. I don't show her or tell her about it cause she's still staring at me, and there's a smile starting.

"Yeah."

"Then why don't you just ask him yourself?"

"Please," which comes out more kid-like than I want. "I have to have his address."

"Ok, ok," she says and she seems softer, like the old Tiffany, for just a second. "I don't have the actual address. But he lives on the other side of the school, past the ValueMart, off Highlands Road. His building is brown and it says Buena Vista. Except, like, half of the letters are missing."

"Thanks, Tiff."

She rolls her eyes and puts her headphones on to tell me it's time to leave. Just knowing where he lives is a relief. I feel like I can breathe again and Mom's yelling starts to quiet in my head.

I walk back to Derek's room, smiling.

"I told you," he says without taking his eyes off the game.

All he wants to play is his new basketball game, but I don't like playing sports games cause they're boring. There's no story. But when it's my turn, I still beat Derek even though all I can think about is being back in Tiffany's room. When it's Sven's turn, Derek starts talking about toys, then aliens. I beat Sven. Then I beat Derek again. It's fun, but now I wish I were somewhere else, doing something else. I want to be sitting on the hood of a car, music bashing into my brain, clutching a cold can of beer. I want to hang out with Tommy Pescadero cause it felt like falling out of a kayak into the rapids—terrifying and magical.

"Why does your sister know where Tommy lives?" Sven asks after we've stopped talking about it forever. This is how he always is.

"Why don't you ask her?"

"Just..." barely slips out of Sven's mouth before he stops.

"Why does she?" I ask cause I'm curious as well, and I know Sven would let it go.

"I overheard her and Shannon talking. By the pool." He's trying to concentrate on the game and the words come out like bubbles out of a soap wand. "Shannon was at a party. At his house."

"Your sister wasn't?"

"She's too good to be hanging out with someone like him." He throws the controller when the game's finally over and I beat him again. "They were talking about how Christina and him were dating. So, there you go, more proof that *she's* an idiot."

"I think she's hot," Sven mumbles and blushes at the same time.

"No shit," I say.

"Well, why the hell is she with Tommy Pescadero?" Derek's bottom lip turns in and his eyes squint like he's mad, but he just looks goofy. "That guy's a douche."

"No, he's not."

"What do you know, Sven? You're a douche too."

"Shut up, Derek," I say, but I wish Sven would stand up for himself instead.

"Why should I? Tommy Pescadero is a douche, one hundred percent guaranteed."

"What makes you so sure?" I ask.

"For one, he stole your gun."

It was in the back of my head but it didn't feel like it could be real until now. I try not to think about Tommy Pescadero stealing my gun, or him shooting me on purpose. I just wanna remember the beer and the music, but that other stuff is there, floating between it all. And I can feel the hole where he shot me. It has its own pulse that when I notice, I'm compelled to squeeze my hand and give it more energy.

"He didn't steal it. We'll go to his place tomorrow, and I'll prove it to you."

"*We?*" Derek says, sitting back and smiling.

"You don't have to fucking come," I snap, tired of him always being like this. He never helps if he doesn't have to, and barely does at all. He weasels out of everything.

"Perfect," Derek says.

He picks up the controller and starts moving up and down through the teams. I hate how easy it is for him to be a jerk. I want to yell at him, or beat him up, but Dad says there are better ways to resolve things. He just didn't tell me how. Derek starts a game by himself.

While he's playing, I start thinking too much. It happens all the time. But it's started happening more. Usually, it's something simple, and before I know it everything is crazy and awful. I was thinking about Tommy's music, how weird it was. How heavy. For a moment I can feel the vibrating of the drums in my chest and it feels good. But then the idea that Tommy stole my gun takes its place. And it's joined by Mom's tired, angry eyes and I can feel the cut of her voice.

"Think I can stay the night?" I ask.

"Probably."

I run downstairs to use the phone. The kitchen is dark and quiet. A glow comes from the living room. Peter and Amy are probably watching a movie in there. Probably cuddling on the couch. Derek thinks it's gross and dumb. They do it a lot. I like it. It makes me happy to know that parents don't have to hate each other.

I dial Mom's work and no one picks up, even though someone must be there since they're open till two in the morning.

"Mom, I'm staying at Derek's tonight," I say after the machine beeps.

I don't call the house, cause if Mom's not home yet I'll have to talk to Brad. I tried to call, which is good enough. She doesn't care what I'm doing, but she makes me tell her where I am so she doesn't have to worry if I'm not home. Sven doesn't even have to do that. He can go days without telling his parents where he's at and it doesn't bother them.

I run back up the stairs and grab the other controller. I'll keep playing Derek's stupid basketball game, and keep beating him. If I stay here tonight, and we can get the gun tomorrow, everything will be fine. We play more games and Derek gives Sven shit and I give Derek shit and Sven even tries to give me shit. I get lost in the fun and don't even think about my hand or the gun, until I hear the doorbell followed by Mom's voice. She sounds tired, which is usually a bad sign.

"Shit," I say.

The stairs creak under her heavy footsteps, and then she's standing in the doorway.

"Time to go," she says.

"I called you earlier. I'm gonna stay here tonight."

"Not tonight, kiddo. Come on." She talks like she's already under the covers in bed. She sounds like this all the time after work, and the mornings after. It's depressing.

She steps to the side and waves for me to come, but I'm not moving.

"We're not doing this tonight."

"Why can't I stay?"

"Because you're in trouble."

My stomach starts to bubble and my face feels hot. "Why?"

"You would know better than me."

"If you don't have a reason, then I can't be in trouble."

"I got a message from Brad."

"What'd he say?

"Get up. Now," she says, sharp with the last bit of life in her voice.

Brad knows I took the gun but she doesn't. Still, she'll believe him without hearing my side.

"I have to get my bike."

"You can get it tomorrow."

"Fine. See you guys later," I say to Derek and Sven, cause if she says I can come over tomorrow it means I'm not grounded.

They don't say anything.

We walk down the stairs and Amy is waiting at the bottom by the door. She's still smiling and perfect-looking and I wish she were my mom.

"Sorry again for showing up so late, Amy."

"Don't worry, Cat."

We only have to drive around the block but it feels like it takes forever cause Mom won't say anything. Brad's car is in the driveway so she parks on the street. Everything is quiet after the door slams, but I can feel the screams waiting inside the house. While she fumbles to unlock the door, I feel the bb. I don't squeeze it, though. Not yet.

Brad's sitting on the couch, in front of the blank TV screen. His cans are stacked in a pyramid on the coffee table and he almost kicks them over when he brings his feet to the ground. He stares at me with heavy eyes, folds his hands, and leans forward. I look down and Mom pats me on the shoulder.

"You need to talk to us, kiddo," she says.

Brad stands up.

"Tell your mother what you did." Each word comes out like an elephant step.

"Nothing," I say.

"Don't lie."

"Take it easy, Brad."

"Tell your mother what you did."

"Nothing," I say. Even though I know he knows, telling him what he wants to hear won't make things any better.

"You little liar. You lying fucking thief." He raises his arm and points at my mom. His veins are pulsing. My throat squeezes shut. "Tell your mother what you did."

"It's ok," Mom tells him.

Why is she always wrong?

"Where's the bb gun, kid?"

"I don't know." I look at Mom but she's looking at him.

"You don't know?" he booms.

"Calm down, Brad." Her voice is low and harsh and I step back but Brad doesn't move.

"You stole it, you thief."

"I didn't steal anything. It's mine."

"Stop it, Brad."

"You want me to be more responsible. To act like a father! Here's where I start. He steals something, he gets a spanking."

"No one wants you to be my fucking dad," I yell.

His chest swells as he lunges forward, massive hands moving toward me. Then he disappears, and my face is pressed against the white of Mom's work shirt that smells like old French fries and is patterned with stains that, even after all the washing, never disappear.

"Go to your room," Mom says and pushes me away.

I back up into the wall. Brad looms just beyond Mom. I can't move my feet or tongue. My hands and chest start to shake and my knees give out. I'm sitting on the cold floor and from down here it's impossible to understand what they're saying but it feels like I'm under a waterfall of hate.

"Oh god, is he crying?" Brad yells and I snap into focus.

"What the fuck is wrong with you?" Mom yells back.

I can't tell if she's talking to me or him. I crawl to my room and each time I press my hand to the floor the shuddering pain overtakes my body. I kick the door and lock it against the explosion of their voices. The room shrinks around me, their screams bearing down. I sit against the door, hoping my weight can keep them out. There's a soft scratching on the other side. I reach over my head, turn the knob and lean forward to let Daisy spill through the crack. I lay on the ground, close the door, and she licks my ear. I climb up onto the bed and she hops up after me and I bury my face in her fur.

I grip my palm until tears fill my eyes and then keep gripping. It's a long time before the voices fade, then disappear into total silence. Brad's truck rumbles to a start and there's a knock on the door. I don't say anything but it opens anyway. Daisy's tail thumps against my leg and Mom sits on the edge of the bed. Her eyes are red and her smile is cracked.

"You doin' ok, kiddo?" she asks in a wobbling voice.

I don't say anything.

"I'm so sorry."

They're barely words when they filter through Daisy's fur. Mom lies down and her arm covers Daisy and me. I can feel the wetness of her tears in my hair and I'm sure Daisy feels the same. No one gets up to turn the lights off, but I wake up in total darkness to the click of the door and the creak of Mom's footsteps. And then I'm awake, waiting to fall asleep, wondering what Derek and Sven's night was like. Or what mine could have been like if Dad was still around. If Tiffany will ever talk to me again and if Tommy really meant to shoot me. Or if he'll even give me my gun back.

I press the hole in my hand and the worry disappears behind a blanket of pain.

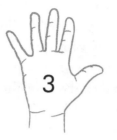

3

THE SUN'S COMING through the blinds, heating up the room, and I have to pee but I'd rather be uncomfortable in here than be out there. I can hear Mom moving back and forth from her room to the kitchen. A lemony-cleaner scent comes in from under the door alongside the usual coffee smell. Daisy's lying crosswise in the bed and I'm scrunched in the corner. She jumps up excitedly and wriggles against the door before I even move.

I push to sit up and it feels like I grabbed a hot coal out of the campfire. I look at my palm. The band-aid's peeled off and there's a black hole, like a vortex opening in the center of my hand. It's crusted around the edges with little bits of brown, but it's still leaky. I can just barely see the shimmer of metal at the center. When I focus on it, the hurting stops even though the pain keeps radiating. It's a weird, good feeling.

Daisy bursts down the hallway when I get up and open the door, scratching and clattering until she gets to Mom. Her tail thumps against the couch like a drum. I close the bathroom door but the trapped feeling comes back, except now I'm in a smaller room with a sink that's still covered in Brad's beard hair. Mom won't let him shave in their bathroom, but of course it doesn't matter that he messes up mine. Everything else of his is gone but that doesn't feel as good as it should. In his absence, I remember more—the smell, the swearing, the fear I had coming home when he'd been drinking. He was always drinking. I remember last night and the gravity of his voice and the embarrassment of my cowardice. I open the bathroom door and walk slowly down the hall. Mom stops talking to Daisy and my ears start to burn, she's saving her words for me.

"Hey, kiddo," she says. "You hungry?"

"Sure," I say, but I'm not.

"What can I make you? Something special."

She speaks slow but high. It's the same way she talked when Grandma died, and when Dad left. It's like she's sprinkling syrup on shit and I remember how I didn't think I could ever feel worse than those days, but today is worse until I squeeze my hand and a soft haze of pain surrounds me.

"We have eggs. Juice. No bacon, though."

"I'll just have waffles."

"You want me to make real waffles?"

"No, I like the other ones."

She walks from the couch to the kitchen table and sits down. She takes a drink from her mug then takes a breath like she's going to start talking again but doesn't. I open the freezer, get the waffles, toss them into the toaster, and focus on the buzzing and the way it glows like an alien ship. The waffles pop up when they're done. I eat without setting them down.

"Will you sit with me?"

I don't want to have a talk, but I sit anyway and she takes another breath like we're in the car, about to go through a tunnel and she doesn't know when it's going to end. I worry this won't ever end.

"Brad and I broke up." She looks at me like she expects me to know something. "I know you didn't like him, and I know he could be difficult." She's always hassling me about how important it is to make eye contact when you're talking to someone, but she turns to Daisy, then the TV, which isn't even on. "Maybe it was unfair to you. It certainly shouldn't have taken something like last night to end it. I really am sorry."

"Why now?" I ask, since it should've never started. Nothing's changed since the first day.

"I don't know if I have a good enough answer for that."

"He was an asshole."

"I don't want you saying stuff like that."

"But he was."

"Yeah. Yeah, he turned out to be. I do think, in his way, he tried. Still, it'll never happen again."

I don't want to hear her excuses. I want to ask how she could even start dating a guy like Brad. How she could be with him but not Dad. I want her to know how wrong it is, and how I'm always the one that has to deal with it, but now she's looking at me and her eyes are soft and starting to get shiny.

"Ok," I say.

"I'm going to need your help," I don't like it when she starts crying and her words come out broken. It makes me feel guilty even when I haven't done anything wrong. "I know it's not fair, but I'll need to pick up more shifts at work and we won't be able to afford to have anyone looking after you."

"I don't need a babysitter. I can take care of myself."

"I know. I know you can. But it's a lot of responsibility."

"I know."

"Sure you do." She reaches her hand across the table and grabs my arm. She holds it with her warm, soft hands. I clench my fist. I should pull away, but I don't. "I love you, kiddo."

"Yeah," I say, and I wish she would stop looking at me and let go. "I love you, too."

"It might be tough for a little while, but it'll be better this way."

She pats me on the arm and leans back. I'm free.

"Yeah," I say again, but I don't believe her. I've heard this before. "Can I go to Derek's?"

"Sure," she replies, letting out a long breath. "That's fine."

It's earlier than I usually go to Derek's, but I have to get out of the house cause all I can think of is Brad lunging at me, and how I curled up on the floor, how cold my body felt and how hot my face was. How Mom trusted him. She let him live in our house even though I told her I didn't like him, and now she wants me to help her out.

When I get to Derek's backyard my hands and forearms are tingling, rubbed raw from scraping against the walls. My bb-hand pulses like a different life-form.

"It's been a while," Peter says from the living room.

"I missed it here," I say.

He laughs, then says, "We're happy to have you back."

He speaks with a warmth I've never felt anywhere else. I walk up the stairs to Derek's room. He's under the covers in bed, playing video games; just his fat head sticks out, like a turtle with a curly wig and braces.

"What are you doing here?" he says.

"Good morning to you too."

"I thought you'd be grounded."

"Guess not."

"My parents would kill me if I did what you did."

"They tried," I say.

I hold my arms out and spin around to convince him how ok I am. There are a lot of times that, even if I don't want to tell the truth, I don't have to lie. I can just talk about them and people still don't want to believe me—it would explode their perfect world, especially Derek's. It's nice, normally. I don't want to deal with their questions. But sometimes it can make me feel like I'm drifting away in outer space.

"Look at your hand," he says. "It's fucking gross."

As ugly as it is, it doesn't look bad to me.

"You hungry?" he asks.

"Already ate."

"Wanna get me breakfast?"

"Get real."

"Fine," he says, pauses the game, and kicks off the covers to show his pale, chubby body that's starting to get weird hair around the nipples. He stops in the doorway like a troll. "Do you want anything?"

"Nope."

"Play for me 'til I get back."

"Nah, I'll just wait."

I don't want to play and I don't want to wait. Being here's better than home but I want to get out, get moving, do something so I can stop thinking. And, even though there's not much need for it now, I want to get that bb gun back.

When Derek returns with his Pop Tarts and orange juice, I stand up.

"Let's get out of here," I say.

"Why?"

"We gotta get my gun back."

"No, not *we*. You keep saying that," he says and flops down onto his bed. The Pop Tarts slide on his plate and a little stream of orange juice sloshes over the edge. He licks the glass clean.

"Come on, man."

"I already told you, no."

"Thought you might change your mind," I say, but I didn't actually expect it. He's too stubborn for that.

"No way, just take Sven."

I try to imagine Sven next to Tommy Pescadero. He might melt into a puddle of sweat.

"It'll be cool," I hope.

"With the guy that shot you?"

"It was an accident."

"So?"

"So, it doesn't even hurt. Don't you wanna ride bikes?"

"Not now. Not there."

"You don't have to go into his house."

I know I should stop. The more I try to convince Derek to do anything, the less likely it becomes.

"Then why do you need me to go with you?"

"I don't *need* you to come with me."

"See."

"You're such a pussy, man."

"It doesn't make you tough to go to Tommy Pescadero's house. It makes you an idiot."

"Why are you so scared?"

32

"I'm not. I just don't trust him. He's not a good person."

"How do you know that?"

"He drinks and smokes and gets in fights and he's almost been kicked out of school multiple times."

"Sounds like fun."

At least it sounds better than sitting in Derek's room and playing video games, doing nothing all day like a little kid. Tommy Pescadero and his friends were out, actually doing something like grownups yesterday. Being with them felt cool even in spite of the accident, in spite of the fear. Like Dad says, *more fear, more fun.*

"You know his dad's an alcoholic."

"Wouldn't it be nice if all our families were as perfect as yours?"

"Fuck you."

"You don't need to come. Sven'll come."

"I bet you can get Sven to come," he says, making a jacking-off motion with his hands and that stupid face with his tongue half out and lip sneering that always goes with it. I can't stand it. I punch him hard. The sting in my knuckles feels good. I focus on that and let the anger fade away, so I don't get more mad.

"That fucking hurt," he says as he grabs his shoulder.

"Good."

I go down the stairs and into his garage to get my bike. He's made up his mind, and if he doesn't want to come, I don't want him to. Everything he says and does makes me angry, and it feels like the blood is exploding in my veins. Not reacting makes him do things less, but it doesn't make me not feel. Luckily, the thoughts get dragged away as I'm riding to Sven's.

His house is weirder when I'm alone and the streets are quiet. It feels more like the horror movies Dad likes to watch. The windows are filled with all kinds of stuff Sven's parents collect. Inside, it pours out of the rooms and into the hallways and wherever I turn, I feel like I'm going to break something without knowing if it's trash or worth a million dollars. I knock when I get there cause their doorbell sounds like it's from a horror movie, too.

"You wanna go to Tommy's?" I say as Sven opens the door.

"I don't know." The smell in the house reminds me of our garage after the rain.

"Come on, Derek already wimped out."

"I don't know," he says again, but there's more hope the longer he doesn't say no.

"It'll be fun. Yesterday was kinda cool, right?"

"But…" Sven starts and smiles, looking at my hand.

I open my palm and hold it up in his face.

"It's nothing, see? So let's go."

I stare at him and he looks back at me with dead eyes. I don't know how Sven gets good grades.

"Do you want any food?"

"No, let's just get out of here," I say. I think he knows I don't like being in his house. That should make me feel bad. It does when people don't want to be at mine, but I don't want to be at my house either. And I really don't want to be at Sven's.

We hop on our bikes and I start out way ahead of Sven, but it's a long ride. Past the J n the B, past the school, past the shopping center. Sven catches up. His legs are so long that it's like he barely has to do anything once they start moving. The cracks in the streets get wider as we get closer to Tommy Pescadero's. They make the bikes rattle, which feels like it pushes the bb deeper. That good pain is becoming a part of me. When we finally get there, I'm hot and sweaty. Sven looks bright red.

The apartment building is two stories and brown with white letters that are supposed to say *Buena Vista Estates* but instead says *Bun Vita stas*. The paint is a different color where the letters are missing, like the carpet at Grandpa's when he got rid of Grandma's chair.

We leave our bikes on the dry lawn out front. Tiffany didn't say which apartment was his, but I can hear the music coming from the first-floor apartment calling me. I turn to Sven, but he's watching his feet. Still, he's moving forward so I feel like I have to as well. I knock on the screen door, but I don't know if anyone could hear it over the music. We can see right into the house. My stomach growls. There's a skate video on TV but no one's watching it. Then Tommy comes out from the hallway without a shirt on. He doesn't play sports, but he has muscles.

"Help you guys?" he squints through the screen.

I rub the bb and a jolt goes through me as the dried blood cracks and flakes off. "Do you have my gun?"

His eyes widen and he pushes the screen door open with one hand and stands against the door for us to come in, but neither of us move.

"Jesus, you're the dude I shot yesterday."

"Yeah," I gulp.

"Shit luck," he says. "Fucking come inside. I'll get your gun."

"Sure," I say. Sven follows me.

"I'm surprised you'd come here after that. Takes some balls."

His smile makes it hard to swallow; my throat closes off like I'm holding my breath underwater. I turn back to Sven and he's smiling.

He leads us to his room, which is messier than Mom would ever allow, clothes everywhere and cups from fast food restaurants. He's got a guitar on the wall beneath posters of bands I've never heard of—Botch and Throwdown—and a paper that looks like a poem printed above his pillows. There's a blue sheet covering the window. With the sun coming through, it's like the ocean. The water stretching forever. It's the only time feeling small ever feels relaxing.

"What're you guys up to?"

"Not much," I say.

"I ain't got shit to do right now. We should go out and shoot this thing."

"Uh, I don't know."

"I said it was a fucking accident. I'm not gonna shoot you again."

"I'll go," Sven says, with eyes bright and bulging and showing more excitement than he's ever had in his life.

"There we go. It'll be fun."

He hands me the gun in its case and picks up a paper carton from the shelf behind his desk. It's copper and white with a pattern like snakeskin, and when he shakes it at me it rattles with the thousands of bbs that are inside. It feels weird, but it's also exciting that Tommy Pescadero wants to hang out with us.

"Where do you wanna shoot it?" I ask.

"That's my guy! There's tons of shit to shoot in the river."

"Ok."

I sling the case onto my back and Tommy brings the carton of ammo. He grabs his skateboard and from the street we can hear his screen door close with a rattle. His wheels sound like a machine gun against the sidewalk. He's fast enough to keep up with the bikes, but he says it's more fun to hold onto Sven's seat-post and cruise.

The river is ten feet wide surrounded by concrete with a concrete ramp sloping down to a flat area on both sides that fills up when it rains, but that hasn't happened in a while. I always assumed this is what rivers were supposed to look like before we went camping with Derek and his family. Mom and Dad were still together then. That river was surrounded with rocks and trees and was the perfect temperature, with rushing water that stopped in spots and was thirty feet deep but you could still see the fish at the bottom. Now, the rush of the cars driving on the 605 is the only thing that make it feel like we're in the rapids, out of the suburbs.

We stop at the top of the ramp but Tommy lets go of Sven's bike and bombs straight down the slope, falling off his board at the flats and sliding to a stop on his butt. The ammo clatters on the ground as his board races into the water. He's still laughing, lying on his back when we get to him.

"Are you ok?" I ask.

"Fuck yeah, that was fun."

He wades into water that barely covers his feet. His bare back is rubbed raw but not dripping blood. The board is lodged up against a soaked pile of sticks and chip bags. He picks it up, shakes it, and throws it back onto the concrete slope. It slides to the flats. The echoes get smaller and disappear and it's like we're in our own world.

Tommy holds out his hand and I give him the case. He unzips it and pulls the gun out by the muzzle. Then, for some reason he hands it to Sven, who glances up, takes it, then starts smiling at the ground. I wanna tell Tommy that Sven isn't gonna know what to do, that I should get to take the first shot—it is mine, after all. But I don't say anything. Sven takes his time figuring out where to aim. He looks nervous and when he looks at me, I almost raise my hands again but before I do he turns toward a green bottle in the distance. It's the same as the beers Derek's dad drinks. It's weird to see something of theirs here, floating around with all the trash. Sven pulls the trigger and the gun spits the bb onto the ground.

Tommy walks the few feet to pick it up and holds it in front of his grinning face.

"You forgot to pump the gun," I say.

Tommy laughs and it rebounds around the whole river.

"Ah man," Sven says.

"Don't forget next time," Tommy says. "Hand me the gun."

Sven does as two bikers ride along the path on the opposite side of the river, like invaders into our world. Tommy pumps the gun. He settles it in his shoulder and aims in one smooth motion, his smile widening as his eyes squint.

"Think I can hit them?" he asks.

I don't want to say anything that will make him actually shoot at them.

He watches as they pedal closer, two football players from Sven's brother's grade. A year older than Tommy. They're just above us, like twenty feet away, when Tommy fires. The bb clangs off metal. I can't believe he would actually shoot at them. My heart pounds so hard I can barely see.

"What the fuck, bro?" one of them shouts as they stop their bikes.

Tommy rests the gun on his shoulder, they pause and everything goes quiet except for the heavy breathing, which I think is Sven's but might be mine too. I try to stand straight. Then I hear the click of feet on pedals, and we watch until they disappear. And I realize I was holding my breath cause it comes out in a gust. Sven doesn't smile but his eyes are enormous and happy.

"Hit your target and get another shot," Tommy laughs, loads another bb and pumps again.

"Heck yeah," Sven says.

But my head feels scratchy, like the TV when the video stops working.

"Why'd you shoot at those guys?" I ask.

"I wanted to see what they'd do. Run or talk shit or fight. And if they want to fight, we can fight."

"What if the whole football team comes?" Sven asks.

"Then we probably get the shit kicked out of us. But there's worse things than getting the shit kicked out of you."

He's looking at me and all of a sudden it's like I disappear behind Mom's stained shirt. The burning in my stomach that came with last night's tears is back but worse, like every lunch I've had to eat cold leftovers added together and multiplied by a thousand cause I hid behind my mom and cried like a baby. Does Tommy know I'd curl into a ball if they came back? Why else would he say that? What else could he know?

"Fuck those guys. They can bring back the whole football team, we'd kick the shit out of them," I say.

"Oh, you're a tough motherfucker," Tommy says. He turns to me. He props the butt of the gun on the ground. He's standing over me. He puts his two fingers together, making a gun, and jabs me in the chest. Hard. "How tough are you really?"

Sven moves to the side to disappear behind Tommy who stands like a statue, eyes staring into me. He knew it. He knows I won't do anything. My throat, chest, stomach—everything feels like it's collapsing.

"I'm just fucking with you," he says and laughs and ruffles my hair. He turns away to take his next shot.

When the gun clicks, it's like a humongous weight gets pulled off me, and I'm even lighter than normal. He misses and laughs and hands me the gun. For my turn I hit my first two targets, so missing on the third doesn't even bother me. It's getting hot and I jump into the water and splash Sven, while Tommy's taking his next shot. Sven splashes me while I'm taking mine and I miss almost as much as he did.

No one comes to fight us, and Tommy doesn't bring it up again, but eventually he says he has to go. On the ride back to his place he tells us we can stop by anytime we want, but to not bother bringing the gun cause he's over it. I feel the gun case tugging at my shoulder and I think he's right. I wish we could keep hanging out. We could do something else. I wish I knew what he was going to do and why Sven and I can't join. I don't want to leave, but he's got plans so we ride back to my house.

We ride slow with nowhere to go and no desire to leave. Plus, it's hot. My clothes are dry and sticky by the time we get back. Mom's putting on her good-luck earrings when we walk in.

"What happened to you guys?" she says.

"What?" I say.

"You're—ugh—you smell horrible."

"Are you going to work?"

"Yeah. I'm working Brian's shift. There's food in the fridge and three dollars for dinner."

"Three dollars won't get anything," I say. Nothing good at least.

"Don't give me that. You can have the three dollars or you can make yourself dinner with whatever's in the fridge."

"Fine."

"Hi, Steven. How are you doing?"

"Good," Sven mumbles and blushes.

"Well, you boys stay out of trouble and if you go anywhere make sure you let me know so I can get you after work."

"Ok," I say.

She leans in and kisses me on the forehead even though I was try-ing to get away, even though she said we smell gross. She only ever does this when someone else is here. Sven's mom never tries to kiss him in front of us.

We eat once she's gone but it's boring here so we bike over to Derek's. It's good to have our bikes in case we want to go anywhere, but it takes longer than just hopping the fences, which we don't do cause Sven's afraid or too weak to pull himself up even though he can almost see over the fence standing.

Walking in through the front door we can hear people in the back splashing in the pool, but Derek's in his room, playing his Game Gear while cartoons are on the TV. His cup is on the ground and the crumbs from a Pop Tart are scattered on the bed. Seeing him makes it so much worse that we couldn't go with Tommy wherever he was going, even if I'm still a little afraid of him.

"Hey, man," I say. "What're you doing?"

"What does it look like I'm doing?"

"How 'bout we go in the pool?"

"I don't want to."

"It's hot outside."

"It's nice in here," he says. It's the truth. Derek's room is always the perfect temperature.

"Well, we wanna see your mom and sister in the pool," Sven says.

I want to laugh but I choke from the shock. Derek slams his Game Gear down on the bed, making the crumbs fly.

"Fuck you, Sven. What are you guys doing here anyway?"

"We just wanted to hang out," I say, even though I have a hard time catching my breath.

"Is that what you wanted to do?" Derek says. He sits on the edge of the bed, staring at Sven.

"Come on, Derek," Sven says. And for a second it looks like he's gonna say more, but now he's looking back down at his feet.

"It'll be fun, man," I say.

"If you want to go, be my guest."

"It won't be as fun without you," I say.

He rolls his eyes and stands up, "Fine."

"Can we borrow trunks?"

He points to the dresser, instead of saying yes, like I didn't already know where they were. I walk across the room and grab a pair for myself, then throw some to Sven.

"Nope. Those are mine," Derek says.

Sven hands them over and waits for me to give him another pair. The only others I can find are bright yellow and look like they'd be small on Derek. I toss them over and his head sinks. He goes to the bathroom, I go to the closet, and Derek changes in the room. Sven comes out in his black shirt and yellow trunks looking like the world's palest giraffe.

"Someone switch with me," he says.

"Why?" Derek says like he's laughing straight at Sven.

"Please? I can't wear these."

"It's just Derek's family, really."

"Then will you wear them?"

"I don't want to," I say, cause Tiffany is probably out there and I can imagine the way she'd look at whoever came out wearing these.

"Don't be such a pussy, Sven," Derek says.

"Why don't you wear them, Derek? They're yours anyway," I say.

"You guys should be happy that I'm letting you borrow my stuff at all."

"I can't wear these."

Sven pulls down on the edges of the trunks but that doesn't do anything. His face is bright red and it's just Derek and me in here.

"You guys are such babies," I say. "I'll wear them."

But when I put them on they're worse than I could have imagined. It's not just that they're short, but tight too. I don't know why Derek would even have them. I wish Sven wouldn't have said anything. He's going to look ridiculous anyway, wearing his shirt in the pool cause he thinks it hides the cave in his chest, even though that only makes it more noticeable.

When we head out, Peter and Amy are lying on towels near the shallow end with their legs dangling in the water. Tiffany is sitting at the deep end with her friend Shannon. My whole body is screaming to turn around, but I clamp my teeth and keep walking. Why did Tiffany *and* Shannon have to be out? Tiffany didn't start getting mean until she was hanging out with her. I guess that's when she knew she could be cool. Shannon is a year older than her and dating the varsity quarterback.

Peter sits up at the sound of the sliding door.

"You made it outside. Oh my, and look at the style master," he says to me.

My face flushes. Amy sits up now to look at me too. She's wearing a red bikini, and the sight of her body gives me momentary relief, maybe too much, and for a second I'm happy the trunks are as tight as they are. I'm safe so long as I keep my dick wedged against the seam.

"How good do *those* look? Derek, why don't you ever wear them?" she says and points at me.

I can feel Tiffany and Shannon's stare too. I don't look or smile. I try to pretend I'm not there, to move slowly, to breathe.

"They look stupid," Derek says.

"No honey, they look amazing."

"I gotta agree with your mom, kid."

"Tiff, what do you think?"

It feels like I got hit in the stomach with a cannonball. Tiffany just rolls her eyes.

"I think you're right, Mrs. Williams. They look really amazing," Shannon says.

I'm trying not to, but I start smiling anyway and my breath disappears and I get lightheaded. I jump in the pool and listen to my heart thud, the only thing I can hear underwater. I look up toward Tiffany and Shannon and even though they're all blurry I can picture them perfectly.

Derek and Sven jump in the pool and I come back up. Peter and Amy lay back down. Tiffany and Shannon start talking to each other at the other end of the pool. Derek splashes me.

"You know you look like a fag," he says, soft enough that his parents won't hear.

"You'd know," I say and splash him back.

"Fuck you."

"What was that?" Peter asks without sitting up.

"Nothing," Derek says.

The only time I've ever seen Peter mad he looked like he was going to explode. He'd overheard Derek call me a fag and he went off, talking about Derek's uncle who's gay. I knew that's what fag meant but we never really used it like that. Still, when Peter calmed down and explained that it's like the n word for gay people I stopped using it. Derek just told him he hadn't said it. He'll never own up to anything he says or does. It's always pissed me off, but seeing his chubby face barely bobbing above the water, I'm not as annoyed as normal.

"So, did you get your gun back?" Derek asks.

"Told you I would," I say.

"We hung out with Tommy again, too," Sven says.

"He didn't shoot you?"

"No."

"What'd you do?" Derek's upset, but he won't admit it so I won't say anything. It's not my fault he was too scared to go.

"We shot the gun in the river."

"That's what that smell was."

"You should've been there," I say.

"Like I'd want to hang out at that disgusting place with Tommy Pescadero."

"He's cool," Sven says.

"What do you know?"

"And he said we could hang out with him whenever we want."

"Doesn't change anything for me," Derek says. He's trying to give us a tough look, but he doesn't wear his glasses in the pool so it's just funny cause I know he can't see.

"Whatever," Sven says.

He ducks underwater, his shirt rippling like a flag in the wind. We stay in the pool until our fingers turn pruney and the day's no longer hot, getting out when Amy says she made dinner: hamburgers and tater tots. After that Sven leaves, and I think about staying but I don't cause for some reason it feels weird with just Derek and me. Especially when I can hear Tiffany and Shannon across the hall.

The bike ride home takes off the last bit of water that a towel can't get. The house is quiet with Mom at work, and empty except for Daisy who's fine being home alone all day. Even though I'm happy Brad's gone, the emptiness of the house feels like a weight. I lie down in the backyard with my head on Daisy's stomach and look into the cloudless night that's supposed to be full of stars. Nothing's there but an orangey-grey. So I look instead at the hole in my hand, the scab around it is wet and brown. There's a little red ring around too, like Saturn, that stays after I close and open my hand again, even though everything else turns pale.

I can still feel the pain, but it makes me think of Tommy and I start smiling. Even though I'm kinda afraid, the universe feels bigger when I'm around him. The longer I sit, the darker the night gets, the more stars start to show. Stars that Dad says are made of the same stuff as me, Daisy, Tommy Pescadero, Sven, Derek, Tiffany, Shannon—even the world and everything in it.

I don't know how that's possible, but it makes my chest feel light.

4

THERE'S A LIST of chores taped on the TV and at the bottom it says, "Thanks, I love you." Mom's always telling me she loves me *after* she tells me I have to do something. I peel the note off, stuff it in my pocket, and turn on the TV. The couch is nice and cold. I shuffle through channels until Mom wakes up. She messes up my hair on her way to start coffee.

"Sorry I didn't get home until so late." She's already on her way to the kitchen. "You find food alright?"

"We ate at Derek's."

"Good. Did you get my note?"

"Uh," like I wouldn't see it right on the TV screen, "yeah."

"So, do you think you can help me out?"

"Derek gets paid for doing chores."

"That's great, honey. Derek's lucky."

She's staring at the coffeemaker, her hands resting on the edge of the counter until Daisy rubs against her leg and she reaches down to pet her.

"And I'm not?"

Now she turns. Now she looks at me. Not like normal though, it's not angry. She looks like she's tired of me and wishes I weren't here. I wish I weren't here, either. But where would I go now that I don't get to go to Dad's anymore? They both said it was for the best, but I don't believe it. They both said he'd come around here more, but he doesn't. I don't blame him.

"Will you please just do your chores? The house is already a sty." Her voice is hard, but quiet.

"Fine," I say cause I'm just over it.

I take out the trash, do the laundry, and mow the lawn, which is kinda fun cause I can imagine it's a machinegun and the blades of grass are bullet shells spewing out as I mow down an invading army. My chest and eyes sting from their bullets. My arms are still humming when I walk back inside. My hand throbs and I clench my fist to get it to stop, try to contain it, but the pain slips through like water.

Mom's putting on her work earrings when I come back in. When I was six, Tiffany, Derek and I were talking about Santa. Derek was excited and trying to figure out what time he would get to their house, cause when he came he always brought so much. That's when I realized that he didn't exist or he would have enough for everyone. Derek tried to fight me. Tiffany hid her smile cause she already knew. When I told Dad, he said he was proud that I figured it out so young. Mom looked disappointed. With her stupid good-luck earrings, I bet she still believed in Santa.

"I brought you a sandwich home from work last night. That'll have to do for lunch," she says.

"Sure."

"And you can use the money I gave you yesterday for dinner if you need."

"That's dumb," I say.

"Yeah, well, that's life."

She says it so easily, like it doesn't take a second of thought. Maybe that life's fine for her, but it sucks for me. When she leaves for work, I hop the walls to Derek's and slide open the back door they never lock. The TVs aren't on and there's no one in the kitchen. I run up the stairs. There's no one in Derek's room.

I stand in front of Tiffany's door, pausing at the Stay Out sign. I can't hear anything moving. My hands are shaky but I open the door. The bed, now red with pink pillows, is perfectly made. The wet, shirtless guys in her posters stare at me like they know I'm not supposed to be here.

I go back to Derek's room and his bed is perfect too. It's never this clean in here. It's like they've been abducted by aliens: they're gone, but everything else is in place. It makes my chest tighten and my fingers tingle until I remember that Derek and Tiffany always go to camp in the summer. And their parents are probably at work.

They always tell me this is my home too, but it doesn't feel like it with no one else here.

I go back to my house, where I expect Daisy to be waiting for me, but she's given up and fallen asleep in her ditch by the fence. She doesn't even wake up when I open the door to go inside. I sit on the couch and turn on the TV and flick through the channels, but there's nothing good on. Tommy Pescadero's offer floats around my head like some kind of magic trick. It doesn't make sense that someone as cool as him would want to hang out with me, let alone me and Sven. He must have better things to do. It's probably a trap. I call Sven anyway.

The phone starts to ring and I pray that his parents don't pick up. They almost never do, but when they do they're mad that anyone called. Like it's someone else's fault they have a phone in their house. Plus, they breathe all heavy and weird. But Sven picks up.

"Hello," he says after forever.

"You wanna go to Tommy's?"

"Yeah," he says, his excitement easing my doubts.

I jump on my bike and head over. He's straddling his bike when I turn the corner onto his street. He rides toward me even though Tommy's house is the other way, passing his neighbors, the Thieson twins, who are in our grade and still playing in the dirt in their front yard. They don't even notice when we ride right by. Sven and I both laugh.

We cruise down the middle of the road through the neighborhood, then cut through the church that's so big it has two parking lots. It's ugly, but at least it's different. Everything else is beige boxes, strip malls with little stores that I never see anyone go into, until we cut through by the power station and ride the along the river. We start laughing thinking about the jocks Tommy almost shot. My hand tingles and my whole body swells with excitement looking onto the river—down there's our world.

At Tommy's apartment, we set our bikes on the sidewalk, rattle his screen door, then wait for a long time. I start to doubt whether we should have been so excited, but then I hear a door open and see Tommy walk across the hallway, then another door closes. The toilet flushes, the door opens, and I knock again.

He looks surprised, and tired even though it's after noon. His hair is messed up more than normal but it looks cool, maybe even cooler.

"Hey," I say, wishing I had something better.

He's walking slowly to the door, rubbing his eyes.

"What's up?" he says from behind the screen.

He doesn't look excited to see us, which makes me feel like an idiot. I want to run away but Sven's standing behind me, blocking me in. His smile hasn't shrunk. I can feel him lean closer, his breath getting heavier. Mom told me once that sometimes you're brave for yourself, and sometimes you're brave for someone else, and that both are good. I try to be brave for Sven. I push on the bb and grit my teeth. The hurt's a little sharper, but the haze more complete and comforting.

"We were seeing if you wanted to hang out?" I say.

"Oh, sure. You dudes wanna come in?"

"Ok," Sven blurts out.

I push him back quickly so Tommy can open the door and we tumble in. There are piles of clothes on the chair and the couch. Tommy sits down anyway, clothes spilling out from under him.

"Just move that shit," he says, waving his hand at the couch. "So, what the fuck is your plan for the day?"

Sven and I push two big piles to the sides and keep one smaller pile between us.

"I don't know," I say, not wanting to admit this was the plan.

"You don't have anything to do?"

"No."

"Fuckin' lucky."

My brain pops. The thought that Tommy Pescadero would envy us in any way is unbelievable.

"What are you doing today?" I ask.

"I'm supposed to work later, but I might just say fuck it," he says. "Tim's having a party. Should be cool."

And it's like some barrier in my head has burned down. Not just cause of how cool it sounds, but that I could do the same thing—that it's actually a possibility. If I don't want to do chores, if I don't want to go to school, I could just say fuck it, too.

"Cool," Sven says even though he doesn't know who Tim is and neither do I.

"You dudes wanna cruise?"

"Yes!"

I'm happy Sven blurted that out, cause I want to go just as bad but this way—when Tommy rolls his eyes—it's not at me.

"Word. Then we're gonna have to get supplies."

"Like what?"

"Let's go to the store, we'll talk about it there."

Tommy gets up and goes to his room to put on a shirt. Sven looks at me and smiles like a kid on Christmas, and I do the same. Tommy grabs his skateboard and paper grocery bags. We ride to the supermarket with him towing along behind me. When we get to the parking lot, he slingshots out in front of us and power slides to a stop. We jump off our bikes. The heat of the blacktop comes through my shoes.

"Alright, we gotta go over some things," he says as he tucks the grocery bags into the top of his pants, under his shirt.

"Ok," Sven and I say.

"Here's the thing: we're not *allowed* to buy alcohol, which is a basic requirement for any party. So, we're just gonna take some." His face is stone and he continues, "It's not stealing because they won't accept our money. But, you take a piece of candy without paying—that's stealing. That's wrong. Soda—same. This, on the other hand, is the only measure we can take as a disenfranchised minority."

We nod. I wonder if Sven understood what he was saying, cause I don't know if I did.

"But, just because what we're going to do isn't stealing, doesn't mean they won't try to stop us. The key for us is confidence. Don't look down, don't look around, don't shuffle your feet. Walk like you're meant to be there. Like you're not doing a thing wrong. Easy, right? You're not doing anything wrong."

He points at me and my head goes fuzzy.

"Ok," I say, surprised I can even cough that out.

"Steve, you're lookout. Make sure there's no security and make sure no one takes our shit."

"Sure."

We walk over and lean our bikes against the smooth white walls. Tommy makes us turn them around so they face away from the building. He takes his skateboard and props it a few feet closer to the door and we walk into the store. I give one last look back at Sven, whose eyes are bulging and scared and I flick my hand to tell him to keep an eye out as the doors slide shut between us.

"I *almost* feel bad doing that, but you can tell Steve isn't ready. You're my man though. You fucking got this," Tommy says.

I feel taller. My steps feel longer. I don't have to try to keep up with Tommy as we walk past the snacks and circle around to the alcohol section. Our steps are loud. The only other noise is the buzzing of the giant refrigerator. I can remember standing in front of it with Dad, and it seemed big then, but I didn't realize how many different things there were cause Dad always bought the same beers that came in a gold and red box.

Tommy pulls out the grocery bags from under his shirt and hands me one. It's creased and warm like a shirt Mom just started to iron.

"These aren't even from here," I say, louder than I wanted.

"No one'll ever notice that." His voice is cool, easy. "Grab a bottle of whiskey, I'll get vodka."

"Which one?"

"Doesn't matter. Make it quick, but don't rush."

"Got it," I say even though it doesn't make sense.

"Just one bottle, but make it big."

"Ok," I say and grab the biggest bottle I can find, put it in the bag, and start for the door.

"This way," he says before I've taken two steps.

We circle back around, past the toilet paper and cleaning stuff that leads straight toward the doors. My hands are squeezing the thin handle of the paper bag, my knuckles turning white. I look left at the registers, workers smiling, talking to people, not looking at us but with a clear view if they decided to.

"You got this. You're my fucking man," Tommy says.

His voice is like a warm blanket. I slow down, and again we're matching step. We're almost there and as much as I feel like a swarm of police will attack us once we hit the door, Tommy is walking calmly and I am too. When the doors part for us, there's a flood of sunlight. And no sirens.

"Oh my god, guys!" Sven yells.

"Calm down," Tommy's voice is quick and sharp. "We're calm. We're going to ride slowly out of here like we did nothing wrong because we didn't do anything wrong. Right?"

"Right!"

Sven grabs his bike and starts riding, but won't stop looking back for us. He wobbles and I worry he's gonna fall but he doesn't. Tommy told him to be calm, but he just can't. I get why we didn't bring him inside. He's turning around with an excited, creepy smile every two seconds all the way to Tommy's.

"You boys killed it today," Tommy says as he opens the screen door. "I think we need to celebrate."

"WOOOOO!" I shout until there's no air left in my lungs and my whole body is ringing.

"I'll grab the coke in the fridge. You dudes want vodka or whiskey?"

"Either. Both. I don't care," I say

"Take it easy, my man. I'm gonna have whiskey."

"I'll have whiskey, too," Sven and I both say.

"Good, vodka's a chick drink."

I didn't realize there was a difference, so it makes me laugh now thinking about Christina's friend telling Derek he would like it. Sven looks at me and starts laughing, too.

"What's so funny?" Tommy says.

Sven stops.

"I was just thinking about Derek drinking the vodka," I say.

"That fucking kid. He a good friend?"

"He's cool, I guess."

"Sure," Tommy says like he doesn't believe me and doesn't care.

He hands us drinks, which look just like cokes but right before I take a sip I smell gasoline. Sven's watching me, waiting. Tommy's not. He's got the remote and he's clicking through the channels, drinking like his is just soda. I know it's not. He's tough enough that it doesn't bother him. It bothers me that I didn't just drink it in the first place, so I take a big gulp and start to cough and gag. My throat feels like it's on fire. My stomach feels like it got punched. Sven's staring at me with eyes like full moons.

Tommy laughs without looking away from the TV.

"Take it easy."

I can't imagine ever having another sip but after a few minutes, when my breathing goes back to normal and my chest feels like it's glowing, I drink a little. It's still gross, but easier. Once Sven sees this, he takes a sip too and snorts. It doesn't look as cool as when we were drinking beer together, but it still feels pretty good.

"You guys got a ways to go," Tommy says.

I try to imagine a future when he might think we're cool. We just have to work toward it. I take another sip, stifle my cough and imagine the party, but all I can think of is being at Derek's birthdays at the end of the summer when we play video games and the Thieson twins inevitably show up and there's cake and pizza and the sad sense that summer's over. I doubt that's what Tim's party will be like. There's still so much summer left.

My mouth feels like it's swelling and I can't stop smiling. I finish my drink and Tommy pours me another. I finish the second one fast and when I have to pee, I stumble into the wall and laugh because it's funny. It's really funny. It should be so easy just to walk to the bathroom, but it's not. Walls shouldn't move but they do. Sven and Tommy are laughing too, which just makes me laugh more until I'm in the bathroom and the toilet's swaying so much that I have to sit down to pee. Derek would make fun of me if he ever found out about me peeing like a girl but caring about that feels like it's on the other side of a force-field.

I've stopped peeing but I'm still sitting on the toilet and I take a deep breath, my lungs are hot, and I smile. It feels so amazing not to worry. Not to pretend I don't care, but to really not care. I look at the bb in my hand, try to see the metal but I can't anymore. It's just crusty dried blood inside an expanding red circle, but I don't feel anything. I poke it and the pain is on the same side of the force-field as Derek.

"I want another," I tell Tommy when I get back to the living room.

"Not right now, dude. You gotta pace yourself."

"What does that even mean?"

"I'm taking you to a party later. You gotta be ready for it."

"I'll be ready for it."

Thinking about the party feels like coming out of the pool and lying down on the hot cement. I melt back into the couch and watch whatever's on TV and when Tommy or Sven laughs it buzzes through me too. Tommy has a third drink but doesn't ask if Sven or I want one. I still have some in my glass.

Then, I look outside and it's dark, Tommy's getting his skateboard and Sven's standing by the door. The cool night air kisses my warm face.

"Let's go," Tommy says. He talks funny.

Time feels weird and each step toward the door is a moon leap. Gravity's different. My bike is a spaceship. We take off flying and before I know it, we're at a party where everyone is older and looking at me. Tommy hands Sven and I beers in the kitchen and I cheer.

Cheers surround me. Open smiling faces. Laughter. Girls. Everyone and everything is cool.

"Dude, how drunk are you?" Tommy says.

"What?"

"Don't make me look bad, man."

"What?"

"Definitely, don't puke."

"What do you mean?"

"And you'd better finish that beer."

"Ok."

I don't know why I can't puke, or why I would puke, or why I wouldn't drink the beer. When I look over at Sven he looks white, whiter than he usually does. I didn't realize that was possible. We both look blurry too.

"Hey, Steve," I say.

"Huh?"

"How do you feel?"

"Uh, I don't know."

"Are you having fun?"

"I think so."

"Yeah."

"Are you?"

"Yeah."

I don't know where Tommy went, but it doesn't matter. I don't know where we are, aside from Tim's. But I don't know who Tim is. The music is bouncy, like Mom's 80s radio music and Tommy's music had a baby. It makes me wanna dance for the first time since Mom and Dad's kitchen dance parties, but everyone else is just standing around. Talking and laughing. So instead I let the music settle in me and bear hug my chest.

Seeing so many people talking and laughing feels good. Being here feels right. I don't know who these people are or where they came from, but they're here, perfectly in their place, I think, until my beer slips and explodes on the ground. It's foaming on the carpet like when Mom cleaned the cuts on my leg. It's splashed onto me and a pair of shoes that stand in front of me. I follow them up, and up, and up until I'm looking at a face in the ceiling and a hand pointing down at me.

"What are you little shitheads doing here?" The voice is like the PA system at a basketball game.

Sven tugs at my sleeve.

"I spilled my beer."

"Why are you drinking my fucking beer?"

"It's good."

"Are you serious right now?"

"If you don't think it's good you shouldn't care about other people drinking it."

"Little fucking punk," he says.

He pushes me against the wall and I drop my beer again. The crash knocks out the rest of the noise in the room and most of the air in my lungs. He moves closer. He gets bigger. His fists clench. Everything is quiet. The magic disappeared.

"You think you're funny, huh kid?"

He grabs my shirt and twists. I punch at his arm but I'm a kid again. Dizzy and weak.

"Ay!" a voice.

Everything stops. Tommy's walking calmly down the stairs. Christina's behind him. MAGIC.

"What's going on?" Tommy says.

"This little shit was mouthing off."

"This little shit is my fucking friend. So, when I bring him to a party I expect him to be treated that way."

"Well, why didn't you say something, Tommy?"

"I didn't think I had to. I thought we were better than that."

"Come on, man. How'm I supposed to know that some dopey little kid wearing his fucking Big Dog shirt and spilling beers is with you?"

I look at my shirt. I didn't even know I was wearing that. I never thought to think about what I wore. But now that I know, I know it's stupid. I can't believe I didn't think about it. That no one told me.

"You spilled your fucking beer?" Tommy turns to me, is staring down at me, on me. His voice is hard and heavy.

"Sorry," I say.

"Don't worry about it, dude. It's a party," Tim says.

"What did I tell you?" Tommy says.

I'm shrinking into myself.

"Tommy, it's all good. See?" Tim grabs a beer out of the hand of a girl standing by him and throws it on the ground. The foam splashes onto me, him, the carpet, the wall, the girl. Anything or anyone around. Everyone cheers but the girl whose drink Tim took and Tommy, who turns and walks back up the stairs. "Let me get you another one, Amy. I'll get one for you too, dude."

Instead of kicking my ass, Tim is handing me a beer. The room fills back with energy. I take a drink and it's magic again, but a little less. My shirt feels itchy. I keep looking up the stairs for Tommy. Sven comes closer, holding his beer with both hands. Christina walks over, her hair a waterfall of beauty and a disapproving smile that feels like home.

"What're you guys doing here?" Christina says.

"Tommy brought us."

"Are you having a good time?"

"Yeah," I say, but I'm no longer so certain.

"That's good."

She looks around the room and smiles like she's happy when everyone else is happy. But there's something in her voice that reminds me of Mom and Dad and all the moments that I don't want to think about right now.

"Your parents don't mind that you're here?"

"I don't care," I almost yell. "My mom's busy working anyway."

"My parents don't care where I am," Sven says and guilt washes through me. It sounds sadder when he says it.

"What about you?" I ask.

"Mine think it's healthy for a young person to make their own decisions and mistakes so they know they can get through them on their own."

"Ok," I say, but I feel bad that Mom does care about me and angry that she doesn't care enough to trust me. And bouncing back and forth between being angry and guilty makes me feel nauseous.

"My parents don't tell me stuff like that," Sven says.

I think this is the most I've ever heard him in front of other people.

"What else do they tell you?" I ask Christina.

"That they don't know what they're doing. So my choices are just as good as theirs and they'll just help when or if they can," she says.

"How can they help if they don't know anything?"

"That is a good question."

Suddenly, a cry of "COPS! COPS! COPS!" fills the room. People are yelling, scrambling and bouncing into each other. Doors are flying open. Red and blue lights flash through the window blinds.

"Y'all were having too much fun," Tommy yells as he skips down the stairs.

"What do we do?" Sven asks.

"How good are you guys at hopping fences?"

I want to brag but don't cause it would be embarrassing, even though the size of my smile is probably just as bad.

"What about the bikes?" I ask.

"We'll get those later."

Flashlights scan through the hallway as we run out the back. Christina hops the fence first, then Tommy, Sven tries but can't and we don't have time so I push him over then hop the fence after. We sprint across a damp lawn, light flooding in when we get to the side. We open a gate and run through the street, toward Tommy's until he veers into another yard. A dog barks and a voice yells at it. Sven's breath is ragged as I boost him over the next fence.

Tommy and Christina stand still in the darkness of a side yard. My heart pumps. I don't know where we are.

"Catch your breath and when we walk out, look relaxed," Tommy whispers.

I try to silence my breath but I can't tell if it's working cause Sven is breathing so loudly. He's still breathing hard when Tommy stands up and quietly opens the latch of the gate. We walk out; Christina links arms with Tommy. My heart beats twice as fast as my footsteps and doubles again when a cop car drives by the street ahead of us.

It passes and we walk back to Tommy's house. My nerves are on edge the whole time, but I keep breathing and there's no more trouble. We sit on the couches and talk and laugh more than everyone at the party combined.

"You guys want another drink?" Tommy asks.

"Baby, I think they've had enough fun for tonight," Christina says.

"Is that right? Have you guys had enough fun for the night?"

We shake our heads.

"I'd like some alone time."

"You heard the lady. We've had enough fun for the night," Tommy laughs and waves us to the door so we get up and walk right back out. He high fives us, then shuts the door.

"Get home safe," Christina yells from inside.

It's a long walk home and the hum and warmth of the night fades slowly. My feet feel heavier as we get closer. Sven is looking over and I sense that he wants to say something, but I don't know if he will.

"Dude! How amazing was that?"

Even when I can tell he wants to talk, he usually doesn't but his voice is bright now, and loud in the quiet of the night. It makes me happy.

"It was awesome," I say.

"I thought that guy was going to kill you."

"I thought we were gonna get arrested! Twice!"

"I wish we could go back now. I never want to leave."

"Me too."

"And did you see all those girls?"

There were girls, older and more beautiful than have ever been in one room at once. I wonder if that's what high school's gonna be like, and for the first time it doesn't feel so scary or bad. Maybe high school will be amazing. Maybe it'll be fun. Not just some all-important period like Mom keeps bringing up, that's harder and more boring than middle school. Thinking about it all makes me wish Tiffany had been there. She could tell me about what it's like. Maybe now that we'll be in the same school, she'll wanna talk to me again.

We're standing at the crosswalk, waiting for the only pair of headlights on the road to pass so we can head into our neighborhood. Except the headlights don't pass. Sven and I both freeze. They pull up and then a spotlight shines on us.

It's the cops. They know everything. I'm going to vomit.

"What're you boys up to?" The officer steps around his car and hitches up his pants. He's got a gun on his right hip. I wonder how many times he's used it.

"Walking home," I say, praying that's all that will come out of my mouth.

"It's awful late out for a couple kids to be walking home."

"We were just leaving a friend's house. We didn't know it was so late."

"Summertime, no responsibility, huh?"

"Yeah."

"And you're just going home?"

"Yeah. Right in here."

We point to the neighborhood, which is only across the street but feels a million miles away. It's cold and dark and quiet, like we're lost in space as the officer decides our fate.

"Ok, then. You kids get home now. But I'll be patrolling the area and if I see you again, you're in trouble."

"Ok."

"Enjoy this time. Summer'll end eventually."

The fear fades when it's clear he doesn't know anything. It's just July, summer has barely started. We walk casually into our neighborhood.

We hit Sven's house first and he goes inside. I'm alone with a few blocks to walk by myself, in a quiet that feels different now. It's not empty cause there's enough in me to fill it out: all the talk and laughter from the party is there, and all the drinks, all the music. I almost wanna dance until I turn the corner and see the blue and grey of Brad's truck sticking out in our driveway. The truck bed down, his legs dangling over the edge. As I get closer, memories of Brad push everything out. He takes a drink of beer, still watching me, and sets the can down on the edge.

"What the fuck are you doing here?" If I could spit the acid that's filling my body, I would.

"Your mom hasn't been returning my calls."

"Good."

"Almost three years, kid. Maybe that doesn't mean much to you." His voice sounds like a trap, a lie. I remind myself of every joke, every insult and scream. Everything.

"Must not mean anything to her, either. It was way too long for me, though."

"God, that attitude, always with that attitude," he says, and takes another drink. "I get it, I was like you, fucking pissed off because I didn't have a dad."

"I have a dad!"

"And I didn't realize how fucked up it made me until I was older and there were fucking people—FUCK, people, you know—that would help me."

"Like you could help me."

His laugh is cold and short. I don't remember ever hearing him laugh.

"Like you'd let anyone, kid. I don't know. I don't. Maybe you're not like me. It was stupid to even—goddammit. *I* was *looking* for help. Not you, though. I shouldn't have even tried. Too fucking late now, huh? Too late." He takes a swig, then chugs until the beer is gone, crumples the can in his hand, throws it into the bed and opens a new one. "I put so much work, so much fucking time, and you—you don't know about either. Fucking kid. Now, it's nothing, nowhere."

He waves the back of his hand at me. He's staring at a streetlamp, won't even look at me, shaking little drops of beer onto his jeans.

"I won't feel fucking sorry for you," I tell him and my body jolts with electricity.

"Christ, kid, I'm not stupid. Of course you won't feel sorry for me. You only think about yourself, you wouldn't even consider," he laughs again but louder this time, "just for one second, about why our relationship ended. Then I want you to think about why your parents' relationship ended. Then I want you to see if you can find the common link."

"Go to hell!"

He hops off the truck and I don't budge. He slams the back gate closed. My fists clench but he opens the driver door, sits down and slams it shut. He smiles red-eyed and the truck rumbles. It's hard to breathe. He backs out of the driveway and screeches away.

I flip off the taillights until they disappear down the street, walk inside the house and slam the door without turning on any lights, heading through the hallway while Daisy scratches at the back. I jump on my bed, my fists pounding indents in my pillow that get puffed out with each punch. I keep swinging until I can't anymore and I collapse and hold the pillow and squeeze, squeeze my eyes closed. And when that's not enough, I jam my finger into the hole in my hand so hard I have to scream into my pillow until my lungs give out.

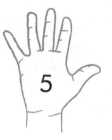

5

I RUN MY finger over the raised, rocky scab in my palm. The red ring around it is spreading, growing like it's part of me. Or overtaking me. I press my hand and the heat travels all the way up to my throat. The bb is still in there from when Tommy shot me. I like that. It is a part of me, the coolest part of me and the reason Tommy Pescadero will hang out with me. I didn't cry. I didn't tell on anyone. I went back.

The warmth of the pain and pride fills my whole body. It feels good against the cool of my bedroom floor, which is dusty even though Mom just cleaned last week. Even more cobwebs are piling up under my dresser, which is scratched and beat up on the bottom. And there's a heart I never noticed with Mom's initials in her handwriting, black outline with scratchy red ballpoint pen filling. She probably did it when it was her room, when this was Grandpa's house.

The other initials are in a different handwriting—KJ. That's not Dad, which is weird cause they started dating in high school. I don't know who it could be. She's never mentioned anything like that. What I do know, is if I wrote on the furniture she'd kill me.

I don't want to look at it, so I roll over. From the floor, the walls look boring and sad. There's nothing on them. No posters or drawings or printed-out song lyrics like Tommy has in his room. I can't stop staring. It's the same depressing color all around, a dirty white like the dentist's office, but even there they have pictures and equipment. My room is a bed and a desk that I've never used. There's a stuffed monkey in the corner that I liked when I was a kid and a closet filled with clothes that all have some stupid cartoons or logos on. They look nothing like what Tommy wears. And everything is boxed in by those boring walls and I feel like I'm going crazy. Then there's Mom's heart on the dresser.

I grab a Sharpie and cross it out. My arms shake as I admire it—little bits of red show, just enough for them to remember what was there. But besides that it's a black smudge. My feet feel light and I float out of the room.

"Morning, kiddo," Mom yells as soon as I open my door. "Why're you so smiley?"

"No reason."

"Hope I didn't scare you coming home last night."

"Nope."

I barely see Mom anymore, which is a relief. I've been staying at Tommy's when I can; I've even stayed at Sven's a few times. That was weird, but I did it cause I don't want to talk to Mom. Even though, when I have to sleep here, I hardly see her. It's only in the middle of the night when she finally gets off work, smelling like spilled beer, and comes into my room to get Daisy. If she doesn't have to work in the morning she sleeps in, so it's easy to get out of the house without talking to her. The more I don't have to talk to her the more I don't have to tell her about Brad and what he said. The more I don't have to think about it, but I keep thinking about it. As much as I tell myself he's wrong cause he's an idiot, I can't help but believe he's right—everything's my fault. Now Mom's here, trying to act casual but wanting to talk. I squeeze my hand and the fuzz blocks it all out.

"Work was crazy, but in a good way. I don't know where the people came from, but we got slammed right before closing."

She puts her palms into her eyes then pushes them to the side. It smooths her wrinkles until she lets go. It's strange, she looks the same as ever but different.

"Cool."

"Well," she says and smiles, but it's not at me. "What did you do yesterday?"

"Just hung out with Steve."

"No Derek?"

"He's at camp."

"Right. His mom told me that. What did you guys do then?"

"Nothing."

I remember Brad's laugh, how it made me feel like a kid again. Like I'll always be a kid. I don't think about these things when I'm at Tommy's, but seeing Mom brings Brad back into my head and he's still sitting on his truck bed. His words still sounding like a door getting kicked in.

"So, you didn't call me last night." She sets her coffee down just to stare at me. One more reason to feel like a kid, stuck, except it just makes me mad. "If you weren't doing anything, then there was really no reason for you to not let me know where you were."

Her eyes are dark and she talks like a computer that's powering down. She leans over the kitchen table, her hair sticking out all over, spinning the coffee mug between her hands, waiting for me to apologize. She makes a sipping noise even though she's not drinking to let me know she's upset.

"I forgot," I say, and I did after a while. Sven forgot too. We were drunk. Tommy's friends came over and they were playing music and I didn't want to think about anything else. When they play it's like I'm lost, but exactly where I need to be. And I can't feel anything, but everything feels right and I don't want to leave there, or even think about leaving.

"That's not an excuse."

"What does it matter where I am?"

She tries to smooth out her hair, but it sticks straight out again, "It makes me feel more comfortable."

"We were just hanging out. And I was home before you anyway.""I'm not asking for much."

"You know I'm not a little kid, right?"

"I know that, honey. So stop acting like a little kid and help me out."

I can never win. Everything always has to be her way. I have to be the one that sacrifices to help her. I have to do all the chores without getting paid, but still she's going to treat me like a little kid who has to call his mommy to let her know where he's going to be. I think about the dresser and almost smile. Tommy saying *fuck it* echoes in my head and I know now that I don't have to do what she says anymore.

"Fine," I say.

"Thank you."

She scrambles eggs and makes toast, and says she's hungry but doesn't eat anything. Says she wants to relax but finishes her coffee and starts complaining that the house is messy and stressing her out. Now I have to help again until she gets tired and decides to take a nap before I can sit on the couch and turn on the TV. My legs stick to the fake leather and I wish I could be in Derek's pool. Instead, I call Sven to see if he wants to go to Tommy's. He sounds like he was waiting for me. I leave the house while Mom's still napping.

Sven's outside when I get there. The heat is brutal. I feel like I'm sweating out alcohol. I have to work hard to keep up with him. When we get there, Tommy's sitting on his couch in his boxers, the fan from his room set right in front of him and running on high.

"What's up, boys?" he says, his voice chopped up by the fan. He sits forward when we walk in and the outside muscles on his arms pop out. "Ready for another trip to the store?"

"Yeah," we say simultaneously.

The store is easier than it was last time. Sven waits outside again while we grab the bottles: rum and gin since Tommy says it's important that we expand our minds. That it's part of our education. Sven's excited when we walk out but doesn't make a scene. It's less exciting for me, too. I can't figure out if that's because it's not new anymore or the people there are clueless or because they know and still don't care. None of those things should bother me, but they all do. Mostly the last.

I stop worrying a little once we start drinking. I don't like gin, but rum is great, probably my favorite. Rum and coke tastes even better than regular coke, and almost as good as cherry coke. Maybe rum and cherry coke would be better than just cherry coke.

Then the door opens and Shane, Dan and Bert enter.

"Yo," Shane says and nudges me on the shoulder.

"Hey," I say.

They were at J n the B the day we drank beers but when we saw them the next time at Tommy's, it was like they didn't know who Sven and I were. Except Shane, he's always been chill. He and Dan sit on the couch. Bert walks into the kitchen.

"Anyone want drinks?" Bert says. He makes one for Shane, Dan, Tommy and even me and Sven, like we're just one of them now.

Tommy's dad doesn't care if he drinks. Christina says he's barely around now that Tommy's mom left. Which is good for us, cause it means we have our own space to do whatever we want, whenever we want, finally. Which feels amazing. But Christina said Tommy's upset that he doesn't know why she left, or where she went. It's hard to imagine him sad, but Christina said she thought I'd understand and I think I do, even if I don't want to think about it.

I have half a drink left when Sven gets up to make himself another and I have him make me one too. It's uncomfortable having those conversations with Christina, and she likes to have them a lot, but I usually feel weirdly better after.

"I can't believe you jacked this booze." Shane says

He sits next to me on the armrest of the chair. I have to look up at him but it's hard to look away from his red pants. Little black hairs cover his chin and parts of his cheeks. His eyes seem to change color, with a look like he's already thought of a joke about me.

"It's easy," I smile too, thinking about Tommy and how this isn't really stealing.

"Good to have you around," he says and I wait for that joke while he smiles, smiles at me, but he doesn't say anything, just tips his cup and sits back on the other couch where they talk and laugh.

At some point Shane brings out a purple electric guitar and a tiny amp. When he starts playing I can't stop smiling. It sounds like a Poison the Well song Tommy showed me, but it's better. I'm in that perfect place until he pauses and I snap back to reality, but I go too far and I'm out of the moment. I'm away from here and all I can do is remember Brad and Mom again. I try to push my cold glass into my hand. It's redder and open again. There's a little ooze coming out, which is gross, so I look away, look around the room. The vibration of pain makes it all a little out of focus, but I can still feel that everyone is having a good time, laughing and talking and singing, enjoying the night. I feel separate, lost. I don't like feeling that way here. It's supposed to be safe. I should be having fun. I take another drink, getting closer with each sip, pushing everything else away, even the music they're playing, which should be loud and fast but sounds like it's underwater. I make myself another drink but run out of coke halfway so I fill it up with more rum.

It tastes sharper than before, but after a couple sips it's ok. And I start to feel fuzzy. Everything's a bit blurry, even without pressing the bb.

"Are you alright?" Christina says.

"What?"

I don't know where she came from. I'm glowing. She is too. I nod. Nodding feels dizzy.

"How's your night been?"

"Hakuna matata."

"What?"

"Huh?"

"You don't look good."

"Wha—"

I sip. Cough. It's crawling. Christina grabs me. Fluorescent lights flick. Warm bathroom floor. Orange ring around the bowl. Dust and hair stuck beneath the seat, on my hands. Hold on. I puke. More than possible. Nothing's left. Still puking. Breath hot. Sour. Breathe.

Christina's on the edge of the bathtub, hand on my back. Her kindness a weight I can't lift. Shane, Tommy, Sven pee in the sink. Christina laughs from behind the shower curtain. Sven calls Mom, leaves a message. I lay my face on the bathroom floor. It's cool now. Dark.

Then it's not. I squint through an explosion of light. I'm sitting in a chair that's grey and squishy but not comfortable. It's Tommy's chair.

Shane's on the couch. Sven on the ground. There's a glass of water next to me. My face is hot, stomach cramped, mouth like glue. I take a sip of the water and it's the first drop into an empty pool.

The laughter from last night is living inside me. I'm nervous, stupid. I hear a flap, and then another. It's coming from the kitchen. I sink down and it flaps again. Shane and Sven are asleep with sheets as blankets. I have a sheet too. The stretchy kind that I could pull all the way over my head and disappear into, but I sit up and see Christina reading a book through the spots popping on my eyes.

"How're you feeling?" she says, setting her book on her lap.

"Uh, I dunno."

"You had a pretty rough go last night."

"Yeah."

"No talking," Bert mutters from the ground. I hadn't seen him behind the couch.

I walk over to the kitchen and sit at the table, still wrapped in my sheet. My skin feels like it was flipped inside out. Christina looks tired, but her eyes brighten when she smiles and I feel less stupid.

"You're lucky," she says.

"I don't feel lucky."

"I'm not trying to scare you straight, but last night is not a worst case scenario." She makes a funny face. My head stops buzzing. "Plus, everyone else had fun. That's probably the more important thing. You won't get to share those moments if you aren't at least a little careful."

"What happened?"

"I'm not exactly sure. I was in the bathroom the whole night, remember?"

My face flushes.

"You guys are still talking," Bert says.

"Deal with it," but it's warm when Christina yells back.

"I'm sorry," I say.

"Please, you're not the first person I've had to help while they puked. And, despite my best efforts, you probably won't be the last. I just hope you *try* to not let it happen again."

"I won't."

"I don't believe you won't, but I know you'll try," she says in sing-song. Then her voice goes back to normal, "Do you need to get home?"

"Not really."

"Your mom won't be worried?"

"I think Steve told her I was staying at his house. Right?"

"If I were your mom, I'd be worried that Steven was the one that called instead of you."

"Yeah, maybe you're right."

"Don't worry, nothing's gonna be going on here for a while," she says and looks around the darkened room at everyone covered up with sheets.

"Doing nothing here is better than anything at home."

"Better, but not nicer. And it won't help you get out of trouble."

I don't want to go home. I already feel bad and Mom'll only try to make that worse. But it's hard to say no to Christina and I'm too tired to even try.

"Ok, I say. "I'll see you later."

She tousles my hair like Dad used to. I walk to the door.

"Wait up," Sven says. He sits up, still under a blanket sheet. "Are you leaving?"

"Yeah."

"Children! Shut. Up," Bert says.

"Bert, you're making it worse," Shane says. "You make everything worse."

"Wait for me. I'll come too," Sven says.

I go outside to wait for Sven cause I'm starting to feel terrible, not like I'm going to puke again, but like I'm slowly imploding and when it's over all that'll be left of me is a pile of embarrassment. Sven walks out in his socks and puts his shoes on by the bikes.

"How was last night?" I ask, not really wanting to hear the answer.

"It was awesome!"

"What happened?" I can't stop myself.

"Nothing really *happened*, I guess. You kinda just had to be there, I mean—technically you were."

He's happy when he says this, and I should feel good for him. I do feel good for him. But it makes me feel worse. The ride home is long but at least it's early enough that it's not hot. Still, I feel like I might pass out. I leave Sven at his house but instead of going home I ride down to the end of our neighborhood, into the park and around the playground. I skid out on the baseball field and send up a cloud of red dust. I pick up full speed, jump off, and watch my bike bumble into the outfield. It falls and I run over and fall down next to it. The grass is dry but cool, the sun's alone in the cloudless sky. Spots float around in my eyes and my head feels light. I'm almost feeling better when a group of little kids and their dads, all dressed in their baseball gear, kick me off the field. One of the teams is silver and black, the Raiders, just like I was as a kid. I thought I was so cool that I'd wear my uniform to school, but now I wonder if I looked just as silly as they do.

I ride to Derek's house after. There are no cars in the driveway. I open the side gate and take off my shoes and socks. I dangle my feet into his pool and feel my legs tingle. I lay back and watch one cotton ball cloud drift through the blue sky. It must be amazing to be Derek and have such a perfect life. But now Sven and I have Tommy and his friends and Derek doesn't. The cloud disappears and the sun gets warmer and I realize I don't belong here. I probably never did.

The realization is so definite that it doesn't even feel bad.

I hop the wall home, the dirt and grass squeezing through my wet toes. I try not to think of what Mom is going to do, listening for her as my throat tightens and my eyes get soft.

I open the back door. The house is quiet. Walking down the hallway my steps smack and creak like I'm on the gangplank. But there's an emptiness in the house. I yell and wait, but there's no response. Mom's not here.

Everything is quiet, which makes me feel so much louder. There's a note in the kitchen that says she's covering for Brian then working her regular shift. That she won't be home until late. There's five dollars attached to it, which reminds me that I didn't eat dinner last night and I puked up lunch. My stomach starts to growl but the idea of food sounds terrible. I feel terrible. The note asks me to call her, but I don't want to or have to. She's at work. There's nothing she can do.

I flop on the cool couch and flip on the TV.

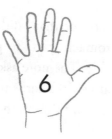

6

SHANE'S FINGERS MOVE around the guitar so fast that I can't
believe they can stop long enough to make distinct sounds. But they
do. I can feel them. It's perfect. And Tommy's humming like a wild
beast, which sounds separate but totally fits with what Shane's playing.
Their eyes are closed but they move comfortable and natural, and it
just looks so cool that my chest starts to shake like I might cry.

They've haven't said anything since Sven and I came in. We don't
say anything and neither do Dan or Bert. The music forms a bubble around everyone, connecting us but keeping us safe and separate.
When it stops, I feel dazed, like I was in a car accident. I start to come
to and think about how embarrassing the other night was. How stupid
and like a little kid it was for me to puke. I can't get out of my head.
The burning in my face and stomach is back and it's worse than that
night. It's like how it felt when I found out Mom and Dad were breaking up.

I miss Dad. Everything was always better when he was home.
There was music in our house then. He and Mom would dance, which
seemed weird cause Derek and Sven's parents never danced, but, looking back, I don't think I'd mind it so much. I wish I could go live with
Dad. I wish I hadn't picked Mom. I wish he didn't tell me to pick her
cause now I know he's not coming back. I don't even think he should
with how tired and cranky Mom is all the time.

Thinking of Dad adds sadness to the other night's embarrassment
and I wish the floor would fall away so I could sink into nothing. Then
I remember KJ, Mom's other love. It's bad enough having to deal with

her boyfriends after Dad; I don't want to think about anyone before him. Instead I reach my thumb to the bb, feeling it before I even get there. I push hard. The pain, like electricity, pulls my shoulders up and back until I let go and ride the mellow hum.

It's started looking gross, so I put a band-aid over it again, but now the liquid comes out of the sides when I push it too hard and soaks it. The fabric gets heavy and feels like it's going to fall off.

"We gotta make another trip to the store," Tommy says as he opens his eyes and smiles. His cool washes over the heat.

It's like nothing even happened for them. They sit around like normal. It looks normal. The sheet I slept under is still hanging over the small couch and the others are kicked under the coffee table. The empty cups and beer cans are right where we left them. Tommy's even wearing the same black shirt with the sleeves cut off he wore yesterday. But I can't believe it could actually be the same. It feels like they're gonna start making fun of me any second.

"Then let's fucking go," I say.

They laugh. I just want to get outside. Even though we've done it a bunch now, I'm ready to prove I'm not just a dumb kid.

"No one's got balls like you, dude," Bert says. It should help, but there's something about the way Bert says things, even if they're the right thing, that sound a little off.

"Is anyone else coming?" I ask.

"You, Steve-o and me. The rest of these guys are pussies," Tommy says.

"It's just—you guys make a good team," Shane jokes. "We'll buy your food."

Then he's looking back down and the music jumps out of the guitar, which makes me wanna stay and watch until I'm able to figure out how he does it, how his fingers can move like that. I want him to teach me. But I wanna go with Tommy too, and that feels like a better way to start making up for last night.

I have a lot of money now that I don't always have to spend what Mom gives me. People buy us food when we get the booze. I keep it in my desk, which is the only time I've used it for anything. I don't know what I'm gonna buy with it. Maybe clothes, which I never even thought about until now, but these guys all look so cool. Except for Bert cause he's too big for his shirts and is always pulling them down to make it look like they fit. They all wear tight clothes and it's almost all black and white. Only Shane wears lots of colors. People make fun of him, but I think he looks sweet. Just not as cool as Tommy. That might not be the clothes, though.

Tommy gets up and it's time to go. Once we're outside and riding, I relax. It's just Sven and Tommy and I on our way to the store. The sun's down and the sky is purple and orange and starting to cool. I ride without the handlebars and it feels like I'm flying. I don't even have to worry about getting the alcohol cause we've done it enough times now. And, as we ride up to the supermarket with its neon lights and stacks of soda boxes outside the door, I start thinking about having a drink back at Tommy's and it makes me even more relaxed.

"Wait," Sven says, as Tommy and I are getting ready to go inside.

"What?" Tommy asks.

"Can I do it this time?"

My heart starts to beat faster. I'm not anxious doing this with Tommy anymore, but the thought of Sven in there, of Sven trying to be calm, makes my throat dry. He does seem different though. He looks serious. That he would even be willing to ask Tommy gives me hope.

"You think you can handle it?" Tommy asks.

"I—I think so."

"Alright, go for it."

"You sure?" I say.

"You two got this."

I can't say any more. Tommy's smiling like he did in the J n the B parking lot and I can see all the veins on his arms when he folds them across his chest. I want to complain and I want to run, but I trust him.

When we walk in, the same tightness I had when I did it the first time is there. I tell myself I've done this enough. I look at Sven; he sticks his jaw out and nods, then follows me inside. His feet shuffle and squeak as we step on the sticky grocery store floor. I keep my eyes locked straight ahead but I can feel him looking toward the cashiers like an alien who just came straight to the supermarket from Mars. I take a deep breath and try to slow my heartbeat. We walk through the candy aisle, around the back and I hand him a bag.

It's cool by the alcohol, but I'm hot, sweaty, and shaking. The beer fridge is humming and I look up and down the aisle. No one else is around but I feel like we're being watched. I remind myself to breathe.

"What should I get?" Sven asks.

"Anything but rum." Just looking at those bottles makes me gag.

"But, like, what?" His mouth is tight. His eyes are huge.

"Whiskey. Or vodka."

"Well..." he starts.

"You get vodka. The biggest one you can find. I'll get whiskey."

I grab the whiskey, stuff it in my bag and head toward the back to circle around through the cleaning supplies. I go slow so he'll walk next to me. As we get closer to the end of the aisle, to the opening in front of the cash registers where the last bit of orange sky is calling us through the doors, I hear Sven's shuffle quicken and thump along with the clinking of glass. My heart starts pounding. I told him just one, but I should have said plastic to be safe.

He's just ahead of me at the end of the aisle. My heart is revving like a racecar ready to peel out. I try to keep my eye on the door, but I can see him getting further away from me. I've stopped breathing, like the smallest difference in sound could be what saves us. My heart still pounds and spots are popping in my eyes as Sven wheezes and lunges, the glass bottles clang like an alarm. He's running, and then I'm running too.

A shout comes from behind. "Hey!" I turn. A man spins out from behind the register and sprints after us. The automatic doors barely open in time for us to squeeze out. I grab my bike from the top, jump on, and jet. Tommy's standing with his skateboard in hand, leaning against a brick pillar. I give him a screaming look to run.

"Nooo!!" Sven yelps.

The man has him by the collar. Sven's standing on his tiptoes over the bike's top bar but I don't stop pedaling, not even when I'm looking back. I'm going faster than anytime I've ever raced anyone. Sven gets pulled off his bike, into the store. Tommy looks at me smiling, then with a shrug turns and follows inside.

I want to go back but my body won't respond. Act casual, I think, but my head is spinning and nerves are fried. I'm halfway to Tommy's before I can even slow down. My lungs burn. The bag of whiskey swings from my right hand.

Sven's scream loops over and over, each time with more force until my head is pounding, calling me to go back but I can't. I should help him, but I don't know how. Hopefully Tommy's got it, now.

I was fine; it was Sven's fault he got caught. He should have just stayed outside like normal. I should have made sure Sven stayed outside. He was stupid for coming in. Now he's probably getting arrested but it's his fault for being so stupid. It worked every time Tommy and I did it. I want to be mad, but I can't stop thinking about the sound of his scream and how scared his face looked when he got yanked off the bike like a puppy by the scruff.

I set my bike against Tommy's building and open the door. Everyone cheers when I walk inside, until they see there's no one else with me. And then I can feel how much my heavy breathing fills the room.

"Where are the other dudes?" someone asks, but I can't look to see who it was.

"I don't know," I say and walk straight into the bathroom and jam my thumb into the wound until it looks and feels like I'm trapped in lightning. I release and breathe steady again. I wipe the tears from my eyes and walk back out.

"What do you mean? What the hell happened?"

"Me and Sven went in."

"Who?"

"Steve. Me and Steve went in, but he started to run so I started to run and they chased us. I got to my bike. I tried to tell Tommy to run, but he didn't. And they got Steve."

It's harder to breathe out here.

"Then, what?"

"I don't know. They took him inside. I don't know. I came here," I say like a coward. The pounding of my heart slips into my stomach and I think I'm going to be sick.

"What about Tommy?"

"He went in after Steve."

"What do you mean he went in?"

They're staring, the room is hot and dark and the air is heavy. I close my eyes, but only see Sven staring at me. Begging for me to come back. The huge hand pulling him up by the collar and his shirt lifting up to show his pale white stomach and ribs and sunken chest. Everyone is staring at me until the door clicks and their heads turn and the weight slips off my shoulders.

I turn and there's Tommy. He's smiling.

"You motherfucker!" Shane giggles.

"What's going on?" Tommy asks as he saunters toward the kitchen table and sets a bag down.

My heart stops.

"You went in after?!" I yell without meaning to.

Tommy nods. "What'd you get?" he asks coolly.

"Whiskey."

"Damn, we doubled up," and it's like he moves across the apartment in one step and punches me softly on the shoulder.

"Steve?" I spit out.

"He'll be fine."

"What about the cops?"

Tommy laughs. Everyone laughs. Immediately I know how stupid it was, but I don't know why.

"They'll call his parents," Tommy scoffs. "That's it."

"Oh."

"Stop stressing out. Have a drink," Tommy says.

"Actually, if he's up for it, I lucked into something that might work a little better," Shane says.

All I want is a drink but Shane pulls out a small container and when he shakes it what's inside clunks around like a single shirt in the dryer. The top pops open and he holds it out to me. I look and all I see is a rolled up ball of grass that smells funny, but familiar.

"You know what this is, right?" Shane asks.

"Yeah," I say, but I can't even think about anything.

"You ready to try?"

"Sure."

"Good. You ever been high before?"

"No. I don't know."

"Well, you're about to find out. Tommy, get your piece, let's spark a bowl for the kid."

"But there's hardly anything in there," I say. "Why do you need a bowl?"

Bodies are falling off the couches and chairs in the explosion of laughter. It's the only thing I can hear or feel and my throat starts to constrict. I don't know why that was so funny. When you know you said something stupid and people laugh you just laugh too, but I don't know what I did and now I definitely feel worse than waking up after puking. I want to get outside. Get away. But I know that if I do that feeling will follow me.

And I don't have anywhere to go.

Tommy hands me a small glass thing that looks like the oversized finger of a jungle frog. He's the only one that's stopped laughing, but I feel like this is still a part of the joke. It's cold and heavy in my hands. I turn it over. I don't want to ask what it is or why he handed it to me.

"That's a pipe. And that scooped out part on the end, that's the bowl," Tommy says.

"Oh," I say, and it feels better to know, but worse that he had tell me.

"Don't worry, dude. You're not the first person, not even the first person in this room to not know what this shit is."

"Who else?" I ask cause I need to know.

"Yo," Shane says.

"Bert won't admit it, but he did too."

"Bullshit!" Bert says.

Dan nods. And I smile.

"It might just've been me that didn't," Tommy says.

"You're such a cool guy, Tommy."

"Oh, Shane. Don't hide your admiration behind a shield of sarcasm."

"You know me so well."

"Whatever," Tommy says and turns back to me. "You ever smoke anything?"

I shake my head.

"Never stole any cigarettes from your pops? Or a Black & Mild from a cousin? No hippie aunt getting you high?" Shane asks.

"No."

"You're gonna cough a lot the first time but don't worry. With weed, that's a good thing."

"Did you cough the first time?" I ask Tommy.

I know I shouldn't ask that either, but it just spilled out of me. Tommy rolls his eyes and looks back to the group.

"Of course. I thought I was a tough guy, so I took a huge hit. Coughed for a fucking hour. That was a long time ago. I was probably a little younger than you," Tommy says and I feel better.

He smokes, then explains how to do the same. Natural breath, he says. Which I think I understand, I mean, I know how to breathe normally. Except I breathe through my nose, unless I'm sick, and now I have to take a normal breath through my mouth. I'm worried I'm going to cough, or mess something up. I'm trying to remember all the things he told me to do, but I can't even get the lighter to work.

Tommy takes it from me.

"Ready?" he asks.

I nod and he lights, and I start to breathe in and it's warm. I thought it would burn but it feels more dry and prickly. Then suddenly my whole body locks up, trying not to cough. I push it down, but it's coming no matter what I do. The first one is like swallowing a hiccup. Tommy takes the thing out of my hands and then the coughing really kicks in.

"Woo!" Shane hoots. "That's a good one. You sound like an angry donkey."

I can't stop, and the longer it goes on the stupider I feel. They all smoke, and none of them really cough, not like I'm coughing. My face, my whole body feels like it's covered in tiny explosions. I know Tommy said it's normal when you first try, but I still hoped it wouldn't happen to me.

When I think I'm done coughing, I start up again.

He hands it back to me and I try and cough less this time. Or it's all part of the first cough. The pipe is going around. I feel like, like my chest should be burning or my hands should be sweating. I feel like something. Or. I feel, I feel nothing. I think I feel nothing in a good way. I smile, but my smile isn't part of me. No one is doing anything but they're having a great time. I'm having a great time, I'm floaty and I like floating. Not off the ground, not flying, but like a cartoon vampire. I look at my hands and I'm not a cartoon. And I look in the mirror and I'm not a vampire, but vampires look like people. I don't think Tommy, or Shane, or Bert, or Dan are vampires either.

They're all laughing. I laugh too. My laugh sounds good, like an ice cream sandwich.

"What are you guys laughing at?" I ask. I want to hear if my voice sounds as good as my laugh but it doesn't.

They keep laughing and I float over to the couch, which feels like a bowl of mashed potatoes.

"Mashed potatoes?" Tommy says.

"What?"

"You said mashed potatoes."

"Huh?"

"Wait," Tommy stares out the window through tiny beams of sparkle-shine. The laughter stops. Everyone is quiet except for their heartbeats. Then the sound of a car engine stopping. Anti-sound. "You guys gotta go."

I stand up but can't float anymore. Darkness crashes around. My steps are heavy and slow, the door opens magically and Dan, Bert, and Shane are walking in front of me. Breathe normally. Is that the nose or the mouth? Neither work. I'm suffocating. Clouds move. Dark. My lungs are half-full and filling and I don't know how. I pick up my bike and the grip feels like shaking hands with a lizard.

Tommy's dad is in the parking lot with the trunk propped open with a hockey stick. It's full of tools, paint, a jar of mayonnaise and a case of beer. Mayonnaise. I laugh. He can hear me. My heart stops. He doesn't look. Maybe I didn't laugh even though I felt like laughing. He takes the beer out and leaves the tools, paint and jar of mayonnaise.

Mayonnaise is what I'm still thinking about when I weave my way to my house and no one's home but Daisy.

The backyard is shaking softly like a tambourine. It's warm even in the shade. I lay down in the grass and it holds me with cool hands. Daisy lays her head on my stomach, her warm breath like a smile. She's happy just to be and I'm happy to be. Mayonnaise. I can't stop laughing.

Daisy licks my hand. Licks the band-aid off. It's cracked and red, but the liquid is white. Mayonnaise. The bb is still in there. It's inside of me. Like a spy. Part of me that shouldn't be part of me. But what should be me? Who should I be? Isn't this the part of me that Tommy likes? That Christina likes? That Shane and everyone likes like I have a superpower. The hum in my hand is like a force that moves me from being uncool to cool, a kid to a grownup. That pushes Brad away. And it only has to hurt a little. Right now I can't even feel a thing. But the pain is everywhere, staring at me, stalking me from the inside. Ripping pieces of me away. It's growing, not just the pain, but the hole. I wonder how long until it'll consume me. Like a black hole. Until I am the whole hole. Or it's me.

My laugh sounds hollow in the emptiness of the backyard, so I stop. I lie back down and hold my hand up to the sky. The hole like a burned-out sun, ugly and frightening like it could end all of life. My chest is cold, and it feels like I can't fill out my body. Like I'm nothing in the universe. I inhale and exhale and pet Daisy to match.

I try not to think.

7

SHANE, DAN AND Bert are sitting on the couch, their knees spread just wide enough that they don't touch each other. Tommy and I are on the kitchen chairs cause the little couch is itchy when it's this hot. The windows and door are open, but the heat is trapped inside and growing. There's no breeze. The only thing coming in the window is the conversation from Tommy's upstairs neighbors hanging out in the walkway. I can't hear what they're saying but can hear when they laugh. And when they smack the iron railing, the whole apartment shakes.

"It's too fucking hot," Tommy says.

His dad is gone again. I asked where he went but Tommy doesn't know. I asked about the mayonnaise too but Tommy didn't think it was funny.

"Where's Christina?" Shane asks Tommy.

"I don't know, dude."

"She doesn't have a pool, does she?"

"I fucking wish."

"We know anyone that does?"

I can see Derek's pool in my head. It's quiet. It feels like summer. I don't think his parents would care, but it's still weird to imagine us there. I don't say anything, just picture being at the bottom of the pool, staring back into the wavy blue world.

"Doesn't Rebecca have one, Shane?" Bert says.

"She's not exactly talking to me right now."

"You should call her anyway," Tommy says.

"Pass."

The door pops open and I arch my back and look over the chair to see that it's Sven. He's higher up than any of us, but still looking out from under the hair that falls over his face.

"He busted out!" Shane yells and everyone looks and laughs at me.

My face burns. It looks like Sven's does too, but it's nothing compared to how it looked when he was getting pulled off the bike. My stomach bubbles and I look away. I wish I was underwater.

"So what happened?" Tommy asks.

"What do you mean?" Sven says.

"How'd you get fucking busted? What happened when you did?"

"I don't know. They just started chasing us. I think they were watching us the whole time."

"No they weren't," I say cause it's a lie, but I still feel bad after.

"No one cares. What happened?" Tommy says.

"I don't know. They took me into a back room and just asked a bunch of questions."

"Tell us what they asked you, what you said, and what happened after. I don't want to have to keep fucking prodding you," Tommy says.

"They asked who I was with. If I'd done it before. They asked for your name. I didn't tell them any of that." It's the longest I've ever heard Sven talk. After he looks around the room like he's hoping someone will say something but no one does. "They said they were going to call the cops, but didn't. Then they called my parents."

"Sorry," I say. I know how angry his mom gets.

"Did you cry?" Tommy asks.

"No."

"Ah! He did!" Bert yells.

"I did not!" Sven is looking down but his voice is stronger than normal.

"Whatever, dude. Keep going," Tommy says.

"That's it. They called my parents and they had to pick me up and they were really pissed off."

"But, you're here now, so are you not in trouble?" Shane asks.

"Yeah."

"That's it? That's fucking tight!"

"My mom would kick the shit out of me if that happened," Shane jokes.

Sven glances at me, then away. He's still standing just inside the door and the heat is coming in behind him. He looks back at me again, then sits down quietly on the little couch.

"You're a bunch of fucking pussies. Worrying about your fucking mommies," Tommy says.

"Let's focus on more important matters, Tom. We need to find ourselves a pool," Shane says.

"What about Derek's?" Sven asks without looking at me.

"Who is Derek?"

"That fucking wad you guys were hanging out with at Jack?" Tommy says.

"Yeah, he's our friend."

"Then why doesn't he hang out?" Shane asks.

"He's at camp," I say.

"So he's not home, but you wanna go there anyway?"

"His parents always say their house is our house," Sven says.

"So we're gonna go chill with this kid's parents?"

"No. They're at work."

"Even better," Tommy says.

No one gets up right away, but it feels like we're going and now my mouth is hot and dry. I try to think about being underwater, where it's cool and calm. But the more I think about it the hotter and drier my mouth is getting.

Tommy slaps his hand on the arm of the couch and dust puffs up. He stands and kicks aside the clothes on the ground on the way to his room to get his swim trunks. He's holding them over his shoulder, standing in the doorway where Sven had been before he sat down, but Tommy fills it out like Sven can't.

"Let's fucking go," he says.

Shane jumps off the couch, and Dan and Bert follow slowly. Sven stands up like his body has twice as many joints as it should.

"We gotta get our shit," Shane says. "Where's this place?"

I look at Sven but he doesn't say anything. I'm staring past him at the empty door with the screen peeling off in the corner, but I can feel Shane waiting.

"I'll skinny-dip if I have to, but I don't think anyone wants that," Shane says.

"Sorry," I say. "It's in the Heights, off St. Cloud. I don't know the address but it's big and white with blue around the edges and it's got a big basketball hoop on the front."

"Like novelty-sized? Is there a giant basketball that goes with it?"

"It's ten feet tall."

"Ok, sounds simple enough. We'll see y'all there," he says, walking out with Dan and Bert.

"Are you sure this is a good idea?" I ask Sven, cause it feels weird going in the pool without Derek. But bringing Tommy and Shane and them feels wrong, not in a bad way, but because they don't fit. Like they're from separate universes, and bringing them into Derek's would forever alter it and I could never really go back.

"We're just going swimming. Chill out."

"This is your idea," I say and wonder if it's already too late.

"I know."

Sven and I hop on our bikes and Tommy rides his skateboard, while Shane, Dan and Bert jump into Shane's car. Tommy calls it a shitbox, but I think it's cool. He's the only one with a car anyway. They drive off to get their swim stuff and we start riding so slowly that they'll probably beat us there. I take my hands off the handles and ride through the wobbles until I'm coasting. I raise my arms and close my eyes, but the bike starts to swerve and I have to turn hard before hitting the curb. Tommy's shaking his head and I'm smiling.

The streets are wide and bright without any cars, but we're riding so slow that I can't escape thinking about Derek's universe. I swoop from one side to the other, jump off curbs and try to do a wheelie but I can't get the front wheel high enough to stay. And I can't keep myself from worrying. Even though no one's gonna be home.

"Take it easy. It's tiring me out just watching you," Tommy says.

I slow down and ride alongside them. It takes a while, but finally we get to Sven's. Tommy kicks at some flowers in the neighbor's garden while we wait for Sven to get his stuff. The Thieson twins are playing outside, wrist-deep in mud down the street. We ride by them. I don't think Tommy notices. They don't move a muscle.

There aren't any cars in the driveway at Derek's and when I knock no one comes to the door. It shouldn't matter, but I'm happy his parents aren't home.

"Can we get inside to change?" Sven asks.

"Just wrap a towel and change here. Or be a man and drop trou," Tommy says.

"I'm gonna go home to get my trunks."

"You're not gonna wear the little ones like last time?"

I stare at Sven but he won't look at me. He said that to embarrass me, which is more of a Derek move. He wraps a towel around his waist and I go home to change. When I come back Shane, Dan and Bert are there. Shane brought his acoustic guitar and set it on a chair. He can afford two guitars cause he works at the music store.

Sven's on the ledge of the deep end in his shirt and trunks. The rest are in the pool. It seems so different hanging out here, lighter, like how summer used to be. There's splashing and laughing and no worries. It makes me miss Derek. I run along the bricks on the garden ledge and dive in.

"Where the fuck did you come from?" Shane says when I pop up.

"I just went home to get changed."

"Fucking ninja."

I dive back down and kick and twist. I forget about everything and start to relax. The water pulls gently at my hair and against my shoulders. My hand starts to sting but the calm, cool everywhere else wraps me up. I stay under until my chest is tight and my throat feels like it's stuck between hiccups. I heave out a breath when I get back to the surface.

Shane splashes out of the water, dries off, and starts playing his guitar. I always thought Derek's house was perfect, but it's even better when there's music. I guess I was wrong to worry.

"What the fuck were you doing?" Tommy says.

"Swimming."

"You looked ridiculous."

It doesn't burn as much as it should. Maybe it's cause I'm in the pool. Tommy turns away, swims to the end, and sits on the steps. He leans back on the ledge, both arms on the bricks like a model from one of Tiffany's posters; he's wet and muscly and he's staring up at the cloudless sky.

"This would be awesome if we had some beer," he says. "But maybe we do."

He dries off and walks toward the sliding door. He turns around and smirks as it whooshes open. "Of course these are the types of assholes that leave their house unlocked."

Everything was already perfect until now, but Peter has beers and I know Tommy is going to find them. He comes out with his hands full of cans and starts tossing them around. One splashes right in front of me then bobs to the top. I can't stop this now, only glare at Sven since this was his idea. But he's not looking. He caught the beer and is opening it already.

It feels like I can only breathe out.

I grab the beer and swim to the ledge. I can see Peter's soft eyes harden with each pop of a can, then get sad. It's uncomfortable to think of him crying. My lips start to quiver so I push them against the cold metal and take a swig. The beer tastes weird.

"What the fuck is this?" Bert says.

"It's an import," Shane tells him.

"It's gross."

"This asshole buys some expensive bullshit," Tommy says.

He chucks the can and golden beer spirals out as it crunches against the planter wall. Foam oozes like a wound. Dan and Bert set their cans to the side. I take another drink. It's bad enough that we stole the beer,

I'm not going to waste it. I try to hear Peter and Amy telling me to help myself, but I know they didn't mean this.

Shane is drinking his and smiling. He sets it down to play guitar.

"Fucking philistines," he sings.

I don't know what that means. Nobody else does either. But we all know that when he sings like that it's to make fun of someone. I laugh even though my stomach is still in knots. When we first got here it seemed like a movie. The pool, the people, it all could've been perfect.

I take another drink cause I'm going to finish this beer, but with each sip I feel worse. Not drunk like normal, I feel sick.

"Let me see if I can find something decent to drink," Tommy says.

"Are you sure that's a good idea?" I ask. My chest thumps. I'm gonna throw up or pass out, which sounds more appealing that saying anything else to Tommy Pescadero. It would be good to stop thinking, stop worrying.

"It's a great fucking idea," he says.

"It's just that, they're gonna know we took their stuff."

"They're gonna know *someone* took their stuff. They won't know that it was us, though."

"Calm down, man," Shane says, but he doesn't tell me how I'm supposed to do that.

"We're gonna be fine. No one's gonna know anything," Tommy says.

"But they could come home soon."

"We're gonna have another drink. If they come home we can just hop the fence to your place, right? So, don't fucking worry."

And this time when Tommy says it, it's final. It's what's going to happen and it's almost better now that I don't have a choice. Like it's just another problem, another thing that's gone wrong in my life. Maybe after this I can go get beers to replace the ones we took but I can't worry about that now. I finish the one I have and dive back into the pool. And while Tommy is inside the house, I can really enjoy being in the water.

There's a splash above me. I look up and see bubbles swarming around Sven. His shirt stretches and waves around his long, pale limbs as he flails toward the surface. I push off the bottom and shoot out of the water. Sven climbs out. Everyone is chuckling. He looks goofy with his shirt clinging to the cavern of his chest. He pulls his shirt away from his body, but it's sucked back like there's a gravitational force inside of him.

"Is that a chest vagina?" Tommy jokes as he exits the house empty-handed.

"Careful Steve. If it is, Tommy'll probably try to fuck it," Shane jokes.

Sven smiles. Tommy smiles too, but it's not the same. Sven's is happy or relieved. I don't know how to describe Tommy's. He kicks my empty beer can into the shallow end of the pool.

"You finished that shit?" he snaps.

"Finally another person with decent taste," Shane says.

"Yeah," I say, even though I didn't like it. But maybe it was alright.

"I thought you were getting more, Tom?"

"Will you take off your shirt?" Tommy ignores Shane to yell at Sven. "That shit looks fucking weird."

"Ok," Sven says, but he doesn't move right away.

Shane gets out of the chair and leans in to whisper something to Sven, who laughs deep and takes off his shirt.

"What did you say?" Tommy asks.

"Nothing," Shane says and dives into the pool.

Sven splashes in after him. His skin is as white as his smile and his ribs stick out like teeth.

"Yeah, well, we should go," Tommy says.

"I was having a nice time," Shane says.

"Let's go," I say and Sven agrees.

It's already getting late. It would be too risky to come back with beers and Tommy's right, Derek's dad will know that someone took his beers but he won't know that it was us. I go home quick to change back into regular clothes and when I get back everyone is ready to go but the cans are still all over the backyard.

"Steve, help me with this," I say.

"I don't think so."

"Just leave it," Tommy says.

"Yeah, just leave it," Sven parrots.

"It'll take two seconds."

"We already waited for you. Now, we're leaving," Tommy says.

"Fine, I'll catch up."

"Whatever."

I hurry around the pool, looking for empties that people had smashed and thrown around. The gate clicks. I don't understand why they wouldn't wait, why they wouldn't help out. But no one cleans up when we hang out at Tommy's except Christina and I start to feel guilty that she does all that work.

I get the cans and put them in the recycle bin next to my bike. I miss the cool hug of the pool as I pedal fast to catch up to Tommy and Sven. They didn't say where they were going but I assume it's Tommy's, and halfway to his house I see them in the distance. Tommy's holding on to Sven's saddle, coasting.

"Faster! Faster!" I hear him yelling when I get closer.

Sven's laughing when I catch up. Tommy releases and for a moment he's going just as fast as us, but then he drifts back and we slow down so we can ride next to him.

"You get the house nice and tidy?" Tommy says.

"You should've brought your maid outfit," Sven says.

"Steve-o, bringing the heat."

I try to stay calm, to not let it bother me.

"Why did you even fucking clean up?" Tommy says.

"It seemed worse if they thought it was a party instead of just some-one taking their beers," I say, still hoping I can replace them before anyone notices.

"That is fucking stupid."

"Whatever."

"Are you upset?"

"I'm not upset," I say but my voice gives me away. I can see it in Tommy's eyes, even Sven's.

"It's ok to be upset. I would be too if I wasted my time cleaning up."

"Shut up!" I yell.

"Don't be such a pussy."

"Yeah!" Sven yells.

"Shut up, Sven."

"You shut up."

He doesn't look down, look away, apologize. His lips are tight. He's staring back at me even as we ride and he looks almost like Tommy. My teeth and lips are clenched.

"Why did you call him Sven?" Tommy says.

"Yeah, why *do* we call you Sven?"

"Fuck you!"

"He tried to ask out this girl, but he couldn't even say his own name so instead he called himself Sven. *And* she said no," I say and my heart sputters out.

"Dude," Tommy says to Sven, his voice sounding like Dad's, "don't worry about that shit. If a chick shoots you down, that's their fucking problem."

Sven is grinning. I want to punch him but Tommy's between us. We get back to Tommy's and the other guys are already there. Christina's there too and it looks like she cleaned up.

"They were saying you found a pool," she says.

"We sure did and it was glorious, but it's nice to be back where we can have a proper drink. And maybe now this kid will relax."

To hear Tommy call me kid, just like Brad, makes me numb.

"Why does he need to relax?" Christina asks.

"He was worrying about some dumb shit."

"Are you doing alright now?" she asks me.

Her smile is bright and her eyes are soft and she seems almost still, waiting for me to respond, able to wait forever.

"I'm fine."

"See? He's fucking fine."

"What were you worried about?"

"Nothing."

I just want it to be over. I want them to stop. The worst place in the world is being stuck between a couple arguing.

"Don't let him make you feel bad about it," she says and looks at Tommy, but he's not paying attention.

"I don't feel bad."

"I'm happy to hear that." Her smile dims, but is somehow warmer.

"I wasn't even worried."

"I know."

And I know she knows that's not true, but it doesn't matter. I can feel the anger in the room fading like a dying star.

"It's just that, we already stole their beers and I didn't want to leave a mess."

Christina leaves her smile for me when she turns toward Tommy.

"You were stealing beers from someone else's house?" she says.

The anger burns back. I wish I wouldn't have opened my stupid mouth. I press my palm and hope I can disappear into the haze of pain.

"Shitty beers from his stupid little friend."

"Fucking philistine," Shane sings again from the couch.

"You were at his friend's house and you stole beers?" she says and it feels like she's getting taller.

"A couple."

"That's not ok."

"Relax."

Tommy leans back and his head rocks up. He's smiling but it's the wrong time to be smiling. Dad smiles when he's not supposed to, too.

"It's ok," I say.

"See? He doesn't even care, and he shouldn't. They had more than enough booze in that fridge, they could do with a little redistribution."

"That's bullshit," Christina says. I almost choke. Tommy scowls. From the couch, Shane laughs. "Stealing from a store is—whatever, we don't need to get into that. There's at least some justification. But from his friends? It's not right putting him in a position where he's the only one that would get in trouble."

"It's really ok," I say.

"Jesus Christina, no one's going to get in trouble," Tommy says. He walks to the kitchen and starts making a drink.

"Yeah, they won't even care," Sven says.

"There's never trouble in summer," Shane sings.

I wanna laugh but I can't cause I feel trapped in the middle again, with so much pressure on both sides that I might burst.

Christina shakes her head and turns back to me. She looks tired and her smile is gone but her eyes are warm, like the blue is getting bluer. She looks at me like she's looking into me. I pick out different points of her face to focus on, everything is soft and pretty: cheek, chin, nose. Her black hair sweeps against a blonde eyebrow. I look at anything to avoid making eye contact.

"I'm sorry these guys did that," she says like it's the last thing she'll ever say.

"It's ok, really. I did it, too."

It shouldn't bother me cause she's mostly upset with Tommy, but I feel bad. A lot of things bother me that I wish didn't, like the way Sven says "supposably." And I wish I didn't feel that grip on my chest when he says something stupid, cause I didn't say it, or feel ashamed that I disappointed Christina now she's angrier at Tommy. I wish I could be like Tommy, who doesn't feel bad about anything.

"Don't worry about her, man. She can be a bit too serious at times," Tommy says and hands me a drink.

Christina stares at him. Her mouth is hanging open. He won't look at her. I can't look away.

"You can be such a prick," she says and storms out the door.

It's quiet. My hand is cold from the drink.

"Fuck," Tommy says. "Maybe now we can have some fun."

He cheerses me. I'm not having fun after the first drink, but after the second everything is mostly back to normal. It's getting dark outside now and the summer air is finally coming through the screen door. Another drink and everyone is laughing and the music is getting louder. I should just trust Tommy since he always knows how to have fun, but I still feel bad about Christina.

I hear Shane's joke, *there's no trouble in summer*, and I try to laugh now that it's all over. But it doesn't feel right. I know it's not true.

8

MY BEDROOM CEILING is mostly all dirty white, but there's a ring that's yellower than the rest. Like someone above me wet their bed. The sun hasn't even come over the wall in the driveway, but it's too hot to sleep. Mom must feel the same cause she got home in the middle of the night but the kitchen already smells like coffee. When I walk out, she's pouring it over a full cup of ice, which is melting before she finishes pouring and disappears completely after.

"Mornin, kiddo," she says from behind her glass with its thin line of separated water on top. Her eyes look grey and her voice is crackly. "I feel like I haven't seen you in forever. Can I cook you breakfast?"

I want to tell her that I can make myself breakfast, that I don't need her to cook for me. But she's smiling like she won't understand.

"Ok."

"What'd you like?"

It's too hot to eat. All I want are Pop Tarts, but she'll get upset since that's not cooking and I just don't want to deal with it.

"Pancakes," I say to compromise.

She rustles through the fridge and pantry. The mixing bowl and frying pan clatter out of the cabinets. She rinses out the dust that's collected on them in the cabinet before cooking. She measures flour and cracks eggs and when she stirs it all together I can see the veins in her forearm, under her skin that's pulled tight but somehow still wrinkled. Butter crackles in the pan and when the smell wafts through, I hear Daisy thud out of Mom's bed at the opposite end of the house.

"How have you been?" she asks.

"Fine."

"Well, what've you been up to?" she asks as she pours the first of the batter into the brown butter bubbles. "Gimme something."

"I don't know," I say, cause I can't think of anything I want to tell her. It'd all get me in trouble.

"Come *on*." She looks up from the pan and the refrigerator behind her hums. "We already blew by the Fourth of July. You've had plenty of summer. Has it been fun?"

"Yeah," I say, but now all I can think about is having to go back to school. Starting high school doesn't sound so bad when I think about hanging out with Tommy and Shane. But Tommy doesn't go to work, so maybe he won't go to school. Maybe I won't, either.

"You'll probably be happy to get Derek back, huh?"

"Yeah," I say.

Hearing his name makes me cringe. I think about how sad or mad his dad must've been when he saw that people stole his beers, even though I've hardly ever seen him sad or mad. My stomach turns. Maybe he knows. Maybe they have security cameras and he saw it was me. I can't imagine what he'd do. I just see the disappointment on his face, which looks like Derek grown up.

Mom flips the pancakes.

"You and Steven haven't just been sitting inside playing video games this whole time, have you?"

"No."

"If you have *anything* you wanna tell me about your summer, I'm all ears. One thing?"

I shrug. There's nothing we have to talk about. There never has been. I could always talk to Dad cause he actually listens. Mom's only ever telling me what to do or how what I'm doing is wrong.

She stacks the pancakes onto a plate and fills the pan with more batter.

"Here you go, kiddo," she says and hands them to me. "I was hoping I could take a couple days off, but I don't know if I can swing it.

Work's been unbearably slow lately. Summer's usually busier, but now with all the regulars going on their vacations it'll only get worse."

She used to complain to Brad, but now that he's gone it goes directly to me. We hardly talk since we never see each other, yet this is all we talk about. And there's nothing that I can say. Her complaints don't make any sense. This time there aren't enough people, but before there were too many, or the people just weren't good enough. It's crazy that she can complain all the time but not quit and go somewhere else. It's like everything is a problem, or a reason to complain but not enough to do anything. And then it's my fault that she has to suffer like this—*she's doing it for me.* But I didn't ask for that. I didn't ask her to be miserable. I tried to tell her to quit but she won't listen to anything I say.

I pour the syrup and cut into the pancakes, which are still gooey in the middle, just how I like them.

"Come on, kiddo. Please, talk to me."

Daisy's sitting under the table with her head on my lap. Her warm breath soaks through my shorts. She huffs for attention. I could give her a piece of pancake, but she wouldn't go away. She'd eat it and look for another. I hand her a bite anyway.

"Don't give the dog food at the table."

Mom'll boss me around and then expect me to talk to her like a friend. I wonder if she even has any. Or ever had any. Dad used to have friends over all the time. Of course, Mom complained about them, too.

"I miss summer," she says and looks out the kitchen window like it's not summer now. "You don't get it when you grow up. It's just a normal time, that's really hot. I miss being able to run around with no responsibility, no worries. Enjoy being a kid while you can."

"I'm not a kid," I say and I drop my fork.

"I know you don't like to hear it, but you should enjoy it," she says like she didn't hear me at all.

"You don't know what you're talking about," I say, making sure she hears it this time, because she needs to stop pretending she knows what my life is like. Like she knows what's good for me when she doesn't know what's good for her.

"Excuse me?" Her eyes narrow and her mouth squeezes tight. I wonder how she even got those words out.

My heart is pounding but my words are slow and clear. "You don't even know what you're talking about." "That's not how you talk to me."

"Don't you even have friends you can talk to?"

"You're being rude. You can go to your room and think about why you would talk like that."

"I thought about it already. It's true!"

Daisy huffs again in my lap and walks off into the kitchen and lies down between Mom and me.

"Go to your room." Mom's voice is deep. Heavy. She stands in front of me and her shoulders widen like wings.

"No."

"Don't make me say it again."

"Say it all you want."

The room goes dark. Daisy's paws scratch. The sweet, smoky smell of burning pancakes floats through the kitchen. Mom grabs my wrist. I try to twist free, but she's strong. She pulls me out of the chair. My whole body is a stack of muscles that she drags through the living room. I grab the wall at the edge of the hallway, but I could rip it down before she'd let go. I'm trying not to pant when she sits me on the bed. Her face is red, her eyes closed. Daisy stands behind her like I didn't just give her part of my pancake. Traitor.

"Stay in here and think about your attitude. You can come out when you're ready to give me a proper apology."

Daisy leads Mom out, who slams the door behind her. The waves rebound into the empty room, getting smaller and smaller, and I feel like I'm getting crushed into nonexistence.

The sweetness of the pancakes has disappeared and now I only smell burning, like a fire that could melt this whole stupid house. Might as well. I could kick through the window and go to Tommy's, until his dad came. Then I'd just wander or hang at the river. But the smell stops. Mom probably turned off the pan.

Now I just sit in this room where I don't have any video games or a TV, or even a drink. There's nothing to do and it's too hot cause Mom won't turn on the air conditioner anymore. It's too expensive now, apparently. I can't tell if my face is burning from the inside or outside.

I think about swimming pools and how good it would feel to be underwater. And I think about Peter and if I were going to apologize to anyone right now, it would be him.

Mom doesn't deserve an apology; she should apologize to me but I don't know if I've ever heard her say she's sorry.

I wish I could disappear. I rip the band-aid off my hand and stare at the hole. The cracked black of the scab gives way to a milky whiteness. I am slowly dissolving. Decaying. I wish it were faster. When I clench my fist the liquid on the edge turns yellow, like acid from a lab. The pain feels good. It's ever-present now. My heart thumps in my chest like the heavy, easy rhythm of a bass drum.

I can hear Mom talking in her phone voice. Walking down the floors that creak like an out of tune piano. I hate being here. I should've just jumped out the window, but when I finally think that I could, she opens the door. The phone is in one hand, the mouthpiece covered by the other.

"It's your dad," she says and hands the phone to me.

I wait till she closes the door, then say "Hey, Dad."

"How're you doin', big man?" Dad's voice is like whiskey and coke. The pain recedes. I feel warm and relaxed.

"I'm ok."

"That's not what your mom was telling me."

"What'd she tell you?"

"That you were talking back. Yelled at her." He gets quiet and my breathing stops until he laughs. I don't want him to laugh but I can breathe again. "Oh man, I've been there."

"I want to come live with you," I say.

"I wish you could too. I do, I do." He says this like it's a song. "But you know you can't."

"Why not?"

"That's just the way it is."

"But it sucks here."

"I know. Trust me, I know. Your mom doesn't always know how to handle situations. She tries, though. But it's still gonna be up to you to deal with it like a man."

I don't know why I have to, though. I don't want to.

"Can I at least come visit?"

"I'll try to figure something out."

"Well—hurry up."

He laughs again and now my stomach is twisting.

"I'm serious."

"I know, I know. I don't mean to laugh. You're gonna be ok, though. You're a tough dude. All this stuff that feels like life or death now—it's fine."

"Ok," I say, and try to believe him. I squeeze my hand again and the pain doesn't even make me blink. Maybe he is right.

"Put your mom back on the phone."

"Ok."

"And go have some fun."

Mom's in her room. Her eyes are red and swollen and she's still got the dog with her. She looks like a fire pit after the fire's gone out. I hand her the phone and she takes it. I walk down the piano hallway and hear Dad's "I do, I do" in my head.

I walk into the living room and sit on the couch. The phone beeps from all the way at the end of the hallway when Mom hangs up. I don't turn on the TV. Instead, I think about apologizing and how little the words would mean. Why should I care if I barf out, "I'm sorry?" It doesn't mean anything to me, but it'll make Mom feel better. And it'll get her off my case. I hear her coming down the hallway and I get ready.

"You're not in your room," she says.

"I'm sorry I yelled and was rude." The words don't feel like mine and I don't feel anything when I say them.

She stops and looks at me like she hasn't seen me before. "I appreciate your apology. And I'm sorry, too. You know—I haven't been around a whole lot and that's not fair. I don't know what you're going through and I—I know you don't want me calling you a kid and believe me, I try. It's just hard to wrap my head around the fact that you're not my little baby anymore."

"Mom—"

"I know. You don't want to hear that. But I don't know where the time went. Where it's going. I wish I could stop it. Or pause it for a second so I could catch my breath but I haven't figured out how that works. Do you know how to do that?"

"No."

"You sure?"

"You're being ridiculous."

"Oh, but what would you expect?" It's nice to see her like this—almost human again. I don't even know how to respond. "I wish things weren't always speeding out of control. Or I was better at handling them. But I'm doing all I can for the both of us."

"I know," I say.

"Good. You're still grounded, though. I talked to Derek's parents and you'll be staying there tonight until I'm off work."

"Mom..."

"Derek's back home, so it's hardly even punishment. You're lucky. I was going to take work off and you'd be stuck here, but no one would cover for me."

Having to see Peter will be way worse than any punishment she could imagine. And I can't help thinking that he knows. Or he's going to find out while I'm there. But he probably wouldn't say anything. He'd be too cool to say anything, just torture me with a look that says he knows about the beer—about everything. He's known all along that I don't belong and he just had to wait for me to prove it.

"Can't I just stay home? I won't even watch TV."

"No." Her eyes pinch. They look darker than normal. She doesn't understand. "Haven't you missed Derek?"

"Not really."

"Isn't he your best friend?"

"I guess."

"Well, don't you want to see him?"

"I just don't want to go."

"Jesus, you're just like—it's only because I'm making you go isn't it?" She turns toward her room.

"It's not that."

"Then what is it?"

I stop myself from saying *Derek sucks*. I don't say anything at all. She waits, but not for long before she starts doing chores. I have to do them too. I clean my room and mow the lawn, both of which seem like the least important things for her to care about. The grass and the mess in my room are always going to grow back but at least it gives me time before I have to go to Derek's, time when Mom might change her mind.

After chores she has to get ready for work. That's when she remembers how tired she is, like sweeping, dusting, doing laundry, vacuuming and scrubbing the entire bathroom was a distraction from feeling that before. Just getting the mower from the garage or picking up the first shirt makes me not want to move. But she's gripping the sides of her head between her hands while she puts on the same good-luck earrings that never work.

"You want me to drive you or are you hopping the fence?"

"I'll hop the fence."

"They'll be expecting you."

"I'm going."

She leaves out the front door and I stare at the back corner of the yard. The sun's barely coming through from behind the trees and the lawn smells like fresh cut grass, which smells better when I'm not doing the cutting. The heat coming off the ground looks like a time portal that could take me into the future, where I wouldn't have to worry about Derek's dad or Derek. Where I'd be older and everything would be easy cause I could just do what I want. I walk through, and when I look back the portal's gone. I hop into Derek's yard and his dad's by the grill, drinking one of his beers. The beer that he probably had to dig to the back of the fridge to get while he wondered where the rest went.

"Welcome to your jail cell," he says as I hop down the garden ledge.

My stomach flips. He sets a beer by the grill. I don't think I can be here but he turns and smiles and his eyes twinkle behind his glasses. Maybe it worked. Maybe I am in the future. Or in another dimension.

"How's it going?" I manage to say.

"Great. Having the kids back brings a little more joie de vivre to the house."

"Even Derek?" I say and he laughs. "Derek will be happy to see you. He's up in his room."

He smiles and nods and I hear the soft scratch of the can lifting as I slide open the door. I run up the stairs but they don't have their usual bounce. Derek's in his room playing video games. Everything looks so normal, like he brought the mess of plates and glasses with him. His old toys watch from the shelves. Something about it feels stuck.

"I heard you're grounded," he says without taking his eyes off the screen.

"Yeah."

"That sucks."

"How was camp?"

"Cool. What've you been doin'? Just hanging out with Sven?"

It feels like when Mom asks cause I know if I tell him he'll be angry. But I have to, even though I can hear that asshole tone he uses when he thinks he's better than something or someone.

"We've been hanging out at Tommy's a bunch," I say.

"Why?" he looks over without pausing the game.

"It's cool."

"What do you even do there?" he says and turns back.

"Hang out mostly."

"Sounds pretty gay."

"You're the one that went to summer camp."

"Which is the opposite. I had a girlfriend there."

"Bullshit."

"She let me put my hand in her pants."

"To touch her dick?"

"That's what you do with your boyfriend, Tommy Pescadero." He says Tommy's name like it's surrounded by pink and purple hearts. I don't know why it's so annoying. But once Derek makes something a bad thing, it's hard not to get sucked in. Even when I think he's stupid, cause I almost always think he's stupid.

He looks chubby and awkward but his eyes are intense. He pauses the game now, and sets the controller on the bed.

"Can I play?" I nod to the screen, not wanting to fight.

"Fine," he says.

It's a multiplayer game, and we're on the same team. I'm a giant who can pick up and throw rocks or smash people with one punch. Derek's an elf. He's fast and casts spells. And he can heal both of us. It's the best combination, which is lucky since these are our favorite players anyway. Derek knows the maps and which people to talk to, but he always gets trapped by orcs and I have to save him.

We've made it through three levels when I hear footsteps coming up the stairs, light and quick. Tiffany stands in the doorway, on the edge of the room. And I can tell it's her, but it's like I've never seen her before; the sun coming in from Derek's window is all around her like we're in heaven. And in it, her green eyes are shining. But when she steps into the room she looks at us like we're diseased.

"Food," she says.

We pause the game. She stares at me as I walk by. I can feel it on the back of my head. I turn and she smirks. Her lips are blood-red and her teeth are just barely showing. I almost trip down the stairs. My face feels hot and my feet don't remember how to move until she stops. The kitchen smells like barbecue. Burgers cooked with cheese on top and on the inside. Amy made potato salad, and there's potato chips and soda out. The good kind, not the store brand stuff that we have at home or buy to mix drinks at Tommy's. Everything here looks and smells delicious but I'm not hungry cause Peter comes inside shaking an empty beer can and Tiffany is still staring at me like she led me into a trap. My hope of passing through a portal to the future or any other dimensions are dashed; it's here and now and I'm going to suffer for what I did.

"You guys ready to eat?" Peter asks.

Derek and his sister both say yes, which masks my silence. Peter is leaning into the fridge like he's trying to climb through the back. He pops out with another beer.

"Wow Dad, you barely made it out of there," Tiffany says.

He laughs and stares at Tiffany for a while before talking. "Had to go way back for that one. I could've sworn I had more."

"You're having another beer?" Amy asks as she walks around the corner.

"Yes, ma'am," he says with a smile.

"I don't know why you have to have any."

"Summer's gonna end before we know it, so I gotta enjoy the BBQ and beer while I can," he says, but there's still so much summer left.

"Well, just don't have too many.""Honey."

Tiffany is staring at me, staring, staring. I miss the Tiffany that wouldn't look at me almost as much as I miss the nice one. Peter and Amy sit down. The food should be delicious but Tiffany's stare is making me taste mud.

"Salad's really good, honey," Peter says.

"Thanks."

Forks scraping against plates sound like blades being sharpened. I wish they'd put me out of my misery. Dinner's finished, but now there's dessert. The one time I don't want it and it's strawberry pie fresh from the bakery. Besides Mom's pumpkin pie, this is my favorite. Peter and Amy know that, so I take a slice and eat it quickly before it rots in my mouth. Too quickly, cause Peter offers me another slice that I have to say no to, which makes me look weird. One more reason to be suspicious. One more reason I don't belong.

When everyone is done, Derek and I run up to his room, but before we can start our game Tiffany steps in like a giant smashing through the first line of defense.

"So," she says and stares and my brain turns into a soup of scared and excited, "I hear you have some new friends."

"Yeah," I try to say but it comes out in a clump. I realize now how Sven felt when he couldn't say his own name.

"He's been hanging out with Tommy Pescadero," Derek says.

"Why would he want to hang out with you?"

"I don't know."

"Why would *he* want to hang out with Tommy Pescadero?"

Derek's words float off somewhere behind her. She doesn't take her eyes off me. "And what is it that you do?"

"Nothing, really." There's no point in saying we hung out here cause I can tell she already knows, but Derek doesn't and he'll be pissed if he finds out.

"Where do you hang out?"

She tilts her head to the side and smiles and my heart is pumping like I'm scared and sad and happy and everything. It makes it hard to breathe even though my chest is swelling.

"At his house mostly."

"Is that *really* all?"

"Stop being stupid, *Fanny*," Derek says but she ignores him even though she hates that nickname.

"We've gone to a few parties."

"What is it you do at these parties?"

She can tell Derek about the drinking and beers. She can tell her dad, too. It would suck, but it would be better than this. Better than her holding it over me.

"Why do you even care?" I say.

I can breathe again, and I start breathing faster. My body feels like it's buzzing.

"I don't," she says and her smile sinks.

"Then why do you keep asking?"

"What's your problem?" she says and steps back and the light dims around her.

"You," I say and my voice feels sharp and it's like a wind is rushing through me.

"You're acting like a jerk," she says quietly.

She looks soft and sad and it's like a force-field opened and all the memories that she wanted to keep hidden spilled out. I remember walking through a park when she was pointing out all the trees and birds. I still remember there are no blue jays in this part of the country; those are scrub jays. Her grabbing my arm before I stepped in poison oak. Making up songs by the fire when our families went camping. When Mom and Dad were still together. When it really felt like we were all a family.

She leaves the room quietly, and now it's like Derek's a different person. I can see him sitting up and smiling out of the side of my eye.

"Dude!" he says.

"Let's play," I say.

"That was awesome!"

He looks so goofy when he gets this excited. I should make fun of him. He'd stop if I did.

"I'm starting," I say instead.

"Did you see that?" he asks, like the only thing he'd rather do than make fun of me is see me make fun of his sister. "You totally shut her up!"

It's been a long time since I've hung out with Derek but he hasn't changed. He's still a kid.

When he goes to the bathroom I knock on Tiffany's door. I don't have much time, so I go in before she answers. She's pulling big red headphones off. Her room feels smaller with the blinds closed. Tiffany looks small too, but I think it's just cause of how big her bed is. It takes up the whole room. The music from her headphones bounces out softly. It's something I've heard Shane play—The Faint. Tommy makes fun of him, says dance music is for chicks. I don't tell him that I like it too. I like it even more now.

"I'm sorry," I say.

"I know about your fucking party here," she says, quiet and angry, but she won't even look at me.

"I figured."

Somehow, every time I feel bad, there's a way that it gets worse. Like that feeling is a bottomless pit and if I'm not falling further down, I'm smashing myself on the walls.

"And I could tell my dad."

"Is that what you're gonna do?"

I want to tell her to do it. I want this feeling to go away, but I could never be the one that tells him. Just imagining the disappointment on Peter's face is enough to make me brush the edge of the bb. The tingling starts up my arm.

"I'm not gonna tattle on you."

"Thanks." I should feel relieved.

"But, you owe me."

"Ok," I say. I don't feel relieved.

"Is it fun hanging out with them?"

"Of course."

She holds a headphone over her mouth like the music could hide her smile. I smile too, with the same heat I had when Tommy, Christina, Sven and I walked through the streets at night dodging cops. It feels just as quiet as it did then. Like something's wrapped me up and everything else is outside, even the sadness. Right now it's just my heart beating and her half-hidden smile.

"Next time you're going to a party, you have to invite me," she says.

"I will."

She smiles again and I bounce back to Derek's room. He's sitting in his chair with the same disappointed look that he's had since I've known him. The same look he had around that campfire when he couldn't think of anything to sing about. Like he's waiting for everything to stop for him.

"What were you doing?" he squints his eyes behind his glasses.

"Nothing."

"You're such a fucking pussy."

We play a soccer game against each other but I'm too busy think-ing to pay attention and he wins. I don't care even when he's making fun of me. It doesn't feel like I'm pretending this time, which is good cause he doesn't stop until I hear my mom downstairs. Her steps up are heavy and slow. She doesn't say anything when she gets to the top. She doesn't have to. I get up and walk with her, wishing the whole time that I could hear Tiffany's door open. Wishing that she would come out to say goodbye. She doesn't, and then we're back in Mom's car even though I could've just hopped the fence.

"Was it nice to get your friend back?" she asks as she pulls away.

"Yeah."

"What'd you guys do?"

"Just stayed inside and played video games."

"Ok," she says and it's quiet again until we're home.

I feel tired, like the energy was sucked out of me. But when I lie in bed I can't sleep. I'm stuck in the dark, in the quiet, with Derek's dad and my dad and Tommy Pescadero and Derek, Sven, Shane, Mom, Shannon all in front of me, like the ceiling is an old movie screen that plays every dumb or bad thing I've done, every stupid mistake I've made alongside their disappointed or disgusted faces.

But then there's Tiffany. And it's a different movie that makes my heart pound and my whole body ache cause we're together. I wish I could be in that movie.

9

THE WATER IN the river is full of plastic bags and old shoes. Almost black, it doesn't look like it even moves while I'm sitting on the concrete slope just below the bike path where those jocks rode by. The bb that hit their spoke probably rolled down into the water here. Now, there's no one around for miles, just concrete and clouds.

Even though it's been almost two months since I was here with Tommy and Sven, this still feels like our place.

Mom left the house early this morning—too early for work—without leaving a note or coming into my room to tell me I'm still grounded. So I left and I'm gonna stay out. She'll have to find me if she wants. I would go to Tommy's but he'll be asleep for another few hours at least. I could go back to Derek's to see Tiffany, but when I think of her eyes and smile, her dad's face morphs around them. I can't go back until I replace his beers.

Thick, grey clouds cover the sky and keep it cool for now. It won't last all day. The heat will sneak through and stick underneath. Hopefully, it'll rain. Hot rainy days are my favorite. It's like being at Grandpa's with Dad lying on the big rocks with his mouth open, until he would laugh and choke and spit water all over. He could always make something boring fun even when Mom and Grandpa were shaking their heads at us. I wish he were here now. I wish I even knew where he was.

A beer can—the same kind Peter drinks—floats slowly down the river and lodges against the pile of trash closest to me. I know it's not, but I take it as a sign. I walk my bike up the concrete slope then ride to the grocery store. I'm gonna replace those beers.

The ride is short and the parking lot is empty when I get there. The red neon sign looks creepy against the grey clouds. The whole store looks like a fortress from a horror movie. I wish Tommy were here, except he would tell me I'm stupid for doing this. I imagine sprinting out alone with a six-pack of beer. The workers screaming, security chasing. Lifting me off the bike like Sven. I won't scream if they do. They'd rip the pack from me and let the cans fall and break. There'd be a pool of beer when the cops come.

My heart's racing, standing in the middle of the empty parking lot, staring up at the buzzing grocery store sign even though I know they won't call the cops. I don't understand the things my brain thinks, but I think I'd rather they called the cops than Mom. I bet Sven felt the same way.

I go in anyway. The store is cooler and drier than outside, but bright like a spaceship. I pass by the alcohol aisle and see someone out of the corner of my eye. I wait by the candy, hoping if I give him a minute he'll be gone. I can't wait too long, otherwise I'll draw attention to myself. But he's still there, slouched in front of the refrigerator, holding the same beers that I need when I go back.

Then my breathing stops. I think I gasp but I can't hear anything cause my brain is screaming to run. It's Peter. It's Derek's dad. He doesn't look over. He doesn't move when my shoe squeaks and stops and sticks. He doesn't move but I'm frozen. It's just me and him and the beers he's holding. Everything else is blank.

He turns and looks right at me but doesn't recognize me. He's wearing his glasses but his eyes don't brighten. They don't narrow. He's doesn't look angry or shocked or surprised. He looks empty.

"Mr. Williams?" tumbles out of my mouth. I couldn't bring myself to call him Peter.

He stands up straight, the beers cradled between his hands. He smiles. My feet unglue and I go closer, but it's not his normal smile. He doesn't say anything. His lips press tight against each other. His glasses magnify his hollow eyes.

"What are you doing here?" I say.

He chuckles and shakes his head and clears his throat. He takes a deep breath and laughs a little more and I feel lost.

"Is everything ok?" I ask even though my stomach is turning in on itself. Whatever he was laughing about, the joke is over. It looks like a tear is starting to form in the corner of his eye and I'm starting to freak out.

"I don't know." His voice scratches like a radio station that's lost its signal.

What? What doesn't he know? And how could he not know?

"I need to buy beer," he says.

He's holding the beer and I want him to just turn and buy them and go.

"Sorry. Not 'I need to.' I want to. But—ah," he takes another breath and starts to smile again. "Amy doesn't seem to want to believe me."

"What?"

"Feels like I'm losing my mind a little." His voice sounds almost like it's supposed to. He runs his hand through his hair. "I'm the one that drinks. Nothing crazy, nothing—abnormal."

The word lingers and he stares at the neon lights above him.

"But Amy hates beer, hates alcohol. Barely tolerates me drinking it and now, now she doesn't trust me. Even though she's around me constantly. Constantly! But I'm starting to wonder if she's right."

He turns and stares at me. Through me. I move to the side but his gaze doesn't shift.

"I swear my beers just disappeared. Which sounds absurd, I know, but the kids were at camp so it wasn't Tiffany sneaking any with that friend of hers. And Amy would have seen if *I* drank them. She's constantly hovering—*doting*, she likes to say—but after twenty-two years I'd have earned a little trust, right? In all those years, how many times have I lied to her? Practically zero. A handful, maybe."

That can't be right. He runs his hand through his hair again and tugs at the back. He looks normal, but nothing can be normal now. "What is wrong with me?" he says quietly.

It doesn't make sense, seeing him this worked up over so little. Amy will still be nice to him. She'll still be beautiful and their lives will only be slightly less than perfect. I'm the thief that stole his beers.

He blinks and loses the tear down the side of his face and it's like a crack that destroys the value of a baseball card.

"It was me," I say.

"Huh?"

My chest is heavy. My feet feel light.

"I stole your beers."

"What do you mean?"

He starts to laugh for real now and I can't handle it.

"I'm sorry."

I'm out like a bolt of lightning. Pure energy. I can't hear anything. The only thing I see is the door that starts to open when I get close but I'm too fast. It's too slow. My shoulder connects, the door rattles and so do I, spinning, stumbling, until I'm on my bike and now the shaking feels like it's inside me. I can barely breathe from how hard Im riding but it's not fast enough to leave it all behind. I pull up in front of Tommy's, the music ripping through the screen door and open windows.

"You look like hell," Tommy says from the couch.

He's slumped from the heat that can't escape, no matter how many doors or windows are open. I can feel the sweat on my forehead, above my lip, under my arms. My shirt is stuck against me.

"What's going on?"

"I saw Derek's dad," I try to hold back.

"You thank him for the pool party?"

I try to breathe in his calm, but the breathing feels like a stabbing in my chest and I can feel myself start to shake harder.

"I told him." I can't hold it. I shouldn't have come here.

"*Wait*," he sits up, forward, his fists press into the couch, "You what?"

"I told him that I stole his beers."

He slumps back and chuckles, "That *you* stole his beers?"

"I had to."

"Well, that's something."

"I had to, he was… like, crying." I can see Peter's cracked face and it feels like I shatter. There's no point in holding back now.

"HA!" The veins in Tommy's neck bulge and his smile is wider than I've ever seen. "What a pussy!"

"Derek's mom and him were fighting because of it. He was upset with himself, but it was my fault." I can't catch my breath. My eyes sting.

"Parents are supposed to fucking fight. If they didn't fight about the beer, it would have been about some other bullshit."

His words sit at the center of a whirlwind of Mom and Dad fighting about the car, dinner, movies, Grandpa, TV. Screaming and slamming doors. It was all so loud. Daisy was a puppy and she'd hide under my bed. Sometimes I'd crawl under with her. But Tommy's being right doesn't make sense, cause Peter and Amy aren't like that.

"What did he say?" Tommy asks. He's looking at the TV now. I can't even see what's on.

"I ran away."

Tommy laughs and a chill runs up my spine.

The screen door swings open and fresh air pours in. It's Christina. She's wearing work clothes, black pants and a black collared shirt and her hair looks tight on her head. She looks like a different person. I would give anything to make myself a completely different person right now.

"What are you doing here?" she asks. "Is everything ok?"

"I don't know," I say.

"Baby, let's go to my room. He'll be fine," Tommy says.

She sits down on the couch. Her eyes look bigger and brighter with her hair out of her face. She's not smiling but she looks happy, like she's saying it's ok to cry, that she expects me to cry. I hope so, cause I can't stop.

"What's wrong?" she asks.

"He's fine."

"Did something happen?"

"No," I say and keep telling myself no, but it's not working.

"Chris."

"Talk to me," she says.

I want to tell her to go. I'm fine. I want to say that, but the words catch in my throat.

"He doesn't want to talk," Tommy says.

Christina puts her hand on my shoulder but that can't stop the shaking. It won't hold back the tears. Why can't I stop? The words pour out. I tell her everything.

"It's ok. That's not your fault," Christina says.

"Christ, kid! Buck up."

"Tommy! Knock it off!"

"But he lied. He lied to her. And I'm a thief. And they hate me now."

"No one hates you."

"Fuck them," Tommy says.

"He's going to hate me cause I told him. I told him I was the one that stole his beers. I'm the reason he's in trouble. I'm trouble and he probably knew it all along. Probably always knew I didn't belong there. But he was still always nice and still I stole his beers."

"It was brave of you to tell him."

"It was fucking stupid."

"I'm so stupid," I say.

"No it wasn't," Christina says. "It was really brave. And kind. You made a mistake. *Other people* make mistakes too, but they don't take responsibility like you did."

"Oh fuck, Chris. Really working that in there."

Her words feel good when her hand's on my shoulder, but I know that feeling can't last. And then I'll slide back into the acid of my stomach. But her hand is still holding me and my breathing goes back to normal.

It stays even when Christina leaves for work and Tommy'll barely talk, until Shane comes over. Then Dan and Bert. Then Sven. It's not quiet anymore, but the noise is all happening outside of me. Everything is happening outside of me. Except thinking about Peter crying, and fighting with Amy. And the pain in my hand starts to feel worse, throbbing. It's there all the time now, but I normally don't think about it. The liquid is thick, almost like mud on the bank of a river. I squeeze my hand and wish it would go away. Wish everything would wash away and just be normal again but it's not working. Now it's just pain on pain. There's no transformation, no protective barrier. It's just me, here, in inescapable anguish.

"What're we doing tonight?" Shane says.

"Tim's having another party," Tommy says.

The word party bounces around my head like I have to catch it.

"Tim's again," Shane says, rolling his eyes like he's rolling them at me. "Super cool."

"What time?" Bert asks.

"Doesn't matter, let's start now." Tommy gets the two bottles of whiskey from his bedroom then grabs a two-liter of soda from the fridge.

"You alright, big dog?" Shane asks.

I shake my head.

"Tell them what's wrong." Tommy's voice fills the apartment as he pours himself a drink. "You've been talking about it all fucking day. Why won't you tell them now?"

"It's nothing," I say but I know that'll only make it worse.

"This guy," Tommy points to me with his cup, "fucking told the kid's dad that he stole all the beers. And then he came here to *cry* about it."

"Why the hell did you do that?" Sven yells loud enough that no one says anything for forever after.

"Well, dude. I'm not sure that was the smartest move," Shane pats me on the shoulder as he walks to the kitchen to make a drink. "I mean, especially considering *you* didn't take the beer. But, mucho respect for unnecessarily taking the heat off the rest of us."

"And you cried?" Sven says.

"And he was saying…"

"Shut up!" I cut Tommy off.

It's bad enough that he told them I cried. I don't want him saying the same about Peter.

"What did you say?" Tommy says and his voice feels louder when everyone else goes silent.

"Why do you have to talk about this?" I say.

"It's important they know you were being a little bitch."

"So," I say and my heart is pounding, "now they know."

"Whip your dicks out already and we can get this over with," Shane says.

Bert and Dan laugh, but stop quickly. Tommy and Sven aren't laughing.

"Jesus Christ, guys," Shane says. It doesn't sound like him. "Let's try to have a good time."

Tommy's staring at me. Sven's staring at me too. He's always been taller than me but until now I'd felt bigger. I'm not. Tommy walks over and pokes me hard in the chest. I try to stand my ground but I take a step back. The spot is like a button to make me shrink and let everyone know that I'm just a little kid. I wish feeling this small meant I could at least hide, but now it feels like everyone's eyes are on me.

"I am having a good time. Let's just fucking drink," Tommy says and goes to the couch.

"Hopefully this party doesn't get busted up."

"Shut up, Bert," Tommy says.

"It will. Just hope you don't get busted," Shane says.

I don't want to go to a party. I want to go home. I want to lay in the backyard with Daisy. I want Dad to bring out his Super Duper Popcorn, which is just the normal microwave stuff with chocolate chips, and Mom could make lemonade. But that home doesn't exist anymore, and I have to go to the party cause I'm supposed to invite Tiffany. That should feel good but I start thinking about her dad again and I get nervous and angry. I cried in front of Tommy Pescadero, all cause her dad cried. I wish he hadn't. Or I wish I hadn't said I was sorry, or said anything at all. Then maybe everything could just go back to normal. At least, if I hang out at the party with Tiffany we can drink and I can stop worrying about her dad. Just stop thinking.

"Tommy, can I use the phone?" I ask.

"No."

"Why not?"

"Why do you want to use it?"

"I gotta call someone."

"No shit, kid. Who?"

"Never mind," I say, and a numb feeling spreads over me. It's probably better to go there anyway. That way I might be able to avoid talking to Derek or his dad first. I get off the couch and make myself a drink. I don't have to go right away and the drink will help when I do.

What's cold in my mouth warms as it crawls down my throat and into my stomach. It makes everything feel better. Sven's feet sound like band-aids being pulled as he walks barefoot across the kitchen. He pours himself another drink.

"I can't believe you told Derek's dad," Sven says.

"What the fuck does it matter to you?" I snap back.

"Well," and his smile disappears, "it does."

"Killer comeback, Steve," Shane says from the couch and raises his cup overhead.

Sven blushes and his lips tighten. His eyes sink and he picks his cup up and walks to the living room where he sits on the floor against the wall. I wish I hadn't done that. I hate when he looks sad like this, like the life has gone out of him. But then everything settles after we've had a drink. The house starts to feel louder even though no one turned up the volume. I start to feel the vibration through my arms and into my hands. Shane's drumming on his knees. His hands bash an invisible pattern onto his red jeans. I try to lose myself in it. "This is what we should sound like," Tommy says about their band as a Taken song plays, and I think he's right.

"Anything you say, Tom," Shane looks up quickly, then his head drops back.

"Yeah, it'd be rad if this was us," Bert says.

"This is totally the tone your guitar should have."

"I'll get on it immediately," Shane says, but doesn't look up this time.

The songs switch and the new one sounds familiar, but I don't ask what it is cause Tommy would laugh that I don't know for sure. I'll try to ask Shane later. The tracks roll along and Tommy picks out a part for Dan to work on, then Shane, then Bert, then Shane again. Drinks are poured and the hum of alcohol and music are in perfect harmony.

Shane is the only one that asks where I'm going when I leave but I just tell him I'll be back later. For the first time it feels good to leave Tommy's. But the ride to Tiffany's house still feels longer than normal. I try not to dodge the thoughts that are there, but I worry about who's gonna be at the house and what I'll have to do.

I ride by and see Peter and Amy in the kitchen. He's sitting at the table and she's standing. Video game gunfire shoots out from Derek's window. I keep going to the end of their block and stand over my bike. My throat burns but I go back and open the side gate as quietly as possible. Tiffany's room is in the back of the house, above the pool, where we all used to jump from until Derek slipped and broke his leg on the bricks.

I jump and grab the top of the wall, dangling for a second before I can use my feet to walk up the side. The edge rubs my forearms raw. And my hand feels like it's on fire. The fresh pain feels better.

I stand on the wall, my toes hanging over the edge, and jump to the roof. It crunches when I land, then gets softer with each step. The blinds are closed and covered in dust behind Tiffany's window. I tap lightly but the sound of my knuckle on glass makes me cringe. Nothing happens. My arms and stomach are burning. I can't feel myself move, but the roof below me is still crunching. I knock again, a little harder this time.

Still nothing.

There's a gap; it isn't locked. The glass is warm from the day's sun. The window slides open slowly with a sound like air coming out of the oven. There's room enough to crawl through, but I wait to see if she'll come first. She must be gone. I'm already here and I have to try and invite her. I'll write a note. So I push the blinds with my foot. A sprinkling of dust falls and the plastic slats chatter. It's low enough that I hop down, but the ground's not where it's supposed to be and I land on my shoulder hard enough that I think I'll bust through to the floor.

"Jesus Christ!" Tiffany yells as she twists up from her bed and rips off her headphones.

She's upside-down. Dust pours onto my face. My shoulder throbs.

"Everything ok, kids?" Peter yells from downstairs.

Tiffany has her hand on her chest. Her eyes are slowly narrowing to normal. I sit up. She smiles. My arms and shoulders and stomach hurt less when she does. But not my hand. I squeeze it and grit my teeth. I don't want the haze of pain now. I want to live in her smile.

"Yeah," Derek yells just louder than the game.

"Everything's fine!" Tiffany yells.

"Hi," I say.

"What are you doing here?" Her voice is quiet and low and it makes me realize how close we are. My mouth is dry. I look down and see that my arms are cut up but I can't feel that.

"I tried to knock, but you didn't hear," I say.

"I had my headphones—why'd you crash through the window?"

"I didn't think I was gonna crash."

She laughs into her hand. "What are you doing here?"

"There's a party tonight. I was going to leave a note cause I didn't think you were home."

"Oh," she almost smiles. "You should've called."

"I know," I say, my face on fire. "I didn't want to, though."

"Well, why didn't you knock on the door?"

"I didn't want your dad or Derek to see me," and I stop cause I don't want to talk about it, but I can see that it's coming anyway.

"I heard you told dad about the beer."

I have to breathe to calm my stomach.

"How'd you hear that?"

"Why did you tell him it was you?"

"It was my fault."

"He said he was going to have to talk to you. He and mom were laughing about it."

Still trying to breathe. My eyes burn. She can tell too cause she starts to laugh.

"No," she says, "it wasn't in a bad way."

All I can think about is her dad. Of course he's not mad. He must have known I would do something like this the entire time. He's been preparing for this moment since I convinced Derek and Tiffany to climb onto the roof and jump into the pool. He didn't like it even before Derek hurt himself. She scoots forward to the edge of the bed and nudges me with her foot.

"Derek is pissed," she says and rolls her eyes.

A cool wave washes through me when I think about the spot where her foot touched me, and it's like a button too, but now I'm bigger than ever before.

"Let him be," I say.

Derek's always pissed, even when I didn't do anything to him. I wonder what it's like to be his sister. To always be around him.

"The party's at Tim's."

"Who's going?"

"All of us."

"So, Tommy and everybody else?"

"Yeah."

Footsteps thump up the stairs.

"Hey Tiff!" her dad calls out.

"I'll see you there," I say.

"Ok, cool."

I duck under the blinds and climb through the window. My chest is pounding and head is dizzy as I crawl and crunch along the roof until I hear her door open, freezing at her dad's fuzzy voice. The roof is hot on my hands. I can see the trees of my backyard; it looks nice from here.

The voice disappears and the door clicks closed and I run to the edge and jump to the wall. I avoid scratching my arms as I lower myself down then drop the last couple feet. The shock runs into my knees but I grab my bike and click open the gate, which slams shut as I jump on and pedal as hard as I can. When I turn the corner, my breathing is heavy and relaxed.

It's still grey out but now it's hot, so I cruise back to Tommy's where they're all hanging out in the kitchen listening to an On the Might of Princes album that Shane says is flawless cause everything is arranged to perfection and I can feel it. Dan smiles the whole way through and then Shane plays it again. The house smells sweet and skunky, which I never imagined could be a good thing. Thinking about smoking makes me smile and Tommy makes fun of me for that, but it doesn't bother me. It's the most simple, easy moment I can remember. They don't have any more weed, though, so I start drinking again and that electric hum comes back into my arms and chest.

"Where'd you go?" Sven says.

"To see this girl."

He doesn't say anything after that and no one else seems to care that I was gone. I have another drink before we leave. Sven and I ride our bikes and Tommy skates with us like usual. It's the perfect temperature for a summer night. The clouds are gone and you can kind of see the stars cause there's no moon, which was Dad's favorite. *Not even the moon's watching tonight*, he'd say, which I didn't get when I was a kid.

This party's bigger than the last. We can barely open the door, there are so many people. Tommy disappears almost immediately. Sven stays close to me. We go to the kitchen where they have drinks and I get two beers. Nicky Severino's older brother watches me take them and I watch him in the polished glass cabinet as I leave the room. It's baking in the house, but no one's allowed outside cause they think that's why the cops came. I don't think it's going to help; the house was buzzing from a block away.

Sven and I find Tommy in the garage. It's full of people I thought I'd only ever hear about from Sven's brother. There's Sean Bartlett, Silvia, Amy Bryan, Sandra Browning, Darius White and a bunch of others. People that'll be our schoolmates next year, which is wild. I wonder why they're here, or why we're here, but I try to act like we belong.

Tommy shakes James Smalling's hand and hands him something. They look strange side by side. Tommy is muscular and tall and intimidating, but he looks tiny compared to James, who's the varsity quarterback and Shannon's boyfriend.

"Sup, young'uns?" he says.

"Nothin'," I say.

"It's cool, they're with me," Tommy says, which blows my mind a little, especially to hear him say it in front of someone like James Smalling. But it doesn't feel as safe as it normally does.

"Word. You guys lookin' for something?" His hands are in the pockets of his baggy pants, and when he shakes his right hand it rattles.

"What is it?"

"Oxys."

"What does it do?"

"Damn, kid. You got a lotta questions," he laughs and smiles and looks like one of the guys from the posters on Tiffany's wall. "It makes you feel like nothing, but like, in the best way."

I look to Tommy. He shrugs and smiles and pops a pill in his mouth and throws his head back to swallow. Then he takes a drink to wash it down. Maybe it's good if Tommy and James do it, but it doesn't sound good to me. I always hated going to the doctor and swallowing pills that feel like they get lodged in the back of your throat forever.

"Ok," Sven says.

"Are they bad?"

"Everything is bad for you," Tommy says.

"Nah, the fucking coaches give 'em to us all the time. Can't be that bad then. So? They're five a pop," he says, and smiles like he knows I'm gonna say yes. Like I'd be an idiot to say no.

But I shake my head even though I have so much money saved up from not having to pay for food that five dollars would be like nothing. Even though Tommy's doing it. Even though James Smalling's looking at me like I'm crazy, but just the thought of the pill makes me gag.

"Word. If you ever get curious," he says and turns to Sven. "How many?"

He's half-looking at the ground, but it's still crazy to see Sven talking to James Smalling. He gives him the money and James gives him some pills and a high five. Before the summer started, he would've curled up into a ball if James Smalling even looked at him. Now they're actually talking, mostly James, but some Sven too. While they do, Tommy wraps his arm around my shoulder.

"You scared?"

"No."

"Don't bullshit me, kid."

"I'm not; I just hate pills," I say too loud. James heard, but he just laughs some more.

"Wow," Tommy says as he shakes his head. "Let's go back in the house."

The noise and the heat explode out when Tommy opens the door inside. All the energy makes my heart pump, makes my smile widen. Shane is at the entry talking to a girl. She's skinny and pretty with big brown eyes and long black hair that's dyed blonde at the ends. He's not looking at her anymore, instead cocking his head at us, or maybe just me, rolling his eyes so I know he thinks we're being dumb, but he's smiling too so it doesn't feel bad. He taps the girl on the arm and walks over to us. She looks confused as she watches him walk away.

"What're you guys doin'?" he says in a fake dorky voice, but not like Derek's.

"Getting over this party," Tommy says.

"And how are you, boys?"

"Good," Sven and I say.

"Good boys."

The front door opens and a wave of cool air ripples through the party. Everyone gets a little quieter. Shannon and Tiffany step inside. They're coming straight toward us. Tiffany's arms are folded over the black shirt that her mom gave her for her birthday. She's behind Shannon, who the whole room is watching. She's wearing short white shorts, a baby blue shirt and looks like she fits in perfectly everywhere she goes.

"What's up, Hot Pants?" she says to me.

I blush and look to see if Tiffany is going to roll her eyes again, but she doesn't. She won't even look at me. Her eyes look less colorful cause of all the makeup around them. But she's still beautiful. I say hi to her, so does Shane, just to be weird. Then Shannon starts tapping her foot.

"Aren't you gonna introduce us to your friends?" Shannon says.

I do, even to Sven cause I don't know if she knows his name. I call him Steve, though. Tommy grins and Shane smirks when I introduce them. Tiffany shrinks a little. It's like everyone is reacting to something different but I don't understand. Then Tommy says hi to Tiffany. She nods and smiles, bright but it's just a flash before it's gone and she won't look at anyone anymore.

"Can I get you a drink, Tiffany?" I ask.

"Um…"

"God, Tiff. Just have a drink," Shannon says.

"Ok."

"I'll take one too, Hot Pants."

It's hard dodging bodies on the way to the kitchen. I try to hurry cause I want to get them their drinks, and cause I just want to be near them. I want to hear what Tiffany has to say. I want to see her smile and feel the warmth of her laugh. But people are getting more oblivious. They're crashing into me and everyone around them. It's fun bouncing around the party even though I'm trying to hurry. The noise of a million conversations makes my head shake and I smile. The kitchen is crowded but I make it to the beers eventually and get three, one for me, Tiffany and Shannon.

"Hey!" a voice reaches out from behind like two hands on my shoulders. I turn around and see Nicky Severino's brother down the aisle that people have made for him. "What're you doing?"

"Getting drinks."

"Who said you could take those beers?"

"I thought this was a party."

The bigger I smile the angrier he looks, but I won't stop.

"Aren't you a fucking smartass?"

The conversations in the kitchen all die. His voice fills the void. His brother once pushed me off the jungle gym while I was hanging upside down. I hit him in the face with a rock and he had to go home cause I broke his tooth. I wonder if he knows that. I wish I had a rock.

"I was bringing these to my friends."

My voice is quieter than it's supposed to be. He's standing above me now. He's twice the size of his brother and his eyes are perfectly blue and clear and I can see that he's going to try to kill me. Let him try, I think. Shannon walks into the kitchen, she's watching from behind him. Maybe she's going to stop it. His arm moves back. I squeeze the beers. The arm moves forward; a meteor is coming. My head is an explosion. Everything flashing clear. I'm lying on the floor. The ceiling dances around. The cans scatter onto the tile. One spins, shooting out a stream of beer. My face, everything, throbs.

"What the fuck, Bobby?" Shannon says.

"Oh, uh, hi, Shannon."

I put my hand on my face. There's no crater, but when I pull back it's covered in blood.

"You ok?" Shannon asks me.

"Yeah," I say for her.

"Good. Pick up those beers." She turns like a whip to Nicky Severino's brother. "God you're an idiot, Bobby. He was getting those for me."

The crowd murmurs, which builds back into the full rattle of conversation. My face is flush with heat but I feel ok walking behind Shannon. People part in front of her long, tan legs as she struts through. Or maybe they get out of the way because I'm covered in blood. Tommy's gone when we get back. I hand Shannon and Tiffany their drinks. Mine was the one that spilled out all over the kitchen.

"Oh my god, are you ok?" Tiffany says and her eyes get big. All their green is back.

"Yeah," I say like my lips are glued together.

"Jesus, dude, what happened?" Shane says.

He puts a hand on my shoulder and another to my face. He does it gently but when he touches me it hurts like crazy. He shows me the blood on his thumb before he rubs it off on the back of his hand. The radiating is going through my body now. I feel shaky.

"Fucking Bobby Severino punched him." Shannon says and takes a drink. "Guys like that, right?"

"Isn't your boyfriend a 'guy like that'?"

"No, Shane. He isn't."

"No? He's here tonight, think he was selling magazine subscriptions or something in the garage. Have you had a chance to connect with him?"

"You're so annoying, Shane."

It's like they know each other already. Shane takes a drink, shaking his head. He goes to the kitchen and gets me a beer, then wraps a napkin around the can and puts it under my nose. It's a cold, sharp pain and I watch the red of the blood overtake the white of the cloth.

"That's a good look for you," he says.

It hurts to smile.

Tiffany is closer now. Her lips are brighter than normal, the shadows darker. A silver necklace hangs from her neck, touching right above where the shirt cuts away, and her skin is glowing.

"Something you want to say to Tiffany, Hot Pants?"

I'm burning as Tiffany turns to me. Pain dissolving in embarrassment. We look at each other in the eye for a second, a long second. I turn away, and out of the corner of my eye I can see she does the same. Shane, Shannon and Sven laugh.

"No," I say.

I take the beer off my face and take a drink big enough that it hurts to swallow. I walk back to the kitchen to grab another napkin and Bobby Severino is sitting in the corner. He watches me with a look like I punched *him* in the face. I fold the napkin and hold it to my nose. There's less blood now. I add him to my list of people to punch when I get older, just below Brad.

"Where'd Tommy go?" Shannon asks when I get back.

"Upstairs," Tiffany says softly.

"I'm gonna see what's going on up there."

"Let us know if you find anything fun," Shane says, chuckling. He has different jokes than anyone else. "Risky business," he mutters.

Shannon walks away, up the stairs, above a sea of eyes that move with her. Tiffany watches her too without following. She's still looking, even after Shannon is out of sight.

"Are you sure you're ok?" she asks.

"I'm fine," but my face stings and my insides feel like they're getting smashed.

"Are you having a good time, Tiff?" Sven asks.

"Yeah."

"How could she not?" Shane says. It's another one of his jokes, but I think I get this one.

Tiffany looks normal again, or whatever normal has been for a long time. It's weird the way people aren't always the same person. I finish my beer and Bobby Severino watches, but doesn't hassle me when I get three more. One for me, Shane and Sven. Tiffany has barely touched hers. I want to tell her that she'll have more fun if she drinks it, but I don't. The more I drink the less I hurt.

It's getting too hot inside. There have been too many people here for too long with the windows and doors closed. It'd be better to have the cops come than to let this place get any stuffier. I want to get outside. It's the perfect night. The new moon. I wish I could walk out into the darkness and have Tiffany follow me. I wish we could walk all the way home. To her house and have it be ours. We could lay on the ground with our feet in the pool and look up at the nothingness in the sky and have everything be perfect.

Before I can walk out, Tommy and Shannon are walking down the stairs. Sven and Tiffany and everyone are watching her, except Shane. He's looking at me with raised eyebrows.

"What the fuck happened to you?" Tommy says.

"Bobby Severino punched him in the face," Sven says.

"What the fuck did you do?"

"Nothing," I say.

"I'd guess you were being a little punk. That's rad."

"Let's get outta here," I say.

Tommy looks around and nods.

"Tiff, you guys could come hang out with us. We'll ride slow."

"Maybe," she says.

Shannon smiles at Tommy, "That's right, you don't have a car."

"Uneven distribution of wealth shouldn't be blamed on those too young to work."

"I thought you had a job."

"*Had* a job," Tommy says and nods.

"Well, I'm curious what you delinquents do over there," Shannon says. "Don't worry about riding slow, Hot Pants, I'll drive my car."

"I'll ride with y'all," Tommy says. "Make sure you remember how to get there."

Then it clicks that she's been there before. Tiffany knew where Tommy's was before we did cause Shannon had told her.

Tommy's headed for the door. Everyone follows him outside, under the new moon. I follow too, into the blast of cool air where Bert and Dan appear out of nowhere.

Sven and I ride, in the cool of the night and it's almost as good as being alone cause he doesn't say anything. Everyone's already there when we show up. We drink whiskey. The music is loud, but it doesn't get trapped in the house. It's radio stuff that we'd normally never play.

The conversations and body heat float out the doors and windows, and the cool air feels good at four in the morning when Sven's snoring on the ground. Tommy and Shannon disappeared. Shane, Dan, and Bert went home. I realize that I never called Mom to let her know where I'd be. But it's too late now. She's going to be mad anyway, so let her. And now, it's just me and Tiffany on the couch and I can't stop smiling. I don't want to walk away from her. The light barely squeezes through the dusty mesh in the corner of the screen door. It makes her face shine.

I lick my lip and feel the soft open cut. The pain is a pleasant shock that I swallow, my throat is warm from whiskey, which I've barely been drinking cause I keep getting distracted having Tiffany here.

"You guys really do this all the time?"

"Pretty much. I wish you would've been here more."

"Me too, though I'm not sure about your music choice."

"Tommy picked that cause we were gonna have mixed company."

"So when it's just the dudes, you listen to dude music?"

"I guess," I say with a grimace. "I'll show you something I like."

"Ok."

I walk to the CD player and put on the Mineral album that Shane just showed me, *EndSerenading*, cause it's too late to play anything heavier. But listening to it with Tiffany is way different than listening alone. My stomach is in knots. My hands start to shake. The music fills in and she's staring off at nothing and I don't think I can breathe anymore, until she turns and smiles with her eyes glimmering.

"I like it," she says.

"I'll make you a copy," I half-yell.

She laughs. And then it's quiet, but comfortable, and we just let the music play. She lays down and I do too. Her hand is so close to mine that it hurts not to touch.

"Did you have fun tonight?" I ask.

"I am now."

I look over and her eyes are sparkling in the light coming through the front door. I want to explode. I want to tell her she's amazing. I understand now how Daisy felt when she was a puppy and she'd get so excited that she'd throw up. I haven't thrown up yet.

Then the door from Tommy's room opens and he and Shannon walk out.

"What is this shit?" Shannon says.

We don't answer. The sparkle in Tiffany's eyes goes out.

"You ready to go?" Shannon asks.

All I want is for Tiffany to say no. But she stands without looking at me.

"Sure," she says.

"Good," Shannon says. "It was a fun time, boys. I'm not sure when we'll be able to do it again."

"You know how to find us," Tommy says.

I can still feel the energy from Tiffany's hand so close to mine as I watch them leave and it's like I'm tearing in two. Tommy nudges me on the shoulder and tells me it's time to sleep, but I can't. I just lay until the album is finished and then in the quiet after, I think about Tiffany.

10

IT'S COLD AND I have to clench my stomach to stop from throwing up again when Tommy shakes me awake. He's bent over me, eyes cracked and sleepy, but he looks scared. He rips a blanket off Sven, who's still in his jeans and shirt. I think he'd be hot but he must be used to it. The blanket whips into the mess of cups on the coffee table. Whiskey and coke pool and trickle onto the ground. Tommy shouts. He's saying something but my head feels like it's in a washing machine. Sven stands up.

I finally understand.

"Get the fuck out!" Tommy yells.

Sven's behind me when we rush out the door. We brush past Tommy's dad, whose tan skin and sunken brown eyes look like Tommy's but more confused at first, then angrier. He mutters something and I think about the mayonnaise in the back of his car but I can't laugh right now. We race away straight into the sun that's just coming over the apartments.

I slow down when we're at a safe distance and now I remember that I have to go home. That Mom might be waiting on the couch where she slept, ready to yell at me. It's almost enough to make me want to follow Sven into his house.

But when I get home, Mom's not on the couch and there are no pillows or blankets, not even an indent to show she slept there waiting for me. It's weirdly disappointing. My anxiety is vacuumed up and I feel empty. I can't hear her in the kitchen or anywhere in our tiny house. She she doesn't call out for me and I wonder if she forgot to be mad at me for not coming home, for not calling. Not that I want her to be mad, but I don't want nothing either.

My steps in the hall echo the emptiness. I used to want to be in the house alone when Mom and Dad's relationship was ending. I'd ask if I could stay when they were doing something I didn't want to do. Like going to visit Grandma in the hospital. They never let me.

I don't remember what it was she was dying from, but I remember the smell. It was like digging for worms in the community swimming pool. And she was connected to all kinds of tubes. She couldn't really talk, so we'd just talk at her. I could never think of anything good to say, so I'd just tell her about my baseball games, which made me never want to play again. And Mom and Dad would usually fight after. He didn't want to go either.

A lot has changed in the years between. I've changed. But even though I feel so different, I still just feel like me. Except now I don't want to be in the house alone.

Daisy jumps up on me as I step outside. I feel guilty that she's this excited to see me and I want to leave, so I pet her. The scratch of her fur makes my hand sizzle, but eventually she settles down. Still she follows me to the corner and looks at me like she thinks I'm never coming back when I climb the wall into the Thompsons'.

When I get to the corner, I pull myself up the wall, stopping when I can just see over. Tiffany is at the far end of the pool, sunbathing with her headphones on. Her bikini top is dark purple and the straps are pulled to the side enough that I can see the strip of pale skin that isn't normally in the sun. My heart pounds.

Derek is in the kitchen making a snack but I don't want to see him. I only want to be with her. I lower myself back down. If I hop into the Wrights' yard, he won't see me and I can walk alongside their wall until I get to Tiffany. They don't like me, though. Once, when Dad and I lost a baseball in their backyard, I went and asked them for it. Dad told me, *they can't get mad at a kid*. But they screamed at me and didn't give me the ball back. He laughed when I told him, saying they were being ridiculous. I laughed too, even though it was scary.

It's still scary thinking about them, but I hop into their yard anyway. I just breathe and tell myself I'm ok, which helps even if I don't believe it. Even when my lungs feel like they're filled with dry grass and I see the Wrights, sitting on their couch and watching TV. They're smoking too. It looks way less cool cause they're old and wrinkled and mean-looking, even from a distance. They don't see me as I walk along the wall, trying to blend in since there aren't any bushes back here. Everything is dead.

I don't want to scare Tiffany again, so I climb up and rest on my forearms.

"Hey," I say quietly. "Tiff."

She keeps bobbing her head to the music as the sun glimmers off the sprinkles of water on her legs and stomach.

"Tiffany," I say a little louder and she opens her eyes and looks toward the house. "Hey!"

She takes off her headphones and looks over, startled to see me. Her eyes are wide. Then a door slides open behind me.

"You! What are you doing back here?" Mrs. Wright yells.

She's running outside, cigarette still in one hand and her loose dress flapping around. I lose my breath between fear and laughter and I hop the wall.

"What are—" Tiffany tries to say.

I grab her hand and she gets up. We run to around the pool, to the living room door.

"You stay out of our yard!" Mrs. Wright screams.

I slide the door open and we sprint through the living room while Derek's still in the kitchen. We bound up the stairs and into Tiffany's room, slamming the door shut.

"What the hell was that?" she says with a smile.

But I can't stop laughing. I try to catch my breath and start coughing. My lungs sting. Spots float and pop around my eyes.

"Hello?" Tiffany says.

I try to focus, try to breathe but it hurts.

"I—" I say and cough and stop. "Sorry."

"You scared the shit out of me. Again," she says but she doesn't sound mad.

"I was trying to *not* scare you."

"You're not doing that good a job."

"I know that now. But it seemed like a good idea."

"To go into the Wrights'? They're awful. And they're always there. Just sitting on the couch waiting to yell at someone."

"Then I did them a favor," I say and she laughs. "What're you up to?"

"Now? I'm stuck in a room with you. I *was* relaxing by the pool, though."

She sits on the bed. One of her purple straps is still off to the side. My whole body feels warm.

"Are you doing anything later?"

"No plans."

"You're not hanging out with Shannon?"

She scrunches her face.

"I don't want to think about her right now."

Once she says that, last night is all I can think about. Sitting around listening to music with Tiffany, while everyone else slept, except Shannon and Tommy. They were up, together. And now I don't want to think about it either.

"You excited for school?" I blurt out.

"No," she says with a laugh. "I'm trying not to think about that, either. It's not even August yet."

"Almost," I say even though I knew it was stupid as I was saying it, but somehow that's never enough to stop me. "At least you're gonna be a junior. You can get lunch off campus now."

"Sure. But there's nothing good unless you have a car."

"Are you gonna get your license?"

"Of course. And hopefully a car, but every time I try to talk to my parents, they just change the subject."

"Well," I stop myself from mentioning Shannon. "Shane has a car. I bet you could ride with him until you get one."

"I have friends with cars," she says, her voice flat.

"Sure, but—"

"Are *you* excited for school?"

I wasn't before the summer started. I didn't want to be the youngest kid in school and get bullied by the older guys, like sixth grade all over again. But hanging out with Tommy and Shane, I think maybe I might enjoy the year.

"I guess, yeah. It can't be worse than middle school."

"I wouldn't be so sure," she says and I can't tell if she's joking.

"It's been cool hanging with Shane and Tommy."

She reaches over her head and pulls a pillow over her face. She groans into it and my heart sinks.

"Is everything ok?" I ask.

"What do you think?" she says, her voice muffled from the pillow.

"It might help if you use the pillow properly. It's supposed to go under your head."

She laughs, but when she pulls the pillow off her face, her eyes are red. I sit down next to her. The bed squishes and warmth still radiates from her body. It's hard to breathe.

"What do you think happened last night?" she asks.

"We had fun."

"Between Tommy and Shannon."

I can feel it, but I don't want to say anything. Like speaking it out loud it will make it real. And making it real would ruin everything. I can see Christina's soft smile and hear her soothing voice, and it's starting to slip away... away. She's going away.

"I don't know."

"You don't think they hooked up?"

"He's with Christina."

"I'm aware he's with Christina."

"So?"

"She's with James. And I told her—whatever. It doesn't matter. They hooked up."

It's real now. It makes my chest sting. But when I see tears silently sliding down Tiffany's face, it doesn't matter as much. I reach over and put my hand on her back. She's colder than I'd thought she'd be.

"It's ok."

"What? No it's not. They're both in relationships. And she made a promise."

"You're right. It's not—I just meant…" No good words will come out, like my mouth is full of peanut butter. "It sucks."

"It does suck."

"I don't know why he would do that."

"Because Shannon is, like, perfect and everyone in the whole school—in the whole world wants her. She gets, like, twenty-five-year-old guys that just buy her things."

That's closer to Mom and Dad's age than ours, which makes it feel a little gross.

"She can have anyone," Tiffany says and leans her head on my shoulder. "Why him?"

"I don't know. I wish I did. Maybe just to piss us off."

"Why are *you* mad?"

"I—It sucks that shitty things happen to people who don't deserve them."

"Seriously."

"Like, Christina is really cool. And she and Tommy were together."

"I know they're together."

"But now?"

"Are you gonna tell her?"

Just like that, I'm getting ripped in two all over again. Why does this happen to me? I don't want it to happen. I don't want to have to choose between them like Mom and Dad. But I'll get stuck in the middle and then I know I'll have to decide.

Brad's words echo in my head, *think about why your parents' relationship ended.* And I can feel it again. This is my fault, too. It didn't just happen that I'm stuck in the middle, I put myself there. I put Tommy and Christina against each other cause I invited Tiffany and

Shannon over. And I split Shannon and Tiffany apart cause I wanted to hang out with her alone.

I dig my thumb into my palm until the pain fills my body, but it stops in my throat. Choking me. There is no release from the thoughts and the pain just builds and I'm going to explode.

Tears start to fill my eyes. I can't escape the feeling of being ripped apart. Or the fact that I put myself there again, cause I ruin everything.

"What're you doing?" Tiffany says.

I press harder. But it won't wash away the thoughts.

"Hey," she says, louder now.

She grabs my hands. My body pulses without rhythm.

"What is that?"

"Nothing."

"It doesn't look good."

"I know."

"Come on, I'm gonna clean it."

She gets up and pulls me by the hands. My body feels weak, but I stand too. She opens the door and pauses at the video game sounds coming from Derek's bedroom, then pulls hard and runs lightly to the bathroom as I stumble behind. She shuts the door and starts running the tap water and pushes my hand under. The stinging is like nothing.

"Jesus," she says. "That's gross."

It's like the first time I've seen it. It's a dark hole at the center, with the soft brown scabs at the edge, then red veins that shoot out like sun rays. My portal to a better universe, now destroyed. It's magical, but hideous.

"Sorry," I say.

"It's ok."

She feels the water that's now heating up.

"Is that ok?"

"Yeah," I say, despite the burning.

She opens the cabinet and pulls out some bottles and a cloth. She dabs the scab off my hand and squirts an orange-red liquid onto my palm.

"I'm sorry. About last night. It was my fault. I just… I wanted to spend time with you and that meant that Tommy and Shannon were alone, but I couldn't think about that because you were there. And when I look at your—"

She puts her hand on my chest and it's like I rocketed into another dimension. She sets the cloth down. The water's still running but she's staring at me and I can't look at her or look away and everything is hyper-clear but unreal. I lean in and kiss her. Her lips are so soft that they don't hurt the cut on mine. Her breath is hot and sweet like a cinnamon roll. I rest my good hand on her hip and she presses herself against me. She pulls away and rests her head on my chest.

"You couldn't stop thinking about me?" she asks.

"You," is all I mutter as I stare at her hair draping down my chest.

Then there's a banging, and we both jump.

"What are you doing in there?" Derek yells. "I have to pee."

"Go downstairs!" she yells.

He bangs on the door harder.

"Get out!"

"Fine!" she yells then turns to me. "He's not gonna leave."

"I know."

"Who's in there?"

"Two seconds!"

She grabs the cloth and dabs at my hand a few more times, then dries it off and gives me a fresh band-aid and a kiss on the cheek and I'm on fire.

"Ready?" she says.

"Yes."

She opens the door and Derek's eyes flare like exploding stars behind his glasses.

"What the fuck are you doing here?"

"I hurt myself," I said.

"We both got hurt," Tiffany says.

"What?" His confusion turns back to anger. "What the fuck are you talking about?"

"Don't worry, Derek," Tiffany says. "We're ok now."

"What's he actually doing here?"

"Don't you have to pee?" she says.

Derek stares, waiting, but neither of us say anything, so he walks to the bathroom. Tiffany giggles and walks to her room. He slams the door shut and she hovers in the doorway with all the beauty in the solar system arranged in her smile.

"I'll see you later," she says.

I nod and she disappears.

The bathroom door clicks open behind me and she shuts hers. Derek shoulders his way past me without a word. I can feel my pulse everywhere, like my heart is overtaking my body. I can still feel Tiffany's lips and smell her coconut sunscreen as I walk down the stairs, and hop the walls back home and lie in bed. It's still just as real and surreal as it was minutes ago. It's hard to believe it happened. I kissed Tiffany. She kissed me. It warms my soul like the heat from a billion suns.

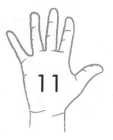

11

THE MUSIC EXPLODES through Tommy's apartment in a whirl
of chaos. I might melt. I could already barely contain myself. I wanted
to scream the second I walked in the door that Tiffany and I kissed.
That she wants to hang out again. That the world finally feels open and
wonderful and I never want this time to end. But, as much as it's bursting in me to get out, holding that rapidly expanding joy inside makes
me feel bigger and better. I want to hoard it like a dragon and its gold.

I wish she were here now. I don't want to wait. Missing Tiffany
makes it hard to breathe. It gives me the chills. I spent all day and night
listening to *EndSerenading* over and over. I tried to get Tommy to put
it on when I got here but he wouldn't. He wanted to listen to Taken,
some band Shane's coworkers told him about. It's good, but not where
my head's at.

"You ready to pick up some provisions?" Tommy asks, shaking the
sad last drops in a bottle of whiskey.

"Can't someone else go?"

I just want to stay here. With him gone I could put the album on.
Plus, I don't even need to drink. Thinking about Tiffany is enough.

"You fuckin' serious? Get up."

"He's pussin' out," Sven adds.

"Take Bert," I say.

"That seems inadvisable," Shane says.

"Fuck you, Shane," Bert responds.

"So you're gonna go?"

"No, but—nevermind."

"Get up," Tommy says, harder and flatter. His face is like stone.

"Fine," I say. "But I get to pick the music when we get back."

"This fuckin' guy," Shane laughs.

"Whatever," Tommy says and he's out the door.

They ride slow and I don't try to go faster than them. It should be easy but by the time they get there I'm coughing and wheezing and hacking up a green glob of grossness that I spit onto the asphalt of the grocery store parking lot. It looks like an alien turd.

"Get that shit out now. I don't want you hacking up when we go in there," Tommy says.

"I can go," Sven adds.

Tommy just rolls his eyes.

"I can!"

"Next time."

Sven's pissed as we stack the bikes and Tommy's board up along the wall. Tommy doesn't acknowledge him. I try to nod, but he doesn't see or care. So, I don't say anything, just follow Tommy inside.

The store is mostly empty. A couple clerks ringing up elderly couples. The baggers standing around more than bagging. I can't tell if the one that caught Sven is working cause I can't even remember what he looks like. I only see Sven's screaming face.

Now all I can hear is the clack of the cash register, the occasional whoosh of a bag being opened, and the squeak of our shoes as we walk down the aisle away from them. No one seemed to notice us, but I know they're on guard, trying to stop us. It makes Tommy mad, pushes him to do it more. It makes me sad. And it makes me feel guilty. I don't know if it's wrong to take the alcohol. Tommy has a point that if we can't buy it, we can't steal it. But I know now that there's someone whose job it is to stop us. I don't know what happens if he doesn't, but I bet it's not right.

Tommy doesn't pause or slow down when he reaches the end of the aisle, turning the corner to the alcohol.

"What're we doing?" I ask.

"Double up on whiskey. Fuck everything else."

He pulls the old grocery bags out from under his shirt, hands one to me and fills the other with the biggest bottle of whiskey on the shelf without slowing down. But I can't. It feels like I'm strapped into a rollercoaster that won't move. I know we're doing something wrong. It's unshakable. I can picture Peter here. No longer crying in the aisle, he just watches me knowingly. This is who I am. Who he knew I'd become. The bag crinkles in my hand and I breathe but the inhale of oxygen is like pins and needles. I start to cough and Tommy stops, spinning from halfway down the aisle and staring daggers at me.

I cover my mouth, trying to keep quiet. Tommy's power-walking back to me.

"What the fuck? Let's go," he says and stuffs a bottle of whiskey in my bag before dragging me by the arm.

My stomach drops out like the rollercoaster is plummeting. Spots fill my eyes. I try to blink them away, but they multiply to the point I can barely see straight. Tommy's a blur of black and white leading me. We hit our stride and I can feel my body taking over. It knows what to do to get out of here. But I hope we don't.

I hope someone yells for us to stop. I hope they throw down their empty bags and rush toward us and Tommy tries to run. I'll let them take me. Call the cops or call Mom, either way, whatever will let me stop.

But no one screams. No one yells. I can hear the clang of the register over the soft laughter after some old-man joke all the way to the door. And then we're outside and the door seals behind us. The sun is bright and hot. Sven doesn't cheer and Tommy doesn't congratulate me.

The spots in my eyes clear and I can see as we ride back to Tommy's. But it's still hard to breathe.

Tommy doesn't let me pick the music when we get back. There's something else he wants to listen to, so I sit quietly on the couch. Sven makes drinks, which I take even though I don't want it, and I set it between the old cups and scattered laundry on the coffee table. I try not to think about the store, about Peter. My insides feel like a stuffed animal that Daisy tears apart until I start thinking of Tiffany and I can close my eyes and she's there.

Her eyes shimmering. The smell of coconut. The taste of sweet cinnamon. It's real, and it sends goosebumps over my whole body to know that I get to see her again at the party. And it doesn't matter what music we're listening to, or what I did, and I don't need to drink to be happy because it feels like she's cupping my heart in her warm hands.

Then the screen door squeaks and I open my eyes. Christina walks in and she smiles and waves and sits next to me, while pulling her hair out of the ponytail she wears for work. The warmth evaporates.

Shannon is coming tonight, too.

"How's your drink?" she asks.

I see the layer of water from the melted ice that floats at the top.

"Good."

"You alright?"

"Of course."

I can see Tommy and Shannon walking out of their room the other night, sly smiles now shattering my heart. I can't imagine how Christina is going to feel. I can't think of anything good to say, or anything at all.

"You sure? Something seems off," she says.

"What're you sitting with him for?" Tommy asks as he walks back from the kitchen with a fresh drink.

"Just weighing my options."

She's joking. I can tell from the tone in her voice, light and easy. But it feels like a paper cut in my ears.

"Come sit by me."

"Maybe."

"I don't trust the kid."

I want to go back. To get out of here. I try to breathe but the coughing takes over. I cover my mouth, but seeing my hand makes it worse. Christina pats my back like she's putting out a fire, but she can't. I'm burning up.

I nod and take a drink but the alcohol dries my throat out even more. The cough sticks in my chest. Christina gets up and sits on

Tommy's lap. They smile and laugh. It looks perfect, the way it's supposed to. But nothing is ever the way it's supposed to be. And I should say something but I can't or don't. I'm trapped inside myself.

It's different than not standing up to Brad, but the cowardice burns the same. I start to push the bb but the pain only doubles, no more disappearing, so I stop. Every part of me is immersed in agony until Tommy decides it's time to leave.

My drink is half full, half water. I leave it even though Tommy will yell at me about fallen soldiers.

Being outside helps. There's space to escape and start thinking about Tiffany again. I try to forget the rest as we ride, but it comes in waves. I struggle to keep up with Sven, Tommy and Christina, who's sitting cross-legged, riding on the front of Tommy's board. I'm gasping and sweating by the time we get to Tim's where Tommy hands me a beer. I hold the cold can against my forehead. Shivers run down my body.

"You gonna drink it?" Tommy says.

"Yeah."

I pop the can and take a sip. Tommy turns away, scanning the room.

"You sure you're ok?" Christina asks.

"I'm fine," I say, but my throat feels dry. All of me is on fire.

Tommy turns back to us.

"Fucking drink up."

"Tom, what do you care if he drinks or not?"

"I don't."

"Then leave him be."

The door opens. Tiffany walks through, eyes sparkling as she looks directly at me and smiles. My face beams like a solar flare. My heart bursts like a rocket. She walks towards us. Towards me. Shannon follows behind her.

"Whatever," Tommy says and walks off, up the stairs.

Christina watches him but doesn't follow. Tiffany and Shannon approach and I sense the impending disaster. But I'm too confused and excited to stop it.

"There you are," Tiffany says.

"Oh god, Tiff," Shannon mutters. "Hot Pants, will you get us drinks?"

"Sure."

"Don't go yet," Tiffany says.

Her cheeks are flushed like she's been laying out in the sun. I can feel her warmth.

"Ugh," Shannon groans.

"I can get you a drink," Christina says.

"No. That's ok, I'll get it myself," Shannon says. I'm happy not to think about her.

"I'm gonna step out for a sec," Christina says.

I think about telling her no, that she doesn't have to leave. But I don't. She heads quietly to the door outside, leaving Tiffany and I alone in the middle of the party, bodies shuffling around us. The joy of her presence is painful. I want to reach out and touch her, just to hold her hand and know that she's here and it's real. But it's like I'm being bear-hugged and shaken. Everything is a chaotic jumble. My mouth is dryer than dry and my hands are soaked with sweat.

"How've you been?" she asks.

It feels like she wants me to reach out, to grab her hand. Her eyes ask, but that can't be right. I know yesterday was real. I think I know she likes me. It makes sense that she would want to hold hands, or kiss, even. But I can't actually believe it.

"Alright, yeah."

"What've you guys been doing?"

"Not much."

There's a quiet between us that's like a scream. I need to do or say something. Anything. I need to reach out and grab her, hold her, kiss her. I need to tell her she's beautiful. That she's perfect.

"So, I guess no one told Christina yet?"

I shake my head. My head's a mess.

Tiffany smiles, waiting for me.

"Do you want a drink?"

"No, thanks."

There's a creak on the stairs and somehow over all the other noise I can know that it's Tommy. He hops down the last step and stands in front of us, hands tucked in his back pockets, muscles and veins running up his arms.

"You're here? Welcome."

"Thanks," Tiffany says.

"Where's Shannon?"

"She went to get a drink. And Christina stepped outside."

Tommy cocks his head for a second then grins. I think if it were me that said that he would've caved my face in.

"If the choice is between having another drink and leaving, I know where I stand."

"She probably just wanted fresh air," I say.

I wish we could leave now. I want to lay with Tiffany on the hot rocks of the desert under the crescent moon and see how her eyes change color, glowing in the darkness.

"She can have it," Tommy says.

He walks to the kitchen. Tiffany watches the whole way. It feels like I'm sinking. Tommy comes back with a beer and he shakes it with a smirk to say he's proving something. But I don't know what. When he pops the can the suds shoot out and he licks them off his hand.

The door opens and I want to turn and see Christina, so they can talk and hug and everything will look normal even if it's not. But it's James Smalling. And when he stands in the doorway it's like all the light and oxygen is sucked out of the room.

"Hey," he yells. "Fish boy!"

Tommy takes a sip of beer.

"Actually, Pescadero means fisher*man*," Tommy says.

James steps toward Tommy, who straightens up. He won't back down despite being half the size or in the wrong. I can see what's happening. I think Tiffany can too cause she grabs my hands and squeezes and the pain is a noose.

She pulls her hand away with a look of disgust. My heart thuds and rattles like a car with a flat tire.

"I heard you fucked my girl," James barks but it's sounds a million miles away.

Then Christina steps into the void of the door. I feel like disappearing.

"Do you really view a person as your property? Seems kinda fucked."

"Fuck you."

"Appreciate the invitation, but I'll pass."

"How 'bout I invite you to step outside?"

"No thanks, party's in here."

"I mean to fight. I'mma whoop your ass."

"Also, pass. As you know, I'm a lover not a fighter."

There's a waterfall of laughter. Christina walks back outside. Away. James Smalling steps forward. I try to breathe, try to calm my heart. No breath, no calm. I have to do something. Anything. I step forward. Try and stop it. But air that can't come out is pounding at my chest and the spots in my eyes fill into one blanket of fog and my legs won't hold me and no one—

12

THERE'S A BEEP and click and squeak of sneakers. It sounds like the grocery store. Maybe it's hell. I can't tell cause my eyes are blurry. Everything is a hazy white and my mouth is dry. I don't feel any pain. I try to move my fingers and I don't feel anything, even though their fuzzy forms are moving like a witch casting a spell over a cauldron.

Somewhere beyond the fog is a voice, familiar but different, comforting and frightening. "He's here, yes. No, he's *not* ok."

The voice pauses. My heart pulses. The beeping quickens.

Slowly, my fingers come into focus and I see the white sheets and thin blue gown that cover my body. I'm in a hospital bed and there are cables connecting me to the beeping machines. If I could feel anything it would feel like I was starting to sweat. I breathe and the air is just there, the mask fogging up as my sight clears.

"He could use his father," the voice says. "I could use *some* fucking help."

The voice is angry but mostly scared, and the fear sits heavier on my chest. The last thing I remember was Tiffany holding my hand and James Smalling going to beat up Tommy. I stepped forward. I want to think that I stopped it or that I stood in the way, at least. But I know I didn't. I collapsed before I could get there.

As the feeling comes back to my fingers, I touch my face to double-check. There's no fresh blood, no bandages save for the one on my palm that covers the bb hole. I have a hard time gripping the tape. Nothing feels or works the way it should. But I slowly peel the bandage back and look under at the orange liquid around the wound that makes it look like a black hole opened in the desert sky.

"Oh god, he's awake," the voice says.

I look up to Mom rushing toward me. Then she's next to the bed, head on my chest. Tears soaking through the thin gown. Hugs tugging at the cables attached to my arm. She lifts her head, her eyes are red and watery and exhausted but shining with joy and my eyes start to water too.

"Thank God. Thank God. Thank... fuck. Oh, you're safe. You're safe."

She squeezes my face and my mask slides over my chin as she kisses me on the forehead. I breathe. I can still breathe.

"How are you feeling? Are you doing alright? Are you in any pain?"

"I'm ok," I say.

"Thank you, thank you, thank you."

She leans back and exhales like she's blowing out birthday candles. She covers her mouth as she shakes her head and sobs. My stomach sinks cause it's strange to see her cry and know it's my fault. It always is.

"You're ok. You're ok," she pulls her hands away to smile through the tears.

"I think so."

She grabs my hand and holds it, palm up. It's like she loses herself in it. Maybe she can enjoy it now.

"What happened?"

"I fell off my bike."

"Is that really your story?"

"I..." I start, but I can't keep going. I feel tired and hollowed out. "No."

Mom brushes her fingertips over the cut on my lip. I don't feel anything, but a pain is still there, somewhere.

"I'm so thankful that you're ok, but what you're doing isn't fair."

"What's fair?"

It feels like someone else said it, but she won't stop looking at me so I glance down.

"What you're doing isn't right."

I squeeze my hand and don't feel a thing. Tears fill my eyes.

"Regardless of what we're going through, you can't do stuff like this. I love you and I care about you and to not have heard from you for days, only to get a call from the hospital telling me you were brought in by some boys that wouldn't give their names... To hear you had alcohol in your system and a cut that was so—to come here and spend all night worrying and crying and wondering if you're ok, is not fair."

She's crying harder. My throat tightens; it's happened too much recently. Her fingertips pressing into her arms go white. I squeeze my hands and swallow back my tears and start to get angry. I don't know why. Angry at myself. Angry at everything. That she's right that it's not right or fair but then nothing feels right now. Or fair, ever. And who's fault is that?

"You're too smart to act so dumb. I hate that I'm not around, but I shouldn't need to worry so much. Because I can't. I can't keep worrying like this and doing everything alone."

She's still so close, looking at my lip, the red in her eyes spreading. I want to tell her that she wouldn't have to do everything if Dad were still around. But he's not. He's not even here now.

"Ok." I just want this to be over with. I don't ever want to see anyone else cry again. I don't want to cry.

"I talked to Steven's parents."

"Ok."

"They told me that he got caught stealing alcohol at the grocery store."

"Ok."

"Do you know why I'm talking to you about this?"

"No."

"They said that you forced him to steal it."

"That's not true!"

"Of course, that's what I told them. I said that was crazy and that they don't get to blame my son for something their son did." Her cheeks get redder. She looks up into my eyes. "Maybe it was because

I was scared at the time, but I used some pretty strong language, language that I've since had to apologize for."

"I didn't make him steal anything!"

My face is hot. My heart is pumping. The monitor is beeping. Mom is looking at me and she won't look away.

"I called Derek's parents last night. I wanted to know if there was anything they knew. Do you know what his father told me?"

"I didn't make Sven steal anything."

That's the last thing I have.

She grabs my fingers and turns my hands up. She's staring at the bandage and then she pulls it back. Her expression unchanged.

"Jesus, fuck," she says and I almost laugh. "How long did you have this?"

"I don't know," I say, even though the whole day is perfectly clear. It was the first time I hung out with Tommy and Shane. My first beer. The last night that Brad stayed with us. But I don't want to bring that up. I don't want to say his name, or think about him, or tell her about how he came back to explain to me how everything is my fault.

"Fuckfuckfuck," she mutters to herself. "You know better than this!"

She yells so loud that the room loses sound. Then there's a squeak of shoes and a nurse sticks her head in the door.

"I see he's awake," the nurse says. "I'll get the doctor."

Mom smiles and nods and her eyes stare off into a distance beyond the hospital walls.

I cough when I try to breathe too deep cause I need to think. I need to know what to do or say. I want to do what's right, to tell Mom the truth. But I can't and I don't know why. The words are scattered in the back of my brain and won't come together. Then the doctor walks in.

He looks around Grandpa's age but he moves a little easier. Maybe it's just that I can't see the way his body works under the oversized white coat. He pats a clipboard with the heel of his hand and smiles.

"Our little Civil War veteran's awake!"

"Just a couple minutes ago," Mom says, getting off the bed and shakes his hand.

They both stand over me.

"Son, you got a staph inspection so bad some of the nurses took pictures."

The nurse in the corner holds back a laugh and steps out of the room.

"It was her, in case you couldn't tell," he says. "Which wouldn't surprise me considering you didn't realize your hand was about to fall off."

He puts his hand on my forehead. It's cool and rough.

"Still got a little fever, but you'll be alright. You're lucky, though."

"I know."

"No, you don't know. Son, that little hole in your hand," he wiggles his pointer finger. "How long have you had that?"

"Since…" They're just waiting for me to lie. Or admit I was stupid even though they already know.

"This is important," Mom says.

"You don't want to say, you don't have to," the doctor says. "I already know the answer is far too long."

"A couple months," I say. "At the start of summer."

"Oh boy," he says.

Mom covers her mouth and turns away.

"It was—it never really hurt. It felt kinda good."

More tears for Mom.

"Yeah?" the doctor says. "In what way?"

"Like a superpower. Like, I could disappear whenever I wanted."

"I was always a flight over invisibility guy," his voice softens. "But here's the deal, as with any superpower, there's a downside. You got to escape for a bit, but it was coming back. That cut got infected and the infection got so bad you got pneumonia. Luckily you're young and strong, otherwise it would've killed you."

The idea of death pours through my insides like lava.

"And you're not out of the woods yet. We're gonna give you some antibiotics that you'll need to take every day. Every *single* day. That sound doable?"

"Yes."

"I should hope so." He writes onto his clipboard then taps it with the back of the pen before pointing it at me. "Another thing, absolutely no alcohol."

"I—"

"Son, before you put up a fight, just know that we did a blood test. Plus, the way your buddies bumbled in here and dumped you was some helpful corroborating evidence. Stupid for them to be the ones to bring you, but at least they got you here."

"Who was it?" Mom asks.

"I don't know," I say and I really don't.

"Listen," the doctor interrupts. "Maybe this is important, maybe it's not, but the bb—that little thing that started this whole big thing—is still in your hand."

"What?" Mom says. "This was all from that stupid gun?"

"I don't know why people think it's a good idea to give kids these things."

He flips over my bandaged hand then grabs the other, guiding it to the back, just under the knuckle of the middle finger where there's a hard bump that I can push and move around.

"We could've taken it out, but it would've been much more intensive, way more costly, and, now that the infection has cleared up, wouldn't have been any safer. You'll just have that little node on your hand forever."

I feel the bb, rolling it over the bone in the back of my hand.

"That alright?" he asks. I wait for Mom to answer but they're both looking at me.

I nod.

"And you remember what I said about drinking while you're on antibiotics?"

"Don't," I say.

"Exactly. And you shouldn't really be doing it at all. Kill you in the long run. But, it'll kill you quicker if you drink now."

"Thank you, doctor," Mom says.

"Not a problem," he says and shakes her hand. He points at me, "You be good."

"Ok."

He walks out and a nurse walks in. She makes me go through a few tests, asks more questions, then tells us that we're free to leave and hands me my clothes in a plastic bag and I realize that some stranger saw me naked. It might be her. I blush, but she doesn't seem to notice or care that we're there. She checks something on the monitor then leaves.

"You ready to get home?" Mom asks.

"Yeah," I say, only knowing I'm ready to be out of here.

She steps out and closes the door for me to change, then we walk down the hall together. Fluorescent lights and nurses rushing around remind me of Grandma. It seemed faster then, and louder. Dad was here, though I know he didn't want to be.

Grandma died in the hospital. She was just there sleeping, then she was gone. It didn't seem real at first, even though that's what we were all expecting. I thought she would just wake back up and ask for more pistachio ice cream. But she never did. Mom kept holding onto her hand for a long time after Grandma died. The nurses worked around her. Mom wanted to be there for Grandma. She held her hand constantly, which Grandma said she liked cause they never did it enough when they were younger. She got weeks of hand-holds before she finally died. Mom cried the whole way home and for days after.

I thought that getting that old seemed scary. Spending your final weeks in the hospital was sad. But last night could've been my last, and I never would've known. That seems worse.

Dad says that when we die our energy goes out into the world, but I know I'm not ready for that.

Out the front door, across the parking lot is the bakery where Derek's mom buys the best strawberry pie. Its green sign hangs over the grey building. It's ugly, but knowing the pies are inside makes it look better. I'd miss the pies and Tiffany. Maybe even Derek. Definitely Shane and Tommy and Dad and Mom.

Mom's quiet on the drive back to the house. With the radio turned off, it's all the squeaking and peeling of the car tires on the road. She looks tired. She won't look at me, not even a glance. Her eyes stare straight ahead and I can't tell now if she's angry with me or just done.

When we get home, there are two open boxes on the doorstep. Inside are Derek's TV and N64 with controllers and games and a note that says, *Hope you feel better, idiot.*

"That's nice of them," Mom mutters.

She carries one box and I get the other, the pain returning to my hand. We drop them in my room. Mom hugs me and holds tight and I start to cry and it feels alright.

"I love you," she says.

"I love you, too."

"You scared the shit out of me."

I would laugh, but she's squeezing me so hard I have to work to breathe.

"I'm sorry."

She ruffles my hair before walking down the squeaky piano hallway to her room. And I'm all alone. And I could've died. I could be nothing but sad energy. I hate pills but I take the antibiotic the doctor gave me. It sticks in the back of my throat before going down. I have to take them every day for a month, which is basically the end of summer. It could've been worse. I could've died.

But the embarrassment of passing out at the party and having to be taken to a hospital, all because of a stupid bb, isn't too far behind.

13

DEREK'S BOXES SIT on the ground by my bed. It was cool for him to let me use his stuff, but I don't care about video games or TV now. All I can think about is Tiffany: her kiss, her smell, her grabbing my hand at the party and recoiling before I collapsed. I hope it didn't all fall apart. But it's been a couple days already and she hasn't come by, even though she has to know I'm home cause Derek brought the games over. I thought he might come, as well. Or Sven, but no one's here.

Mom's been checking in on me before and after work. She tells me I can go outside, that I'm not grounded so I don't have to just lay around listening to music, but that's all I want to do. Partly cause the only places I can think to go are Tiffany's and Tommy's. Both of those thoughts make my chest cave in. Tommy and everyone will just make fun of me for passing out. And Tiffany's—I can't think of a good reason not to go other than she hasn't come here. That she *should* come here first. And I'd look like even more of a loser if I showed up at her place now.

So Tommy's is the only real option, but I won't be able to drink there. And they'll make more fun of me for that, on top of passing out at the party.

I'd rather lay here and wait for Tiffany to show up. To walk in and tell me she misses me. We would lay in bed together, her coconut sunscreen forever scenting my sheets, while her head rests on my chest and our breaths sync to the opening track of *EndSerenading*, which just began again. And it's true that she might never know how much I love her. But I want to try to tell her. I will when she shows up. How long can I wait, though, I wonder, as the hallway floors creak and cut into the rhythm of the song. Then a soft, offbeat knock at the door and before I can answer it's opening.

"Hey, bud. We gotta get you outta the house," Mom says in a way that makes me sad and mad cause I can tell she feels sorry for me. "I have a plan—which you probably won't like—but it'll do something. You're comin' with me to work."

I want to tell her that I don't want to leave. That I can't leave. That if I'm not here when Tiffany shows up it could ruin everything. I want to tell her that I'm happy in here, just listening to my music. But before I can, she starts again.

"I get that you're freaked out. It freaked me out too. And I think it's good for you to focus on the fact that you almost—that, yeah. Because it'll help you take your medication and make better decisions. But you can't stay in here scared forever."

I sit up, shocked by the reminder. Surprised that I've hardly thought about it. But she's right. I almost died and I should be freaked out. I feel the bandage on my hand. The pain is back, even though I've been taking my pills. It's crazy that dissolving pain was me dying, that something so little could've almost killed me.

Still, all I really care about is Tiffany. But I don't want to tell Mom that.

"Anyway, we have about a half hour 'til we have to leave. That work?"

"Sure," I say.

Mom steps out with a tap on the doorframe and a smile. The hospital flashes in my head, with its smell of industrial strength cleaner and death. But I'm in my room now, with the hole in my hand that hasn't gotten smaller. And if I keep taking my pills, I'll stay alive. If I don't drink, I'll have more time with Tiffany.

I lay back down and close my eyes, my heart beating hard. I rest my hand on my chest and imagine the weight is Tiffany. And we're talking about classes next year, how we can see each other between periods. She'll come hang out with me and Shane and Tommy and Christina.

We'll walk home together and she'll know the best way to get back with places we can stop and kiss. In the middle of which, Mom walks in and I snap up.

"You ready?" she says.

"I guess."

"It won't be that bad," she shrugs. "I'll meet you at the car."

She leaves and I swing my feet off the bed. Tying my shoes is hard with the bandaged hand. The lace keeps slipping out from my fingers, so I just stuff them into the side. While I'm down, I see the scribbled out heart at the bottom of the dresser. The one that had Mom's initials with someone else's—*KJ*. The outline of the heart is still visible behind the pen marks. Who's KJ, I'm wondering when Mom honks the horn and I get up and walk outside, locking the door behind me. Mom taps the steering wheel and she looks like Mom, same as ever. But she was my age once. And she was in love enough to draw on the dresser even though Grandpa would've been pissed. She was in love before Dad, which makes my head buzz.

In the car, her same old music is playing—Echo & the Bunnymen, I think. Shane played it for me. Tommy made fun of him. She's been listening to this since forever, before Tommy, Shane or I were even alive.

"I'm glad you're comin' with me," she says.

"I didn't know I had a choice."

She smiles, then it's quiet. Her music fills the gaps. It's not as bad as I remember. Still, we've been in the car way too long before we finally pull into a strip mall that looks like all the other white boxes we passed along the way.

She grabs a rolled up black bundle from the back seat and we step out and walk to a door that says Mr. Q's, where a large man sits on a stool wearing a shirt with the same name. He's got a ponytail that puffs out the back and tattoos around his arms like the Grim Reaper's blades. Tommy says he's going to get a tattoo soon, which I think is awesome, but wouldn't look as tough as this guy's.

"What's goin' on, Cat?" he says, and opens the door. When he talks I see the shine on one of his teeth. It's made of gold.

"Got a friend today, Troy."

She points to me.

"I.D., big man."

He's looking at me. He's standing up and looking down on me. He's three times bigger than anyone I've ever seen, and he's grabbing his wrist, like if he doesn't hold on tight his muscles will send his arms flying back.

"Huh?"

"I'm just playin', man. Go on in. Be good though, I don't wanna have to come in there and get you." He smiles and his gold tooth glimmers off the setting sun.

"Ok."

His laugh is high and girly, though I doubt anyone's ever told him that.

Inside, it's dark cause the windows are covered. Half the lights aren't even turned on and the neon lights covering the walls barely do anything. Mom unrolls her fabric into an apron, folds it in half, and ties it around her waist.

"This is gonna be your little corner," she leans over and her good-luck earrings glow in the light. "I can get you a coke or something if you want and I'll get you dinner a little later, but this is where you hang out. Ok?"

"Ok," I say.

I sit underneath a buzzing Coors Light sign, which is what we drink at Tim's parties. It just reminds me that I can't drink, and so I can't really hang out at Tommy's. I have nowhere to go, except home. I wonder if Tiffany came while I've been gone.

We've been here for less than fifteen minutes when the seats at the counter fill up with old men. They all came separately, but they look like they could be brothers. Once they're in their seats, it's hard to picture what the place looked like without them cause they fit so naturally in the rundown setting. Mom smiles back at each of them, bigger and brighter than anything I've ever seen from her. It looks unreal.

"Jesus Christ," one of them blurts out.

His shoulders are so hunched his neck can barely support the weight of his head. He leans into the bar toward Mom and sticks out his hand. His bony finger bends, summoning her like an evil wizard.

He waits to talk until she's close.

"Did you know there's a goddamn kid here?" he says, still loud enough for the whole bar to hear even though Mom's right in front of him, earrings dangling like a magician's charm. They laugh.

"Yeah, Ron. That's my kid."

"Jesus, Cat! We don't want to know that shit," another one says. His oversized stomach pushes against the bar to hold him up.

"I've already told you guys."

"And we chose *deliberately* to ignore that. A girl like you couldn't have a kid that old."

It's funny to hear someone call Mom a girl.

"That's sweet, Bill."

"What's he doing in here?"

They talk like I can't hear them, like if they don't acknowledge me then I don't really exist. Old people do this all the time at parties or restaurants, at baseball games or movie theaters. If they don't look at me, they don't have to see me, and I hate it.

"I came here to drink," I shout.

Ron and Bill laugh, and Bill turns to his fat neighbor and he laughs too. There's a chain reaction of pauses and laughter all the way down the bar. I can feel a glow, which would be brighter if the laughter weren't all in the background behind Mom, whose smile has completely disappeared.

"Because we're worried about him. He's been drinking and making bad decisions that almost got himself killed." Her voice was fast at first, but softened at the end.

"Well, he's in good company," the guy with the belly says.

"I would've guessed it by that face," Ron says and I can't help but lick at the cut on my lip. "But Cat, I gotta be honest. Seems like a bar is the wrong place to bring a kid like that."

There's another blast of laughter along the bar. But it feels hollow watching them. Mom still isn't laughing.

"It gets him out of the house. And maybe it'll be informative."

"Let us buy him a drink, Cat. We can show him how to do it responsibly," another one says, wearing a baseball hat that doesn't have a baseball team on it and a shirt with a cartoon golfer.

"You wanna pay for his coke, go for it, Stan. But you gotta prove you can drink responsibly before it goes further than that."

Stan leans forward and slaps down a five-dollar bill. His hand stays on the edge and when Mom slides it out from under his fingers he whispers something to her.

"There ain't rules against this?" the oldest one says.

"I talked to the owner. He was fine with it."

"That's not a no."

"I'm not a lawyer though, as y'all might have guessed considering how much of my time I spend with you."

Mom squirts a coke into a glass and sets it down for me then picks up my plastic cup that's twice as big.

"What'd he whisper?" I ask.

"Nothing."

"Stan! What did you whisper?" I yell across the bar.

"Oh come on!" Mom huffs at me, but it's almost playful. She's different here. "Stan, were you gonna tell him?"

Stan shakes his head and his chin waggles along.

"Should I?" Mom asks.

Stan shakes harder. The door opens and the light from outside cuts across his face.

"Everything alright in here?" Troy says in a way that couldn't have come out of his smile.

"Are you going to behave?" Mom waits until she's standing over me to ask. I'm stuck between her and Troy.

"Ok."

"Yeah, everything's alright."

If she doesn't want me to talk, then I don't have to say a word. I watch the TV, some old piece of junk with scratches and pops in the picture that looks like it weighs a hundred pounds even though it's only like five inches. It's soundlessly playing a baseball game, with the music from the jukebox playing out of the speakers synced up to the same scratching and popping, like little explosions from equipment that's too old to even kill itself.

The men stare from the TV to my mom, their hands rap the bar to the beat and their saggy old mouths lip sync the words until there's a break in the singing or they're ordering another drink. They laugh and smile when she gives them another, and they watch her when she reaches down to grab them from the fridge. It's all so simple and easy, but the artificial looks and smiles make my stomach turn.

Not so much so that when Mom brings me a basket of chicken strips and fries, my stomach doesn't growl. The food is better here than when I have to reheat it at home. Some of the guys eat, too, as they sink into their seats. The most any of them have moved is to go to the bathroom. They're getting louder, laughing harder, staring longer. Mom's still smiling, it's etched in her face.

I'm done eating and now the room smells like cold french fries in a hospital. The thought of which, along with the heat, makes me sweat. I'm starting to get claustrophobic. I can almost feel the tubes connected to me and I can't breathe.

I push away from my chair; the squeaky hinges sound the same as whatever old, awful song is playing. Mom's leaning over the bar to talk to Bill. He's watching her mouth. Everyone is looking at her. It's just a few steps to the door. I open it slowly so it doesn't creak too loud and step out into the coolness of night, inhaling so hard I get dizzy.

"Where you goin', boss?" Troy says.

He's leaning back against the window. He doesn't turn to look but he can still tell it's me.

"It's hot in there. And it smells like shit."

He laughs, "It's a bar." "Do they all smell like that?"

"Nah, man. Each one got its own unique stink. So," he turns to look at me and it's like his full weight presses down on me, "why you causin' trouble?"

"I'm not causin' trouble."

"You seen your face, man?" he laughs again, high and girly. I want to say something but I don't.

I lick my lip and my face flares. I have to stop myself from doing it again cause he's still watching me. He hasn't even blinked.

"You're getting into shit, makin' your mom worry."

"She doesn't have to."

"Man, cut the shit and be glad she does."

The car is right in front. There's a scratch on the right bumper that Derek put in and Mom still hasn't noticed.

"You think it's all her fault?" Troy says.

"What?"

"Whatever bullshit you goin' through. You think it's just her to blame?"

"It's not just her," I say, which doesn't sound as good as I want it to. And he doesn't seem to care.

He laughs.

The door swings open behind me with a burst of heat and the same hospital and french fry smell, which is stronger than the fresh air.

"Jesus," Mom says and puts her hand to her chest. She's breathing heavy. She closes her eyes. "What're you doing out here?"

"I got my eye on him, Cat."

"I wasn't doing anything."

"Thanks, Troy."

"It's boring in there."

"He doesn't like the smell either."

"Oh god, I wasn't even thinking about the smell. Thanks, guys."

"I'm tired. Can't we go home?"

"They don't just let you leave work for being tired, boss."

"Just a little longer. Come on, let's get inside."

She opens the door and Troy nudges me on the shoulder.

"Get on in there," he says.

No one has moved and nothing's changed. The song sounds the same as every other. The picture on the screen looks identical. The smell seems worse. Even though everyone is drinking and enjoying themselves, this isn't what I imagined a bar would look like. It's kinda depressing. I think—I hope—it's just cause they're old and they don't have anything better to do than smile wide when Mom comes back in. She's still smiling for the rest of the night, even when Ron asks her out and the whole group hoots and laughs. I peel back the gauze and look at the hole, still a little red. I wanna get out of here, but I can't just disappear anymore.

I don't say anything else from the corner until they've all been kicked out for closing time. When they're gone, Troy tells me they'd stay here all night if they could. He's vacuuming the maroon and grey carpet that has so many stains it looks like a pattern. Mom is wiping the counter tops with a rag and putting caps on the bottles. When Troy's done vacuuming, he puts the chairs on top of the tables. He doesn't look like he wants to be here. When they're done he says bye and walks out the back. He looks so tired it makes me yawn.

Mom looks tired too.

"Ready?" she asks.

"Yeah," I say. I just wanna get the hell out of here. I hope, even though it's so late, that Tiffany will be waiting at the house when we get there.

Mom's smile is gone when we get to the car. It's back to her old music, her old self. I leave the seat reclined but I can't keep my eyes closed even though it's past two in the morning; I wish I could've been with Tiffany tonight, if she'd have come over. I wish I could've been at Tommy's, if I could drink. I wish I could've been anywhere but that depressing bar. But, now that we're leaving, it makes home sound better.

"You tired?" Mom asks.

"Yes and no."

"I know the feeling. I'm usually up another hour after I get home even though I'm exhausted," she says and cracks the window to let some cool air in. "So, you have fun hanging with the boys tonight?"

"Do they come in all the time?"

"Pretty much." She puffs her cheeks with a breath and blows it out slowly. "Are they your type of people?"

"They seem weird. It was… I don't know."

"Depressing?" she says with a laugh.

"Basically, yeah."

"Yeah. It's not how I would live my life if I had my choice, but they're good people."

"Couldn't you get a better job?"

"Probably, but finding a new job is basically a full time job and I'm already so strapped for time now that Brad's gone and everything."

Hearing his name makes me wanna throw up.

"I could stay at Dad's sometime. Would that help?"

She runs her hand over her hair. The air whips the strands right back in front of her face.

"It's more the financial factor. Certainly, you've proven you could use some supervision, but I don't know if you're gonna get much with him."

But I still don't understand why he can't watch me. Why I never get to see him and the only time I ever talk to him is when I'm in trouble. It sucks knowing that he's around, and having no say in getting to spend time with him when we have all these problems, but he can't help.

Then I remember my hospital room. The emptiness of waking and hearing Mom's weary tone as she talked on the phone. It's the voice she often has when she's talking to him cause there's a problem and he's not there to help.

He wasn't there at all. The thought lands like a punch in the stomach. He hasn't been by in the days I've been home, either. He hasn't even called.

"Did you tell Dad I was in the hospital?"

"Your dad…" she starts and stops. The freeway hissing through the crack in the window magnifies her silence. "Yes."

"Why wasn't he there?"

The blurred lights on the side of the freeway become clear as Mom slows the car, buzzing over the bumps as we stop on the shoulder. Her eyes close and her whole body starts to shake. Cars fly by on the freeway behind her. Energy builds but there's nowhere for it to go in this tiny car. Mom takes a deep breath like she could suck it all up.

"I don't know," she says, her voice fizzling out.

"What'd he say?"

She's shaking her head, pulling at the steering wheel like she's trying to pop it off. There's no stopping now. My heart is pounding and my head is buzzing and everything seems so loud.

"The same things he always says. How he *wishes* he could be there. How he *wants* to help. It's just not a good time, like there's ever a good time. Ever!"

She screams and it feels like the car will fall to pieces from the force. My ears hurt, my head is full of blood and my stomach feels empty. She leans against the steering wheel and honks the horn with her forehead between sobs and I breathe deep, trying not to cry too.

"It wasn't a good time for you!" she yells. "It wasn't a good time for me. Is it ever a good time when your fucking son almost—almost fucking dies."

And then the unavoidable wave crashes over, and the tears pour out making the passing cars look like spaceships at warp speed. And we're stranded in space, alone. I put my hand on her back and the waves of her sob run through me until she's holding me and I breathe, breathe through the tears.

"I'm sorry," I say and we squeeze each other tight.

"It's ok. It's ok. It's ok."

She says it like she can convince both of us. Maybe she can. She stopped crying and I did too.

"I'm alive," I joke. "That's good."

"It's a start."

"And I've been taking my pills, even though they go down like Grandma's cooking."

"A few more weeks and you're free. I did it for eighteen years."

"I can tell."

And she leans back laughing and looks at herself in the rearview mirror. She rubs her makeup-stained face with her sleeve, the black streaking the white shirt. I press my palms into my eyes, forgetting for a second the bandage that scratches at my cheek and I laugh, laugh harder and we're both laughing like idiots. Mom shakes her head, and through fits of laughter that come and go, we drive home.

14

MY REFLECTION IN the bus window is bouncing, so it's hard to tell if the scab on my face is gone. When I lick my lips, it feels like it might be. At least there isn't any more of the goop that Mom made me put on, which turned the scab a pale, yellow-green. It tasted bitter but I still couldn't stop licking it.

I put the same stuff on my hand, even though I'm taking the doctor's pills everyday. It makes the hole look like the universe on the other side of a time portal. It's vanishing before my eyes. I can feel its absence when I squeeze my hand and the pain is almost gone and the world outside still looks clear. I turn both of my palms open and still can't imagine what it'll look like when it's fully healed.

The constant stinging was me dying, which freaks me out when I can't sleep at night. It felt bad and good at the time. I wonder if that's what real death is like. I know Dad says we just turn to nothing and our energy goes out into the world, but it's hard to believe there's not any pain. Maybe I'll ask him, but I doubt he has an answer.

I lick my lip again. I hope I don't do it in front of Dad. He'd make fun of me, tell me it's gross. It used to feel fun even when he was making jokes about me, but thinking about it makes me mad. I want him to try today. I want an excuse to yell at him, tell him it's been over a week since I was in the hospital and he hasn't even called.

The longer I'm on this bus, the hotter it gets. Just one living, breathing person is too much here but more people are getting on.

The last time I took the bus was with Derek and Sven to the new skate park even though none of us skated. We'd heard Sven's brother and his friends talking about it and we decided we had to see it. The ride was hot and slow and smelled like the bathroom at the baseball field and when we got to the park, the skaters we watched weren't any good.

We were only there for a little while when Amy showed up. Everyone stopped skating to watch her walk up. So the whole park was staring at us when she made us leave, then dropped me and Sven at my house. He was gonna stay but Mom was pissed. After she kicked him out, she yelled at me for going too far away without telling her anything, but when she wasn't looking Dad high-fived me.

That still feels good, which feels wrong. I try not to get stuck between those kinds of feelings thinking about Dad, but it's hard not to.

This bus looks and smells like the last one. The seats are blue plastic with blue cushions that have pink and green confetti. They're are too many people on the bus, but enough empty seats that it's weird when an old woman sits right next to me. She has flabby, spotted arms that bulge out like cooked marshmallows from her sleeveless, pink shirt. Her teeth are weirdly white when she smiles; I smile back, then look down at my scrap of paper with the directions to Dad's.

Mom asked if I wanted her to drop me off, but I wanted to do this on my own.

"Hope you're enjoying your summer," the woman says, her voice like the scratching of the TV at Mom's work.

She's smiling in the window. I nod.

"Keeping outta trouble, I'm sure," she says and laughs like one of Daisy's squeaky toys.

I don't want to talk. I don't want her to talk to me. I wish I could just be at Dad's already.

"When my son was your age, he sure was gettin' into trouble. Fightin' all the time with the other boys in town. And drinkin'." She scrunches her face and snorts out her nose. "Looks like you might be doin' a bit of that."

I lick my lip again.

"Then the drugs. I hope you don't do that, too. No no. It's not good. Thank the Lord, he got over that."

"Ok," I say. James Smalling and his oxys pop into my head. Sven and Tommy don't talk about it, at least not around me. Definitely not around Shane. He hates them, hates James. He says the people that make oxys are just looking for future patients and the assholes that sell them are only helping. I just always hated taking pills, and it's worse now that I have to take the antibiotics every day.

"Doesn't mean I didn't cause my own trouble. I used to sneak out of my room to go to dances with my girlfriends. We'd drive all the way out to other towns. Or we'd just drive around until the sky was starting to get light and I'd race home to get into bed before my parents came to wake me up."

She laughs again and the squeak makes people turn and stare. I don't know why she's talking to me. It's almost like she's not.

"Something about that age. Being bad is so exciting. You don't care about the consequences. My parents whooped me when they found out what I was doing. No words, just the belt or the branch. That's how I learned discipline. Didn't really work on me. I did it anyway. Didn't really work on my son, neither."

"So why'd you do it?" I ask.

If she's gonna keep talking, I at least wanna know why she'd do the same dumb things her parents did. I think of Mom, with her initials written on the bottom of the dresser, and I can feel the way my chest would shake whenever Grandpa would yell.

"It was what I knew. And I turned out alright, so I didn't try to think of a better way. My husband was the same."

"Even when your son was doing drugs?"

"Well, we didn't know he was, at first. Then, it was so late, it was out of our hands."

"So, how'd he get off them?"

"He went through hell, but figured it out on his own. It still kills me that we couldn't do anything for him earlier."

"He made it, though."

"Yes, indeed."

She smiles awkwardly and turns back and doesn't say anything anymore, just stares out the front of the bus. I stare out the side and at the paper with Dad's address. I know Mom would've yelled at me for putting Tiffany and my initials on the furniture. I know she would've if she caught me drinking sooner, just like Grandpa would've yelled at her. I know she hated it. I just don't know why we all do the same things.

I wonder what hell was like and I lick my lip. I want to ask the woman if it's like having Brad scream and threaten you. Or getting so drunk you throw up all the time. Or holding your heart in your hand waiting for Tiffany to come over, and she never shows up.

I should be used to it. I haven't really been talking to anyone lately. I've hardly left my room, or wanted to. At first, it was waiting for Tiffany listening to *EndSerenading* but she hasn't shown up. So I started listening to other stuff cause Mineral makes my heart hurt. Refused, Botch, A Fall Farewell, On the Might of Princes—they're my favorites. Shane dropped off some other stuff, like Bright Eyes and Braid and Texas Is the Reason, which I like too.

When I listen to it, I don't worry about what's going on. I don't think about what's happening at Tommy's. Or why Tiffany isn't there. Or how Dad didn't show up and Brad was awful and how everything was my fault. I don't think about what happened with Tommy and Christina. I don't even miss the disappearing hole. Everything could be falling apart, but the music is a forcefield around me.

When I get off the bus, the old lady waves bye with her wobbly arms. I wave too and stand at the bus stop, waiting to transfer. Wheels kick up dry dust in the gutters when it arrives. I hold my breath. It feels hotter inside this one, but I'm not on it for long before Dad's stop. I have to scan the area for his apartment. That his home is unfamiliar makes my feet heavy. I should've brought music with me.

There's a Popeyes on the corner across the street so I know I'm close; Dad used to bring popcorn chicken to my baseball games. He always talks about how we'll go when I visit. That it's so close, it's practically like his own kitchen.

His building is grey with blue around the edges and on top of the roof there are chairs. One's knocked over and it doesn't look like anyone's up there. The metal handrail up to the second floor is rough with rust and wobbles when I grab it. Dad's screen door doesn't fully close and when I knock, the wood feels soft. He doesn't come right away and my breathing gets fast, my hands start sweating. Then, the door swings open.

The air is heavy with that weed, sweat, and alcohol smell that fills Tim's house at all the parties but I don't hear or see anyone else in the room. Dad stands in the doorway.

"Holy fuck," he says. "What are you doin' here?"

He looks shocked, almost scared, and smaller than normal but with a belly that presses against his tight, white shirt and over the elastic of his sweatpants. I want to tell him to put a shirt on. The stomach reminds me of Derek. His face is different too. It looks like a month-long sunburn. All the features of Dad are there, but tweaked enough to seem like I'm seeing a stranger.

"Hey," I say.

"Sup, big guy. Like, fu—genuinely big guy. What's going on?"

"I just wanted to see you."

"Does your mom know you're here?"

"Yeah."

"Ok, ok." He looks at the door then shakes it a little and the whole thing rattles. He looks lost, staring at it and then snapping back to me. "Well, do you want to come in?"

It doesn't sound like an offer. He seems to actually want to know, which makes me unsure. I didn't really plan what I was gonna do when I got here, it just felt like I had to come. I needed to see him. To tell him that… what? That I hate him? That he's an asshole for not coming to the hospital? Or not even calling after? That I want to see him *more*? But do I?

"Yeah," I say anyway.

"Cool. Alright."

He steps aside to let me in. His apartment looks like what Tommy's would if Christina didn't always clean up. There's a pizza box popping out of the trash. The coffee table is piled with empty beer cans and two ashtrays. Dad walks to the kitchen. His socked feet leave lint stuck after each step.

When he comes back, he hands me a soda then pushes aside a pile of clothes on the couch and sits. The pop of his beer is like a mini explosion in the small room. I can't stop staring as he sips. It seems even more depressing than watching Mom's customers.

"Let's do something special here," he says and holds the can to me. "Try this. Seems like something a dad gets to do, give his kid their first sip of beer."

"I've already tried beer." I don't mention that I can't have any right now. That it could kill me. I'd rather not think about dying, but now, I can't stop.

"Goddamn," his mouth hangs open and he's staring at me with cloudy eyes, "really? Shit, no, that makes sense. I was like eleven when I had mine and you should be... older than that. I mean, I know you're older than that, right?"

"I'm thirteen, starting high school soon."

"Holy moly. High school? That'll be fun. You'll like it."

"Yeah?"

"Yeah, man. High school was—what a trip. It was good times. And you had your first beer. I wish I—man, I can still remember how gross that first one tasted." He looks up and now his eyes sparkle like they used to.

I think about how he used to write stories just for me. Like the one after we went camping where I found a magic ring that let me live underwater. When he'd read them, he'd do all the characters—frog princes and snail warriors and owl messengers—with different voices.

"My old man gave it to me after he caught me trying to steal some. He thought forcing me to drink it would teach me a lesson, but I finished the whole thing without complaining a bit. At least not to him." He laughs into his chest.

"I got in trouble for stealing beers," I say and can hear Tommy telling me how stupid it is to tell him. For a moment I'm falling to the bottom of my bottomless stomach.

"Mom know?"

"Kinda."

"If she knew, you'd know," he chuckles.

"She knows," I say, waiting for him at the bottom of everything, but I don't know what I'm waiting for. It should feel good that he's not mad at me. But that isn't enough. I want more than jokes. I want answers. I want him to tell me why he wasn't there, why he hasn't been. I need him to promise he'll be there next time, cause I can't remember the last time he was.

Dad leans back on the couch as he takes a sip of his beer. His belly hovers over him like an alien blob.

"Well shit," he says. "I'm surprised I didn't get an earful."

My heart pounds like a machine gun. I try to squeeze my cut but it's just a dull pain and the crinkling of the bandage. There's no going anywhere but here so I breathe. I take a deep breath of what little oxygen is left in the room.

"She probably assumed you wouldn't care."

"What's that?"

"Where were you?"

"What? When?"

I hold up my hand between us. Focus. Breathe.

"Shit, yeah, that. Man..."

He looks at his can, pinging the tab and flicking beer onto his stomach.

"What do you want to hear?" he says and stares at me, his eyes like a lake that's so glassy you can't tell if there's anything below.

"The truth."

"I don't even know how to figure that out."

"Can't you try?"

"Hospitals, man... And having to see you like that. And your mom. And, fuck, I just. I tried, I swear. I really did."

"I've been home for over a week."

"I know. I know. I know. I fucked up."

He keeps talking and I fall into the rhythm of his voice, but I don't know what he's saying or why he's saying it. Nothing makes sense.

"Add it to the list, man. Add it to the list of my mistakes. It's a long one."

"But…"

He puts his hands on his head and stares up at the ceiling, his arms flared out to the side showing his patchy armpit hair and cracking elbows. Then he starts humming and I close my eyes. And I can remember him, us. We're warm and lying out on the rocks at Grandpa's after dark. And it's him, Dad. And it's him when I open my eyes, somehow. But instead of getting up and hopping from rock to rock as he sings, he's rocking back and forth on the couch and clouds of dust play in the sunlight around him.

"You deserve better, man," he says, but he's still staring at the ceiling. "When your mom and I split, I had this plan. I'd take a couple months, get everything together. Get a job that paid good money and had some flexibility, and then I was gonna get a place—not like this."

He waves his hand and it's like the mess comes to life.

"A place you'd wanna hang. Where, like, you'd want to have your friends over. I'd be like a real dad. Not like mine, I'd be cool and fun and… Fuck, I'm nothing like my father, but I don't know if that's a good thing anymore."

He leans back into his chair and takes another sip of beer. He pulls the tab of the can off and loads it onto his fingernail, like he showed me how to flick it when I was a kid. I lick my lip but he doesn't say anything.

"What was your dad like?" I ask since I never got to meet him.

He leans forward and digs his nails into his legs, leaving red scratch marks up his shin. When he sits back down, his hands rest on his knees, but the nails still make white indents on his thigh that'll be red after.

"Honestly?"

"Yeah."

"He was a cunt."

And it's like when someone cusses in class, but even crazier. I'm too stunned to laugh.

"Why?"

"Why or how? He was cold and cruel. All he cared about was success; he wanted to be able to talk to his coworkers about our accomplishments, not us as people. When I realized I could never live up to his expectations, I just stopped trying. Why he was like that, I have no idea."

"Then why would you wanna be like him?"

"Ughhh," he groans and I somehow dig deeper into the pit of my stomach. "I don't really think I do. I just wanna be less like me," he says with a laugh.

"I think I know what you mean," I say as my fuck-ups loops in my head.

"No, no, no. You're great, dude. Plus, much as it pains me to say this, you got a good woman lookin' out for you. You're gonna be alright."

But something about him saying it, in this apartment, after everything, makes me feel hollowed out. All my emotions and anxiety disappear. And it's not like being drunk or high or listening to music even. It's all there, and so am I, but none of it matters.

"Hey, man."

His words get lost, sucked up in the vacuum of space. I don't smile or shrink. I don't feel anything or even lick my lip.

"Fuck me. Listen, I know this sucks but maybe it'll make sense when you're older."

"I understand now."

He reaches over and pats me on the leg. His arms are long and pale, different than the ones that would pull me up and throw me onto his back. He's still shaking his head.

"Then you're a step ahead of your old man."

He points around the room with the beer in his hand. At the kitchen counter covered in dishes. The open cupboards. The window blinds that hang down on one side. The dusty couch and chair and cobwebs in the corners and his papers that cover the coffee and kitchen tables. He holds the can up to his mouth, sips, and his eyes are clear again, just like they're supposed to be.

"Someday, *I'll* get it. And I'll get a place that you can live at. Where you'd be stoked to bring your friends. For now, this is as good as I can do."

"You could call, too."

He laughs, slow and heavy.

"Yeah, I can do that."

And it's like he's on the other side of the universe.

"Are we always going to be miserable?" I ask. The words formed without thought. The feeling of dread pummels me as they pour out.

He takes a long drink and sets the can back on the table, watching it from when he picks it up to when he puts it back down. I wait for him to look at me. To say anything. My heart swells and shuts off my throat. My whole body is battered and starting to shake. I breathe, but breathing can only do so much.

"I should probably get you back home," is his only answer. My shaking stops and instead I shut off, everything numb. "Gimme a second and I'll go get the car."

"I'll just take the bus."

"You sure that's cool?"

"It's how I got here."

He stands up to give me a hug and messes my hair. When I was little, I loved when he'd do this. Then at some point I started to hate it cause it made me feel small. I don't know how to feel about it now, or if I'll ever feel anything again.

Outside, the sun is higher in the sky. The buildings are clearer. Lines of heat come off the blacktop. A woman walks past me with her dog. It barks but she doesn't say anything. The bus stop is empty and so is the first bus. There are people on the next one, but no one sits by me. I arrive at my stop and it still feels like I'm outside of Dad's—lost.

I head toward home, walking by Sven's house on the way. There's no sound or movement. All I can see is his parents' pile of junk that's creeping up the window.

Past Sven's, the Thieson twins are shouting and throwing clods of dirt at each other. They get quiet when I get closer and don't say anything to me as I pass. When I turn the corner, they start to shout again.

Down the street is Derek and Tiffany's house, with its unused basketball hoop mounted to the front. I turn toward it like I'm walking into a blazing fire.

Their parents' cars aren't in the driveway and I don't hear anything from outside. The front door is unlocked, as always. I walk in and up the stairs that creak more than ever. When I'm close to the top, I see that Tiffany's door is wide open and no one's inside.

I hear a scrambling and squeaking of Derek's desk chair. The door is closed, but doesn't have a lock on it. I open it as he's grabbing the Game Gear. His face is red and his glasses are crooked. He's pressing the Game Gear down into his lap.

"Hey," I say.

I can picture him making the same sneering, tongue-out face that he makes with his fake jack-off motion when he's doing the real thing. It's a funny image but I can't laugh or smile. I should make fun of him cause he would do that to me, but I don't want to talk. I don't know why I'm here.

"What's up?" he says, his voice heavy.

I shrug. He's embarrassed, otherwise his first comment would have been about the beer.

"You didn't come through the back."

"I walked here from the bus stop. I went to my dad's."

"I thought you weren't supposed to take the bus by yourself."

"I can now."

"Are you ok? You sound weird."

I nod without looking at him.

"Why'd you go to your dad's?"

Derek and I talk about a lot of stuff, but we never really talk about my parents. He just couldn't understand. And he's never asked about it before. I don't know why I'm telling him now.

"I just wanted to talk to him. He never came to the hospital, never called. I thought maybe he'd have an answer."

Tiffany's room is empty. She's not there. She hasn't visited either.

"Sorry, man, that sucks. Parents don't know shit."

"Yeah."

"You don't know what you're doing either."

"Sure."

"That's why you've been spending all your time with Tommy Pescadero, stealing my dad's beers."

His eyes and mouth harden, but his glasses are still crooked. It's almost nice being back to normal.

"Sorry about that," I say, even though I know that won't do anything. And while I mostly don't care, there's a part of me that feels like he's right and it grows when he stops talking.

I don't belong here. I never have, his parents were just too nice to tell me. Derek's not. But I realize, I have nowhere. My heart sinks, squeezing my lungs. I can't breathe, so I leave. Down the stairs, into the living room where it's painfully bright even though there are no lights on, through the kitchen and outside.

"Hey," I hear Tiffany say as I walk over to the planter ledge.

I push up onto the wall. My legs swing around and I jump down to the Thompsons' backyard with a thud that would normally send stinging waves up my legs. I feel nothing and duck through the bush and walk along the concrete edge of their lawn, then hop over into my yard and surprise Daisy. She scrambles up from her hole by the wall on the other side of the backyard. And when she runs over to me it's like a switch of emotion gets flicked on.

My chest feels like it's ripping apart as I open the door into the house. Daisy's nails scrape along the floor after me. My hands are trembling when I get to my room to the point I can barely turn on the music before I fall onto the bed. The music is a wall of noise that keeps out my thoughts. It's loud and fast and my heart starts pounding. The song is building and I stare at the ceiling, starting to feel safe. It's starting to work. I'm starting to breathe normal when I hear Daisy's collar jingling just outside my room. There's a knock and the door cracks open. Tiffany's standing in the doorway. She's barefoot, wearing her bathing suit top and a pair of shorts, and petting the dog. Everything crashes down.

"Are you alright?" she asks softly from behind her hair, like the words might break me.

"No."

"Can I help?"

"I hope," I say without knowing what it means.

The tears start to fall and my chest starts to heave. Tiffany doesn't say anything but she steps forward and holds me.

She feels like home.

15

THE FEELING OF Tiffany holding me, of being home, is still there when I close my eyes. But it's starting to dim. Again, she hasn't been back in days. I've even gone to her house, but it's like she's hiding and now I don't know what to do. It's getting harder to sit around in my room. Even the music isn't working like it used to. I've stopped listening to *our* album cause hearing it hurts as bad as the bb, except there's no disappearing and it only makes her absence clearer.

The hole in my hand is gone, too. Now its skin is soft and pink, almost like it's wet all the time. When I press on the spot the bb bulges out the back of my hand without pain. It doesn't make sense that something that hurt so much it could totally transport me can just disappear. Especially when I can still see it.

I can still smell Tiffany's chlorine and sunscreen hair, but is she gone too?

I wonder what this summer would have been like if I hadn't taken the gun that day. Tommy wouldn't have shot me, or taken the gun after. I wouldn't have almost died.

It is scary that a little thing like that can get so far out of control, but I try to remember that if I hadn't taken the gun, Brad would still be around; I never would have met Shane and Tommy or found their music; I'd be spending all my time at Derek's without Tiffany even looking at me. Maybe that would be better than the way it feels to have her disappearing.

My brain feels like it's spinning a million miles an hour. It's all a whir of faces and feelings and there's nothing to hold onto. Until I breathe and hold my head in my hands and stare at the dresser where Mom and someone's mystery initials are crossed out. I imagine who KJ is, but the image of young Dad pops into my mind. It's faded like the old photographs of him, but what if KJ was totally different? Different from Brad, too.

What happened to them? Where did KJ go? Why did they end? Do all relationships? Then Tommy and Christina and Tiffany pop back into my mind and I have to get up, get out of my room.

I can hear movement in the kitchen and the TV is on. Mom's sipping coffee at the sink and turns to me while I walk by to the freezer. She says good morning but I can tell from her voice there's more. I reach in to grab some waffles and the cold air makes my chest and face tingle.

"Your father actually called *me*," she says.

I close the door and put the waffles in the toaster. *Why now*, I wonder as the numbness from the ride home spreads through me.

"Ok."

"How're you holding up?"

"I'm good."

"You sure?" And it's like she's digging in the sand at the beach, the numbness like water filling the hole back in. "He sounded pretty rough. Very apologetic."

I used to dream about them getting back together. Now, I know it's impossible. I hear Brad's words and all I can think about is that in all these relationships that end, I'm the common link. Except Mom and KJ. I can't tell if that's good or bad.

"Cool."

"Look, I'm taking the day off today. Do you have any plans with your friends?"

"Not really," I answer even though she already knows.

She grabs a broom and starts to sweep the dust on the floor into a little pile. The toaster is buzzing. She sets the dustpan on the ground, but when she tries to sweep the pile she only gets half at a time. Even when she's done there's still a line of dust on the ground. The toaster pops and I grab my waffles.

"I was thinking about going to see your Grandpa today. Would you maybe want to come with me?"

Things have been better with Mom, but spending half the day in the car with her is never ideal. Sitting at home doesn't sound good either though, and she has a weird smile on her face that makes it hard to say no.

"Ok."

"Yeah? Ok. Great."

She claps her hands, nods, and picks up the broom and dustpan but sets them right back down walks over and hugs me. I close my eyes. Her french fry-smell sends a flash that clears the numbness and I can see the night Brad left. But he's already gone and it's Mom and Daisy and I curled up together in the dark. It doesn't make sense that it was this summer. It feels like so long ago. But when it was happening I thought it'd never end. Now it's just a mix of anger and sadness and embarrassment and appreciation as I wait for the numbness to come back, but it doesn't.

"Well, we'll leave in an hour."

Mom lets go and picks up the broom and dustpan again as I walk to my room shaking.

I put On the Might of Princes' *Where You Are And Where You Want to Be* on, and lay in bed. I want the pulse of guitars and the pound of drums to beat my brain into submission, to stop my heart from hurting, to make the thoughts of Brad and Christina and Dad and Tommy and Tiffany all go away. I want it to leave the good things. The new friends and the feeling of home. The things that it feels like I'm losing. I haven't seen Tommy and Shane since the night I passed out. I haven't seen Tiffany in too long. And I can't go back to just hanging with Derek and Sven.

I'm slipping into obscurity and maybe that's right, maybe it's what I deserve. But it's not what I want. Especially starting high school.

Before I know it, the album is rising to its end and Mom's knocking on the door, telling me she'll meet me in the car. I roll out of bed and sit with my head in my hands, waiting 'til the end of the album, which stops sharply and drains the life from my body. I stand up like a zombie, stop the stereo, grab a mixtape Shane made me and walk out to the car.

Mom's wearing regular clothes, stuff I never see cause she can't wear it to work but won't wear it when she's just at the house. She looks different, but it's not just the clothes. She's smiling enough that I start to worry I made a mistake.

We get into the car and Daisy jumps into the back before Mom can get the blanket spread across the seat. She's trying to protect it even though the whole car is falling apart.

Once we're driving Daisy rests her head on the center console, her warm breath leaving a wet spot until Mom makes a hard turn from the 605 to the 5 and she sits back into the crumpled blanket. We keep going, past the city until even the strip malls start to disappear. Off the freeway there's a quarry with water at the bottom and huge bulldozers and a conveyor belt carrying rocks up that reminds me how much longer we're going to be in the car. I haven't let go of the mixtape. Mom's still playing the same old music and with each beat I feel more like we're gonna be stuck doing the same thing forever, until I can't take it.

"Can we change this?" I ask.

"Oh," she seems surprised. "Sorry, I didn't think about it. Is there something you want to put on?" she says as she looks at the CD.

"Yeah."

She probably won't like it, but I have to do it anyway. She pulls out her music and stuffs it in the center console without putting it in a case, and when she closes it Daisy moves her head back.

"Go for it," she says.

I slide the CD in without changing the volume and it sounds way louder. I think about turning it down, the extra volume is like a gnawing in my head but Mom's smiling more now. The music's faster, more

violent. Violent: that's how Tommy describes it and I finally understand what that really means. It's thrashing around the car like a wild
animal.

"When did you start listening to this?" Mom asks as the double
bass rattles the doors.

"This summer."

"How'd you find it?"

"It's what Tommy and Shane listen to. Shane made me this."

"I am seriously out of the loop," she says, shaking her head. "Who
are they?"

"They're my friends," I say, hoping that's still true.

"I see," she says with a chuckle and looks over at me. "And these are
the boys you've been getting into trouble with?"

It doesn't feel like a trap. She already knows. It doesn't feel like she's
mad either.

"I guess? Yeah. It didn't feel like trouble when I was with them,
though."

Her smile hangs loosely like she's ready to laugh. She nods, looking
straight ahead even when she's changing lanes.

"Sounds familiar."

"Like Dad?"

She takes a deep breath and another and I imagine what it might
feel like in her chest and how she's trying to slow the spin of thoughts
in her head.

"Not just him."

"You used to get into trouble? Like what?"

She shakes her head, "I'll leave the details to Grandpa."

"Was it with KJ?" Saying this sends my stomach into a tailspin.

"Who?" she asks, genuinely confused.

"I saw it on the dresser. Your initials and KJ in a heart."

Her eyes go wide. I picture young Mom in her room, my room.
The brown stain on the ceiling isn't there yet. The plastic floor isn't
warped. She's there scribbling on the dresser with someone next to

her, knowing Grandpa would kill her if he found out. It's fun, hopeful almost, even though it ends up like this.

"Oh my! That is—yeah."

"Did Grandpa get mad at you for writing on the dresser?"

"He… well, he never saw it. I used to leave my shoes in front of that dresser. It was our little secret."

"You would've yelled at me if I did."

"I—would I? Yeah, probably."

I smile so wide that she purses her lips and shakes her head until I start to laugh.

"Don't you laugh," she says, but her voice is light like Shane's when he jokes. "I would've been mad because it's not a good thing to do."

"So, who's KJ?"

"Ugh," she squeezes the steering wheel and glances back at me with a grin. "He was this boy, Kyle Jacobs. My first—do you really wanna hear this?"

I nod.

"My first crush. My first kiss."

I try not to make a face at the thought of her kissing. She's not looking, anyway.

"What was he like? How old were you guys?"

"We'd just started high school and your grandpa finally thought I was old enough to be at the house alone, which thinking about it now, I'm realizing how much of an error in judgment I made this summer."

"It wasn't so bad, aside from me almost dying."

"Don't. You don't get to joke about that for at least five years."

The car is quiet but without the usual pressure buildup. I wait for her to start talking again but she's staring straight ahead.

"So you were at the house alone?"

"Yeah. And not at the house. I'd go out a lot, that's how I met Kyle. He was really sweet, almost nerdy. He played the keyboard, like before it was cool. And, unfortunately, even longer before it was uncool."

"Maybe it'll come back. The Get Up Kids use it. Same with The Anniversary."

"Well, you'll have to show me that. But Kyle would hang out at the house a lot, sneaking in at night too because I made him. We'd listen to a lot of music and it was just nice."

"Why'd it end?" I ask without knowing if I actually want to know.

"His dad got a job across the country and they moved. We wrote letters for a while, but that slowed and came to a stop."

"Why?"

"Life? It's hard keeping something going, especially when it's not there. And then I met your dad."

Which only brings up more questions that I can't help but ask even when I know better.

"What was Dad like when you met him?"

"He was, like, the coolest person I'd ever seen." She's laughing, but it's different this time, like she's trying to swallow her laughter. "He'd drive around in his old—well, it was new then—Mustang. You remember it. Not the same as I do, I'm sure. It was something back then. Ugh, and he would drive around with the top down blaring his music. He listened to punk and dressed the part, too."

We're off the 58, winding around on small streets through rows of tan houses. Mom stops talking when we get to the big hill before Grandpa's neighborhood. She leans forward as the car creaks all the way up. She was cursing the last time we drove up this hill, and the car had an easier time then. We make it up and then the car is just coasting after. Daisy sits up. The houses are more and more spread out and she can see through to the desert behind them. I remember Dad and I, exploring through the rocks and cacti, but in my head he's like I last saw him.

"What happened?"

My heart hurts. Everything hurts.

Mom's quiet and the edges of her eyes are filling with tears as we turn into Grandpa's driveway.

"I wish I knew," she says as the car comes to a stop.

Grandpa's sitting on the white bench on the porch. He sets a drink down and walks toward us and opens the door for Mom, steps back, smiles, and kicks the front tire.

"These things are bald."

"Hi, Dad."

He's looking at the car while he and Mom hug. Daisy spills out Mom's door and runs toward the house.

"You gotta get 'em changed. Let's go to town, I'll buy you some new tires."

"I'll do it later. I haven't had a lot of time lately."

"That's why we'll do it now. You shouldn't be driving around on these. Especially if you got the little…" He stares at me when I get out of the car. "Jesus, you grew. How long's it been since I saw you?"

"Not that long, Dad."

"Come over here. How tall are you?"

I walk over. It's hotter out here, dryer too. The car is steaming and clinking. Grandpa grabs me by the shoulders and looks down at me. He smells the same way he's always smelled. Damp even though we're in the desert, with a sharp smell that I now realize is whiskey.

"You look good," he says to me.

"Thanks, Grandpa. So do you."

"Ha. Get back in the car, we'll go to town and get this thing fixed up."

"Relax, Dad. We're going in the house."

As soon as he opens the front door, Daisy races through the house, out the back, and into the red and orange hills. There are rocks as big as trucks everywhere, with lizards and snakes climbing all over them and cacti jutting up into the sky between. We drove a long way, but we could've driven another day and it wouldn't make sense that we could be somewhere that feels so different from home.

I used to pretend it was another planet and the animals were aliens. When it got dark, and there were a million stars, Mom, Dad and I would try to find earth. *Which one's home again*, Mom would always say, and we'd just point to a different star each time and Dad would make up a story about how we were gonna get back. But I wonder if it was even real. If that Dad was just a figment of my imagination. If that Mom and Dad ever actually existed even as I see the pictures of them on the walls.

"It's sure nice of you guys to come all the way out here to see me."

"Of course, Dad."

"Have you seen your brother or sister?"

"Not since Christmas."

Grandpa draws out a grunt, like he's deciding if he should be mad.

"You should see each other more."

"We'd like to."

The house is all wood and so is most of the furniture. It smells old. There are pictures in the kitchen and living room of Mom with Aunt Becky and Uncle John when they were little. The color on the carpet where Grandma's chair used to be is now almost the same as the rest. It's so close that I think I only know it's there now cause I knew it was there before.

"And what about you?" Grandpa says. "You doing good?"

"Yeah," I say.

"You, Kitten?" Grandpa asks Mom.

Mom sighs, "We're fine."

"Hmm."

I wouldn't know what to say either.

We sit on the patio and drink lemonade, watching Daisy run from rock to rock, chasing lizards. It's not just a little kid thing, it really does look like Mars. The clicks and chirps that come from the desert still sound like an alien language. The hills are so empty you can imagine you're the only one here. Mom says Grandma and Grandpa moved here to get away from the world. It's a good place to do that.

"You keeping busy?" Mom asks Grandpa.

"Sure."

"What've you been doing?"

He shrugs.

"You don't get lonely out here?"

"You worry too much."

"I wonder where I get that."

"It's my job to worry about you."

"I know, Dad."

"I worry less since you left that loser." He takes a drink. "You sure got a way of pickin 'em."

"Let's not start," she says, and she doesn't look or sound mad. She just keeps looking out.

"I just want you to learn from your mistakes."

"Someday."

I want to ask if she will. If we will. But it's not the right time.

The rocks glow under the sun. I used to stay out so long my lips would blister. It never felt hot while I was out there, but now I'm sweating just sitting here while Mom and Grandpa have stopped talking. We're just sitting, drinking, looking at the desert.

"Grandpa, what was Mom like when she was a kid?"

He flinches like I poked him in the face. But then he starts to smile as he glances at Mom.

"It's ok," she says. "I told him he could ask."

"How much do you want him to know?"

"Well, now I'm curious how much you knew."

"More than you realized, that's for sure."

"Start big picture, then."

"She was a troublemaker," he says, squinting at her with a sly smile.

"How?" I ask.

"Wouldn't listen. Runnin' around with boys. Out partying all hours."

"Not all the time, Dad."

"So, she was bad?" I pinch my mouth shut, trying not to smile but it's coming up at the corners.

"Bad, no. She was young and stubborn and really didn't like to be told what to do."

"All these," Mom turns to me with a tilt of the head, "are family traits."

Grandpa rolls his eyes and takes a drink then leans forward and grabs my knee. His fingers are knotted and his hand is spotted and veiny, but huge and strong and rough. He squeezes gently.

"You been givin' your mom trouble, I hear."

"No more than she's been giving me."

"She has it coming to her," he says with a chuckle.

"Thanks for the support," she says. "Do you want to tell your grandfather what trouble you've been getting into?"

"Not at all, no."

"Ha. Your mom already told me."

"Are you mad?"

I've only ever seen Grandpa yell at Mom, but when I close my eyes I can hear how deep and rough his voice gets when he's angry.

"No," he says.

I open my eyes to make sure I heard him right. Mom looks surprised too.

"I'm not mad." He must have noticed. "Too old to be mad. In fact I'm happy you're alright. I don't know what your mom or I would've done if you would've died, how we could've handled it. And from a stupid thing like that. God, what an idiotic thing to let happen. I know we all do stupid things when we're young, but that takes the cake. Hopefully, you're smarter now."

Mom rubs my shoulder. I try to breathe.

"You are smarter, yeah?" he asks.

"Yeah."

"Good," Grandpa says with another sip. "Hard not to go up from there."

"Where was this when I was a kid?" Mom asks.

"That's different."

"How is it different?" "How do you react when he's gettin' in trouble?"

"That's..." Mom starts.

"Exactly," Grandpa says. "Maybe you can learn from my mistakes."

"Is that..." Mom starts, then her eyebrows curl into question marks. "Is that an admission of fault?"

"I may not have always been *perfect*."

Mom laughs as she wipes the drops of water off her glass with her finger and rubs it onto her neck.

"I was only ever trying to help, Kitten," Grandpa says.

"I know."

"So if Grandpa makes mistakes and you make mistakes, does that mean I still have to listen to you?" I ask, mostly joking.

"Do you listen to me now?" Mom asks, her voice soaring out into the desert.

"Pretty much."

Mom laughs again. This time for real. Grandpa's just watching her until she's quiet and wiping her eyes.

"You don't *have* to do anything," she says.

"You'd be an idiot not to," Grandpa adds. "Listen, and you might not have to learn everything the hard way."

"Isn't the hard way the best way to learn?" I ask, cause it's something Mom always says.

"It's the best way not to forget. But you'll learn more, and it'll be easier, goddammit, if you just listen to someone that knows. Maybe she won't be right every time, but your Mom's gonna tell you what she knows is best, just like I'll always tell her what I know is best, and we'll get pretty close. She'll hope you listen, like I hope she listens."

"You could stand to listen every now and then, Dad."

He smiles. "Let's get some lunch."

Daisy runs back when we open the door. She jumps on the couch and I join her. Mom opens the fridge and tells Grandpa he needs to do more shopping and he waves her off. She finds a pizza in the freezer and when she pops it in the oven the smell fills the house. Grandpa sits in his fuzzy, green lounge chair. When Mom's not looking, he adds whiskey to his lemonade. He doesn't see that I see. Or think that I know. Mom stands over him with her hand on his shoulder while she waits for the pizza to cook. She smells his drink and scowls. I guess she really can smell it. I wonder how many times she smelled it on me without saying anything. I wonder why she didn't say anything. Maybe she was too tired. Or maybe she didn't want to yell since it never did anything to her and she knows it wouldn't work on me.

While we eat, we take turns playing Gin Rummy. The first time I ever played, Mom and I both cried. It was right after Grandma died. We'd always played Hearts before. That was Grandma's favorite game, but without her we didn't have enough players. It felt wrong to play but there wasn't anything else to do. The three of us were here and it was silent, no one talking and Grandpa doesn't own a TV.

Mom and Grandpa are laughing now. I wonder if they're thinking about Grandma too.

Grandpa wins the first three hands, but I came really close the second time. Mom wins the next two and scores enough points to catch up to him. I'm in last place, but it's fun cause they're having a good time. We stop playing before there's a winner and go watch the sun set beyond the hills. The ground turns orange and purple and red. It feels easy up here, but I know that probably isn't true.

Grandpa walks us outside and gives both of us hugs, squeezing tighter than when we got here. The alcohol smell is still there, but it's not as strong as the regular, old Grandpa smell. He opens Mom's door and kicks her front tire again, but doesn't say anything this time, just winks. Mom laughs, and shakes her head.

"Be smart," Grandpa says to me or Mom or both.

I nod and open the back door and Daisy jumps in and falls asleep before Mom's started the car.

"Thanks for coming with me," Mom says once we back out the driveway and start down the road. "Grandpa would never say it, but he gets lonely up here."

"I like coming here."

"Yeah, me too."

"Has he always called you Kitten?"

Her laugh rings through the car.

"It's stuck around a long time. Since sixth grade. I was going to my first dance. He drove me and my friend Ellen in his big, beige Oldsmobile and he pulled up behind the gym where all the parents were dropping their kids off. He asked me to give him a hug—which I only learned about years after. I was so excited I was out the door before he even stopped the car. He says it just popped into his head the way I bounced out, so independent. So, he leaned out the window and yelled, 'You be good, Kitten!' If he'd done that when I was in high school, I would've been devastated, but I was too happy to worry then."

It's dark and slow outside. It feels like we're gliding through space. My music's still playing but it doesn't fit the atmosphere.

"We can put on your music, if you want," I say.

"Oh yeah? I would've killed to have my music in Dad's car. That old Oldsmobile never played anything but Merle Haggard or Hank Williams."

"Did you ever ask if you could play your music?"

"Alllll the time. I was obsessed, but—his car, his rules."

She ejects the CD and hands it back to me before sliding hers in. The silence feels like living in a painting.

"What did you want to listen to?" I ask as the music comes on: a song by The Smiths that I only know now cause Shane likes it.

Mom grins, embarrassed.

"This."

"You're still listening to the same stuff?"

"Don't give me that look."

"But there's so much new music."

"Well, I've heard some new stuff today and as good as it is, I'm not sure I'll be listening to it on my own."

"Oh yeah?"

"It's all a bit—aggressive."

It doesn't feel bad that she doesn't like it, when she doesn't like what I like about it.

"That's not what all new music is like," I say and Tiffany pops into my head.

"I know that! I put the radio on sometimes when I'm bored with what I got, but I keep listening to my old music because I love it. This is what spoke to me when I cared most. When it defined who I was and wasn't. And it's comfortable to have it still, even if that feeling has faded. It can take me back—like, I remember sneaking out of the house in the middle of the night to see your dad. He was waiting in his car down the block and this song was playing when I got in. I don't know where we were going or what we were doing but I can see how his face lit up when I sat down and how this song made everything feel perfect."

"Dad liked this too?"

"It was one of the few bands we could agree on but he'd never admit that to his friends."

She chuckles.

"What was Dad like then?"

"Oh wow," she says. "He was the same as always, but different. It's an odd phenomenon how much people change into the people they always were. He was charming and stubborn and self-effacing and smart. He's still those same things but that balance has shifted. The self-effacing turned to self-doubt and the stubbornness, when he's stopped trying, makes him a pain in the ass. But I can blink and still see the first time we met and feel that feeling, just fainter. He hopped the fence to talk to me during my softball game, while it was going on."

"Do you hate him now?"

"I know I'm not supposed to. I mostly don't, but there definitely is a part of me that does. That wishes he could've taken all the parts of himself and turned into someone that would help us. That's pissed he doesn't want to help us. But people change in ways we can't keep up with. Like you." She looks over and smirks. "Don't make that face, it's true. I swear I was just wrapping you up in a blanket and carrying you to your crib. Now we're here."

My first memory is of a pool. Mom was in the water. I could only see her head, and her hands that were waving me on. Dad had my hands, his smile upside-down when I looked up as my toes touched the water. It's strange to think that someone could remember my life longer than me.

"I'm afraid to blink again," Mom says.

So much has changed since that first memory that it's just a thing in my head, not something I lived.

"What's it like getting older?"

The more time she takes before answering, the more I feel she's going to say it's awful. It's disappointing to work a shitty job and have a shitty kid. To keep having people change and let you down.

"It's not even close to what I imagined it would be." She's staring out the window like she doesn't even have to think about driving the car. "But it's actually pretty cool."

She sounds convincing when she says it but it's hard to believe her. "How?"

"Obviously, I don't make it look cool," she laughs, which makes my stomach tighten. "I had a lot of fun when I was a kid, and the good times are these really crystal-clear moments. But, when I think back, in between *those* moments, I was so anxious all the time. I was scared of what my mom and dad would think. Scared of what my friends would think. Scared of what people I didn't even like would think. I never felt like I had a chance to be myself because I was always trying to be what someone else wanted."

"And you're not scared now?"

I wonder what I'll be afraid of when I'm Mom's age. Or Grandpa's age. I want it to be nothing, but I don't know if that's possible, so I hope it's not something stupid. Maybe it'll be dying. It didn't seem that scary when the doctor told me about it, but the more I think about it, the scarier it sounds. I worry it'll just be more suffering, like moments waiting for Tiffany to show and she never does. I wonder how much Mom or Grandpa think about dying now that they're older.

"I hope I'm getting better. When I was younger, I dated guys that were way worse than Brad or—well—yeah. I would stick around because I was afraid to break up with them. Because then someone would have something bad to say about me. Afraid I was nothing on my own. And I would cry, I would be inconsolable, when they broke up with me even though I didn't like them."

I can remember Mom and Brad fighting, his beer cans on the table, his voice loud and deep. His hands come out from the black windshield to swipe at me. Mom's driving, but she's defending me too. And then Brad's voice softens until it sounds like Dad's voice. It's all the same words, same tone, reminding me that everything is my fault. It's me, and it sucks how even the parts I hate about me are still me. There's no escape.

"Brad came by the house," I say.

"What? When?" She leans into the steering wheel, her eyes flashing from me back to the road, as the car speeds up.

"A long time ago. You were at work."

"Why didn't you tell me?"

"I didn't want to talk about it."

"You should've—I wish you would've told me." Her voice is low. The car slows. She looks straight out the window and her lips hang open. "What did he say?"

"I don't know," I say, but it's all there, spinning around my head.

"Please, kiddo. You can tell me."

"It was my fault." As terrible as I feel, it's a relief not to think, not to have to come up with my own words. I open my mouth and his words pour out. "I'm the reason you guys broke up."

"That's what he said?"

"You guys had something good. It was me that ruined it."

"Don't believe that," her voice snaps.

"It's what happened. It happened with him. And Dad. And it happened with Tommy and Christina too. It's me."

"It *absolutely* was not your fault."

"Then whose fault is it?"

She exhales loudly.

"We make this life so much harder than it has to be." The car blurs. "It's no one's fault. You can't blame yourself or anyone else. These things just happen and they're terrible and awful, but they happen and you won't get anywhere by blaming someone. You just—move on. Do the best you can to move on." She smacks her hand on the steering wheel. "And Brad is an idiot. He's an asshole for trying to blame you. Really, if there was one person to blame, it would fucking be him."

"Why does it still feel like it's my fault?"

"Because that's easier. God, you probably get it from me," she groans. "It's easier to blame yourself than it is to accept that sometimes things are completely out of your control. It feels better in the moment but, trust me, it'll only make life harder."

"That sucks," I say, my throat choking, voice breaking.

She's crying and smiling. I try to apologize and she waves me off without saying anything. She laughs, which leads to more tears, and each time she waves me away again. I tell her I'm sorry but she won't hear it. I tell her I think I might actually be ok, and she will be too. We both hope it's true.

It's early enough when we get home that I could go to Tommy's. I'm off the antibiotics so I could drink again, but Mom puts on a movie that I remember watching with her and Dad when I was a kid so I stay. She makes popcorn while the credits start, like we used to in days that are so far away. At some point I fall asleep then wake up to one of the songs that's always playing in her car and the credits are rolling and she's passed out on the couch next to me with Daisy on top of her. It's too comfortable to want to leave, so I close my eyes.

16

SVEN'S BIKE IS propped against Tommy's building. It's copper-colored with white letters and handles and it almost matches the apartment. It should make me feel better, but it doesn't. I wanted to talk to Tommy alone, but now I know that everyone's gonna be there. Sven's bike looks gigantic when I set mine against it. As I'm standing there, I realize I don't hear any voices.

I walk in and it's just Sven and Tommy sitting on the couch watching an old skate video, listening to new music with no one else. They both nod without looking away from the screen. I can't stop staring at Sven. He looks totally comfortable sunk into the couch like it's Derek's parents' mashed-potato couch. He should be melting in a puddle of awkwardness. Instead he stares back at me.

"What?" he says.

"Nothing," I say. "What're you guys up to?"

Tommy laughs, "You haven't been around in a month and you're just gonna stroll in here all fucking casual?"

"I was sick."

"I know. We dropped you at the hospital after James fucking Smalling clocked me in the face."

"He couldn't see it coming because we were all looking at your dumb ass," Sven says.

Everything has changed here. Was I right not to come or did it change cause I was away? Can it come back or is it gone? The pit inside my stomach grows under their glares.

"Whatever," Tommy says. "What the fuck have you actually been up to?"

"Nothing, mostly."

"Bullshit," Sven says as he takes a drink.

My mouth goes dry.

"I heard you went to hang out at Derek's," he says.

That day's a blur, blended together with bus rides and images of Dad. Of disappointment stacked on disappointment, except for seeing Tiffany and holding her. It's the last time I saw her.

"Yeah, once."

"No. You've been back more than that."

He looks like he's ready to laugh as he leans back into the couch and arches his eyebrows, waiting for a response.

"Fuck," Tommy barks. "Who the fuck cares. Shannon told us you've been going around to see Tiffany."

"But how—"

"Tiffany was there, she just didn't want to talk to you," Sven smirks.

The words land like a punch in the throat. His smile is dissolving behind a curtain of water but I breathe and keep the tears at bay. I want to curl into a ball but I keep breathing and it keeps me together despite the battering of embarrassment.

The door swings open, and in comes Dan, Bert and Shane, who walks straight toward me and grabs me by the shoulders. He shakes me and I might just fall to pieces.

"My man!" he hollers. "We missed you. The boys tell you about tonight?"

"No," I mutter, my tongue like a dead fish.

"We're playing our first show. It's gonna be—well it'll probably be awful, but also awesome."

"We're gonna crush," Tommy says.

"Crush," Shane jokes and the pieces of me slowly come back together.

Bert hands me a drink without asking and I take a sip out of habit. It's harsh going down my throat and makes me think about dying, and there's part of me that wishes I were dead. That I could just disappear into nothing and never have to feel this way again.

"I tried to find you, but this doofus," he points to Sven who sneers, "didn't know your address."

I nod.

"We're low on booze," Bert says.

"Need me to go?" I ask.

"No," Sven says. "We got this."

"Developed a nice little two-man game at a store on the other side of town," Shane says. "Let 'em go."

"Pussies," Tommy says and finishes his drink.

Sven gets up behind him, moving with a rubbery looseness as he shoulders past me to the door. Then they're outside. I don't know where I am. I don't know what I'm doing. I hate that I hate it here and wish I never came. Why did I care if he and Christina were getting back together? What did I think I could do or say?

Shane turns off the music and in the crush of quiet I think I might crumble, but he pulls out his guitar and starts playing.

"So, you're coming, yeah?"

"What?"

"Come on. We could use one fan that's not Steve."

"What about Christina?" I ask.

"I do not think she will be in attendance, now or ever. But I'm guessing you saw that coming."

"What happened?"

"Fuck man, she bailed. The right call on her part. She's too good for that bullshit."

"Shannon?"

"That bullshit."

"And Tiffany."

"Her too."

My heart stops.

"You alright, dude?"

I don't have anything close to an answer. Any time I think I might, it dissolves in my hands. I'm alive. I'm in pain. I feel like an idiot again.

"Not really. I almost died and my dad didn't show up. No one showed up. I love Tiffany and now she's avoiding me." The words spill out and with them come the tears.

"Fuck man, that's heavy."

My chest shakes and aches and Bert's laugh is like an icepick in my side.

"Shut the fuck up, Bert," Shane yells.

He stops playing too. The room is silent and my slobbering taunts me from all sides.

"It's all good, dude. You're gonna be ok. And I'm sorry, I would've tried harder to find you had I known."

He shakes my shoulders again and is staring straight at me. His face starts to clear up.

"What you need," he says through a smile, "is to listen to some shit music and just rage. I think that's your cure-all."

"Yeah?"

"I mean I'm not a fucking doctor, but it couldn't hurt worse than the rest of that shit."

I laugh and so do they. Shane sits back down and starts to play and I close my eyes and try to sink into it, just breathe and not think of anything else.

Tommy bursts into the door like the leader of a circus. Sven's right behind him with the bag.

"Get ready, boys." Tommy says then looks at me and points. "We're takin' shots."

There's a cheer but it's not as loud as normal cause I'm not part of it. I do take another sip, though. It burns less with all the ice melted but tastes worse. Sven pours shots into plastic cups. He shoves one in my chest, the plastic crackling as a few drops of whiskey fling onto my shirt. He doesn't say anything. Just hands out the rest of the cups and stands at Tommy's side.

"This is it. First show of many to come." Tommy raises his cup and everyone follows. "Drink deep, motherfuckers."

Sven hoots.

I take the shot, the heat sliding down my throat, settling into my stomach like lava. I can remember how good that once felt, but I can't enjoy it now.

I'm done with my antibiotics, so I don't worry so much about dying. Instead, I think about the bb and almost dying, about Christina and Tommy breaking up, about Tiffany never talking to me, about whatever's going on with Sven and Dad and everything. I feel lost here, which is scary cause high school is about to start and if I can't hang out with them I'll probably be alone.

Tommy turns music back on then sits onto the couch. Shane plays along to the song as Tommy pulls out a stack of papers, his lips moving as he reads and his finger picking at the pages like a scab. He doesn't move from there, locked in total concentration, until he jumps up just before it's time to go.

"One last shot for the road," he shouts as he walks toward the kitchen, pausing in front of me. "And finish your fucking drink. You'd hate to put my boy and me through all that effort just to waste it."

He doesn't move, just stares at me. I don't know why he cares. Or if I do either, but I drink up anyway. And I take the shot he hands me after. And when we all get ready to leave it's like my body's adapting to the gravity on another planet.

It barely feels like we left, but we get to Tim's house and walk around the back, where there's old dog poop on the rocky side of the walkway. Shane, Dan and Bert materialized to meet us—they're setting up their instruments. There's no stage. Bert's drums are pushed up against the house between two sad tomato plants. Their small amps are leaned against the awning. Still the party is coming out to watch. The crowd parts for Tommy, Sven and me.

But as they do, people stare and snicker. They nudge each other and point at me.

"That's the fucking kid," someone says.

And someone laughs, "The one that collapsed in the living room."

My face burns and I look down to hide it, trying to follow closer to Tommy, but he's moving fast and I'd have to run to catch up.

Across the backyard I see Shannon and Tiffany. Our eyes lock and I can't look away. As we hold contact, I can feel my heart expanding until it might burst. Shannon taps her on the shoulder. Tiffany turns and my head is spinning like a tornado.

"Thanks for showing up," Shane says.

"I'm not the only one," I say and he chuckles. But I don't know why I showed up or what I'm doing or if I should leave and if I leave could I ever come back.

Dan plays a few notes on the bass and smiles. Tommy grabs the microphone.

"Hello," his voice booms, the party goes quiet. Tommy turns. "Ready?"

Bert responds with a few clicks of his drumsticks.

Then the music is smashing and clattering. Bursting bass and whirring guitar. It's different and the same as the music we listen to. It's chaos. It's incredible. Tommy's singing until the veins in his neck look like they're about to explode. My feet are frozen to the ground until I'm bumped from behind. There's a mosh pit, just like the videos, big guys circling, pushing and slamming against each other and I crash into the center and everything that's going on is going on directly inside of me, all meant to be there, all that chaos now like a laser that bursts out of me.

Sweat's dripping down my forehead, stinging my eyes. It hurts to keep them open, but I can barely see regardless. It's all a whirl of hands and feet and elbows. Something hits me in the chest, forcing me back but I press forward. My heart racing. The music propelling me through the turbulence. Like the time Mom and Dad took me to the beach and the waves dragged me down and I thrashed until I was back above the water. I don't know which way is up or down. When the song ends, I struggle to catch my breath and have to squint to see that Sven's staring at me like I'm crazy. Tiffany won't even look at me. But my heart pounds and my hands tingle and my head feels clearer than it ever has.

The mosh pit swirls without coming to a stop, waiting until the music blasts through again and it's hands and feet, pushing and kicking. Blurs of light and slaps of sweat and I don't stop until the music does.

When it's over my chest aches and my head feels light but I'm all smiles. There's a crowd around Tommy that includes Sven, Tiffany, and Shannon. I walk over toward Shane.

"You stole the show out there," he says.

"You guys were amazing!"

"Could've gone worse."

As we're talking, Tommy moves toward us and everyone follows.

"That shit was epic," Tommy says.

"Yeah, good job, man," Sven says quietly.

"A little too aggressive for my tastes," Shannon says.

Shane chuckles. "Thanks for the feedback."

Tiffany stands next to me. My heart was pounding but now it's going to blow up like a foil ball in the microwave. I glance over but her head's turned away. If we just weren't in the group, if I could just talk to her alone, I could figure out what's going on and we could get back together.

"Hey Hot Pants, how come you've been skulking around Tiffany's?" Shannon glares at me, but turns away before I can respond. "Little perv. Let's go inside, Tiff."

She opens the door to the house and Tiffany follows her. It feels like my heart's a grenade and the pin is attached to her. Watching her walk away, it explodes.

"Are you coming, Tommy?" Shannon stands with her hand on her hip, blocking the doorway.

"In a second," he says.

She goes inside with a flick of her hair and he just rolls his eyes.

"Dude," he says, punching me in the shoulder. "You were a maniac out there."

"Yeah, thanks," I say. "Should we go inside?"

"You sure you don't want to stay out here? You look fucking sweaty," Sven says.

"Let's go inside," Tommy says, and that's it.

The sliding door opens to the kitchen. People are slapping Tommy and Shane, all the guys, on the shoulder. I look around, hoping to see Tiffany but can't find her in the sea of bodies. Then Tim stops me, wild-eyed and arms raised.

"Dude!" he screams and the whole room looks at us as he hands me a beer. "That was something. Fucking something!"

"Thanks."

He points to the beer he just handed me.

"Don't drink too many of those," he says, his voice cracking with laughter.

"Sure."

I take the beer and keep moving in the path that Tommy makes. I figure if he's looking for Shannon, Tiffany will be there as well. But Tommy heads for the garage and Sven with him. Shane holds back and as the door closes I see Shannon and Tiffany coming down the stairs.

"Did Tommy come inside?" Shannon demands.

Shane nods his head toward the garage and Shannon groans. She stomps past us and out. Tiffany stops and stares at the door like it's the haunted woods we camped at as kids.

"I'm gonna grab something," Shane says and walks back toward the kitchen.

And in the swirling chaos of the party, it's just Tiffany and me. But she won't look at me.

"I tried to come see you."

She doesn't look up.

"Sven said you were there," I say.

"Are you sure you should be drinking that?" she says, pointing to the unopened beer.

"I'm not."

She looks up with an eye roll.

"How come you didn't come see me?" I ask.

"I—" she starts but the garage door opens, the noise pours out as Shannon and Tommy and Sven pour in.

"This party's fucking busted," Shannon blurts and the crowd around her turns to stare. "We're going to Tommy's."

"Can you drop me off at home first?" Tiffany asks.

"No."

"It's not far. And it's on the way."

"Then you can walk, can't you?" `

"Seriously?"

"Seriously."

"I'll walk with you," I say.

"There you go, Tiff. Hot Pants will escort you," she laughs and my face burns.

Tiffany's shaking her head, glaring, but she says, "Ok."

"I'll grab my bike."

I run through the crowd. Tim hoots again when I pass, out through the sliding door and down the poop-filled sideyard to grab my bike just as Tiffany's stepping into the cool night air. Tommy, Sven and Shannon walk by to Shannon's car.

"Have fun," she jokes.

Tiffany rolls her eyes and folds her arms. She's silent as we start the walk. It's dark and quiet—a new moon. I smile cause we really are all alone. When we can't hear the party any more, the only noise is the clinking of my bike chain and the occasional hum of a car driving slowly down some other street. Her hair waves at the corner of my eyes but I keep looking ahead. My breathing is blocked by all the worthless words that want to race out.

"You never answered," I finally let slip.

She glances over and back.

"Why you never—"

"I know."

"Well?"

My chest is squeezing me, like it knows I shouldn't be asking these things but I can't stop myself. I look over and she won't look back. I always thought she looked exactly like her mom, but she has the same eyes as her dad, the ones that make you feel welcome even when you're not.

"I didn't know what to say."

"You could've said anything. I just wanted to see you."

"That's not true. You say it is, but it's not."

She finally turns to me. She looks sad and angry.

"It is, though."

"No!" she snaps.

Her voice cuts and rebounds in the emptiness around us. A light flicks on in the window of a house and an old man peeks through the blinds.

"It's not," she says softer now.

It's quiet again, the clinking of my chain counting the time but it no longer feels like we're alone. We walk in silence as we reach the neighborhood. My throat is tight and my chest is caving in and I focus on breathing but that just helps time go faster. We turn the corner onto her street.

When I was a kid I thought her house was a castle, the best place in the world. It doesn't look like that anymore, mostly cause a lot of the houses on her street are the same size now, but also cause I know now that it's just a house. The place is no longer magic, but she is.

She stops at the walkway, where the grass snakes to the front door, her arms folded, eyes behind her hair and mouth pursed. I can feel every thought and emotion inside of me pressing against my skin, aching to get out.

"I almost died."

"I know. I'm sorry."

It's as quiet as it's ever been here. I wonder how much longer it'll take before I know what to say or do to fill this silence. But all the possibilities, and the fact that I'll probably never know which one is right, make my heart hurt. I squeeze my bike. My hands are hot and damp with sweat.

"I love you," I say with a shot of happiness and anxiety that overrides everything.

She looks up. Her eyes are all I ever want to see. My whole body shivers as she steps toward me but turns her face just as I try to kiss her. My lips press against the soft warmth of her cheek. Her arms wrap around me, holding back my exploding heart.

"I'm sorry," she says.

Her body untangles and springs toward the house and she's gone.

It's so dark and empty without her.

17

I COULDN'T SLEEP or breathe last night. I just sat there, staring at the ceiling in the darkness, seeing Tiffany's green eyes shining like home as she turns away from me and peels my heart like an orange. Still I laid in bed until morning, after Mom left, cause I couldn't drag myself out.

But the longer I lay there, the more I feel trapped. The worse her not loving me feels. The more inescapable her image is. And if I don't get up soon, it's going to smother me.

I roll out of the covers and sit on the edge of the bed and see the faint outline of Mom and KJ's initials in the heart scribbled out. I get up and grab a pen to write Tiffany's and my initials together. My chest pounds like I'm going to get in trouble even though I know Mom won't be mad about this.

I don't circle our initials with a heart, though. Not yet. I stare at it and imagine there must be a way we could still be together. But I can't think of one and it makes my insides boil.

I have to move, get out of the house. I snag a waffle and leave Daisy scratching at the back door while I grab my bike and start to ride. The sun is shining and the breeze is cool. I take a bite of the waffle but can't taste it and my stomach can't handle it. I toss it into the gutter and pedal until my lungs start to burn.

Just riding bikes is kid stuff, but it's the only thing I can think to do, so I keep going. I remember racing Derek from his house to mine and back. It was before we knew Sven. Tiffany would start us off and wait at the finish line with a bandana for the checkered flag.

I turn the corner down their street now and I can see the red and white bandana in her hands as I race toward her. But as I get close the garage door opens. I grip the handlebars and pedal hard until I'm way past their house, around the back way. I pause and turn to see Peter back out the driveway and drive away. It sucks being scared to be seen there after it had been better than home for so long. But after everything that's happened this summer, everyone in that house must hate me.

When I start riding again, I try to get the image of Tiffany cheering and waving the flag back, but it's gone and I go slow as I leave the neighborhood. I don't know where I'm heading. I pass J n the B, and pass school—now my old school. I ride by Tim's neighborhood and I pass Tommy's where there are no bikes or cars, but I don't stop. I ride until I don't really know where I am and then I see the restaurant, the one with the same black and red logo that was on Christina's work shirt and I pull into the parking lot. An old man is hanging out behind the restaurant smoking a cigarette. He flicks it on the ground, still burning on the concrete, and goes in the building through the side.

Then I see Christina through the glass front, standing at a desk. She laughs when she notices me. I jump off my bike and set it against the building as she opens the door, looking left and right and behind her.

"How's it goin'?" she asks.

I didn't realize that I missed just hearing her voice.

"Not great," I say and she frowns. "Maybe you can help, though?"

"I'd like to try," she says, her voice calm and easy. "Can it wait 'til after work though?"

"Um…"

"Am I paying you to stand around and talk to friends?" a voice booms and then I see the smoking man's reflection in the glass behind her.

"Sorry, sir," Christina says.

She turns to go inside and my heart sinks, though I don't know what I was hoping for. Or how it's even possible to be hopeful anymore.

As the door closes she pauses and turns back, saying, "I'm off at three. Come back then."

I nod and smile cause she looked happy still, normal. It feels good to know that's possible. But now that she's gone, I'm left with the image of Tiffany last night on a loop. And each time it goes around I feel worse. So I grab my bike and start to ride. I can't go home or to Tiffany's. I could go to the river but it's too far. So, I go to Tommy's even though going back seems strange.

It's still quiet when I pull up. I can't hear anyone when I open the door. There are empty cans of beer covering the table and tipped over on the carpet. It smells a little like the space on the side of the dryer where Daisy used to throw up. I call Tommy's name and his bed creaks, feet shuffle and his door clicks open. His eyes look crusty. He tugs on his hair and it sticks straight up.

"What's goin' on?" He walks by and high-fives me before collapsing onto the couch.

"I don't know."

"How fuckin' mysterious."

"I was just riding my bike and didn't know where to go. And then I saw Christina—"

"If you came to talk about Christina, it's too early."

"I didn't."

He rubs the crust off his eyes with his palms.

"So, then, what's really goin' on?"

"I just..." I stop. In my head Tiffany is smiling, laughing, then walking away from me and the beauty and the pain rip me in two. "I don't know what to do about Tiffany."

"What's there to do? You guys kissed and now she doesn't want to see you. Move on."

"But I don't want to."

"She made that choice for you, though."

"So there's no hope?"

"Hope is in all the other girls out there," he says and turns on some music I haven't heard before. "Why do you want to get with her if she doesn't want to be with you?"

"Why doesn't she want to be with me?"

The thought rockets my soul into a black hole. He stares at me and pulls his hair back.

"I don't know that she doesn't, dude. Maybe she does. But is it worth all this shit to figure that out?"

"I feel like an idiot."

"Why?" His sincerity startles me.

"It was stupid to think she could like me. She's two grades older, she's smart and beautiful and—"

"She fucking kissed you! Maybe it's not you that's being stupid. Maybe it's her."

Tommy looks at the door like Daisy when the mailman's walking up our yard and I hear the rattling of his dad's car. Tommy slides off the couch and onto his feet, staring out the front door. He doesn't say anything.

"Should I go?" I ask.

"If you want," he says. His jaw is clenched so tight his lips go white at the corners. His hands curl into fists.

I stay and we watch the door silently as the engine grinds to a stop. A car door opens and slams. Steps start and get louder. The footsteps turn to hard slaps. He's an oversized shadow when he reaches the screen door.

"The fuck is going on here?" he says as he steps inside.

"Nothing," Tommy says, as cool as he can.

Tommy's dad's shorter than him, but his arms are wound even tighter with muscle. He's holding a twelve-pack of beer and his veins are exploding out of his dirt-crusted hands. He stares at Tommy with Tommy's eyes, only a little darker, colder. He looks at me while he waits for an answer. I don't move. I don't flinch. I stare back silently.

His dad looks around, the wrinkles get deeper as he sees the empty cans on the table and floor.

"I don't like you having friends over to my house," he says, still softly, but with an anger that coats the walls.

I look at Tommy and I can feel the breath in his chest. His dad turns away, pulling out a can as he walks toward the fridge.

"I live here, too," Tommy says. His voice a deep growl that doesn't sound intimidating.

"Because I let you. Don't make me reconsider."

I can feel Brad when he talks, even though they look nothing alike. I get why Tommy never talks about him.

"What's it matter to you? You're never here and when you are you're too wasted to care?"

"I'm here now and I don't fucking like what I see," Tommy's dad says as he closes the fridge.

"Why? Huh?" Tommy's voice gets louder, sharper. "What does it matter to you?"

"It's my house! Mine!" The words burst apart the room. "That roof over your head, those lights in your room, that's me. My work, my time. So when I'm here I'll do what I want and you'll do the same."

"So where do I fit in?"

"You choose to or you don't."

He pulls a beer out, sets the case on the ground, pops open the can, and takes a sip. His veins pulse. He runs his right hand through gelled black hair, pressing it down hard so it sticks to his head.

"This place is a fucking pigsty."

"It's cleaner than you've ever left it."

"Don't start with me!" he snaps, then cools. "I'd hate to show your friend what a little boy you are."

He sets his beer on the counter and walks toward us. Inside his steps are louder, heavier. His eyes get darker as he gets closer.

"Hey," I say, and Tommy and his dad both glare at me but I clench my teeth and try to find any words that could help. "Let's get out of here, Tommy."

"Who the fuck are you?" Tommy's dad says with gravel and anger.

"I'm his friend," I say. "Come on. Let's go."

My feet feel like they're about to fall through the floor but I keep moving. Tommy's dad doesn't yell, doesn't say anything. He doesn't move. He barely even notices me now. He focuses all his attention on Tommy, who walks slowly past him, returning his glare. All the violence in all the songs we listen to barely adds up to their stares.

The house is creepy quiet when Tommy walks into his room until he starts rustling. I can hear the quick scratch of him tying his shoelaces. He's silent as we walk out, letting the door rattle closed behind us.

I grab my bike and, as I turn, I see Tommy's skateboard hurtling toward the middle of the street. It lands with a crash. When we get to it, he picks it up and the nose is splintering off, but I'm shocked it didn't totally shatter. I don't understand how things survive what should break them.

We don't ride or talk. We don't know where we're going. We just walk. My body feels shaky but light and I keep turning around to make sure his dad's not coming after us. The fear starts to fade as the apartment disappears in the distance.

We're a ways from the house when Tommy stops. His arms press down and his chest sticks out as his chin points to the sky. He screams, "FUCK," with a force that shakes me to my feet.

"Asshole," he says, quieter.

Maybe it shouldn't have taken so long for me to realize why Christina would talk about Tommy's problems with me. Or why Tommy would never talk about them. I don't like talking about them, either.

"My mom's old boyfriend was an asshole, too."

"Who fucking cares."

"When he was around it didn't feel like I had a home. I would dream about running away."

"Why the *fuck* didn't you?"

"I guess I was scared. I mean, what would I do? Where would I go?"

"Anywhere," he says.

I shrug cause I don't have an answer, but I know he doesn't either or he would've left his house a long time ago. We start walking again. Still no discussion of where we're going, just moving to move.

"So, what happened?" He breaks the silence. His fists clench and unclench without looking at me.

"He was always saying shit, cursing at me. Sometimes he'd throw his empty cans at me. One night he got drunk—he was drunk most nights. But this time he tried to attack me cause he was mad when I wouldn't tell him where the bb gun was." Tommy's quiet. "So, I guess it was kinda your fault."

He laughs and grabs the side of his head, runs his hands through his hair and looks like he's going to pull it all out, then laughs again, "Fuck you."

"I forgive you," I joke. He looks like he might punch me, not in a mean way, but one that would hurt still. "It sucked, but it got my mom to break up with him. If that didn't happen he might still be living at our house."

"So he's gone now and life's back to normal?"

I think about hanging out at Derek's with Sven. Going home to Mom and Dad, then Mom and Brad. Daisy in her hole by the wall. Grandpa alone in the desert. Tiffany and her dad and mom in their perfect-looking house around the block from Sven's parents and their junk.

"I don't know what normal is," I say.

Tommy doesn't respond. He probably wanted a better answer. So do I.

We keep walking through neighborhoods where the houses all look the same. If they're a different color it's only slightly. The blues look like the greys, look like the browns. But I bet they just look that way from the outside.

"He wasn't always an asshole," Tommy says.

"What was he like?"

"A dad. Fuck. I used to have friends over all the time and he never cared." He stops. "Maybe it was just my mom. She liked it when they were there. He probably barely tolerated us. Now that she's not around, there's no one to keep him from acting like an asshole."

"Where did your mom go?"

"I don't know."

"I'm sorry."

"Whatever, I'm fucking fine."

"I know," I say, but I don't. "I know where my dad is. That doesn't help."

He laughs again.

"Never have kids, I guess."

"Or just don't be like our parents."

"If that's even possible."

"I hope it is."

There's a stop light ahead and now I know where we are. The high school is just to the right. That doesn't make me feel better. Compared to my old school, this one is enormous. Big, white blocks of buildings like prisons with no one outside. It'll probably be scarier when it's full of people and I have to figure out where I'm going, what I'm doing and who I can actually hang out with. My mouth goes dry. I hope I can hang out with Tommy and Shane. Maybe even Derek too. I hope Tiffany will spend time with me. And Christina would be there instead of Shannon.

I realize it's time to talk to Christina.

"Hey," I say. "I have to go."

"Where?" he says softly.

He's looking at me like we're both lost and I'm crazy. I don't want to tell him where I'm going, cause I know he doesn't want me to talk to him about Christina. But I don't want to lie. I take a deep breath and start to feel a hint of calm.

"I'm supposed to talk to someone, to Christina."

"Why?"

"To talk about that thing, you know, about Tiffany. I tried before I went to your place but she was working."

"Oh," he says and it sounds so normal even though it's Tommy Pescadero. "She'd be a good person to talk to."

"Do you want to come?" I can't believe I ask.

"She doesn't want to see me."

"You don't have to."

"Whatever, if you want me to go, I'll go."

I don't say anything, just start to hop on my bike and he gets a running start before jumping on his board.

Now that there's a destination we ride with purpose. Cars pass and we catch up at stop lights. A green Suburban is packed with high school kids that Tommy knows, who I've met at parties but I barely remember, which is strange since I'll have to deal with them next year. That doesn't seem bad as Tommy laughs and flips them off. But if he wasn't around, it wouldn't be so easy.

Tires squeal as they moon us and drive away. Tommy grins like a madman until we cruise up to the parking lot outside of Christina's work where he stops and sits on the curb at the far edge of the lot, out of view from the front of the restaurant.

"You go talk to her. I'm gonna hang back here," he says.

"You sure?"

"Positive."

I ride up to the door and Christina is smiling. She points toward the back, where her boss entered earlier. I barely press the pedal, trying to coast as slowly as possible to the spot. The bike starts to wobble when I'm close and I jump down. The door opens a few minutes later and Christina exits, shaking her hair out of its ponytail.

"So, what's going—wait," Christina pauses and nods toward Tommy, her expression serious. "This isn't about him is it?"

"No, I promise. I just—after I talked to you I went to his place. And then his dad showed up and we had to leave and we were walking around and I told him I was going to come talk to you. He didn't even want to come."

"Of course he didn't."

"No, it's not like that. He just—I mean—he didn't want to come cause he thought you wouldn't want to see him."

If Tommy can feel her stare, he's still not showing it. He's looking toward the TJ Maxx on the other side of the parking lot where nothing is actually happening. Christina gives me the same face Mom does when I forget to pick up after Daisy.

"What is it you wanted to talk about?" she says, like she doesn't believe that it's not about Tommy. Her eyes are kind anyway.

"It's about a girl."

"Who?" she asks, and now she's smiling again.

My face starts to burn and I forget why I'm here. Reliving everything, saying it out loud, will almost certainly make it worse. My stomach is raging and I'm starting to sweat. I try to breathe but it feels like I'm being crushed. Still, I tell her everything about Tiffany.

"What are you hoping for?" she says when I finally finish.

"That she'll love me. That she'll want to be with me."

"Ok, so?"

"It was…" I stop, wishing I could just melt into a puddle and slide into the gutter. "I passed out at a party."

"What did I tell you about drinking like that?"

"It wasn't that. I passed out from an infection. The doctors said I got pneumonia. That I could have died."

Saying it reminds me of how bad it got. How close I actually came to dying. How stupid I was. Christina hugs me, her breath choppy. When I pull away she has tears in her eyes, which makes me feel worse for her hug making me feel better.

"Are you ok, now?" she asks.

"Yeah," I say and look at my palm; the dot still there but that's not what hurts. "I told her I loved her."

"What did she say?" Christina asks softly, her eyes turning sad.

"She's sorry."

"Oh, no," she says. "That's—that's—wow. I'm so sorry."

I should have known better than to come here, but Christina hugs me again and it feels like maybe I won't fall apart just yet.

"What sucks is that I think she does like me." My words are muffled in her shoulder. "I know she does."

"She might. She should. I mean, she did kiss you."

"So what can I do?"

"I don't think there's anything you can do right now. Give her time. Give her space. I mean, you already gave it your best shot, right? Now she's gotta come around."

I nod. It's all I can manage.

"Ugh, I'm sorry," she says. "I know that feeling, like you're totally hollow except for the pain and embarrassment like shards of glass jabbed into your heart. It's a car crash in your chest. It's terrible."

She glances at Tommy and I pretend not to notice.

"Yeah."

"But, you're gonna be ok."

"Sure," I chuckle cause I trust her, but it also sounds absurd. "You too, right?"

She laughs, sweet and sad, then sighs and her head and arms go limp until she snaps up and pulls her hair back tight into a ponytail.

"I don't know why it has to be so hard," she says.

"My dad told me once that if life's hard, it's because it wants you to earn it. I don't know why, but that always stuck with me. Now it just seems like a bad joke."

She laughs hard but her eyes are soft and light and her smile's thin when she gives me a hug. I miss having her around. Even if she and Tommy didn't get back together, I wish she could still hang out with us.

"I was gonna offer to walk with you, but..." she nods toward Tommy, "another of life's difficulties."

"I get it."

"You do, and I appreciate that. Don't be a stranger."

"I won't."

We hug once more and I head back toward Tommy at the end of the lot. He stands up when he sees me coming and picks up his skateboard. He takes two quick steps and hops on, one push and his mouth is pinched as he skates past me toward Christina.

"Hey," I hear him say when he gets close to her, but that's all.

His hands dance around silently, pointing and opening and running through his hair. She's shaking her head and rolling her eyes. She laughs. They're standing close but not touching. And in my head I can imagine their conversation so clearly. He's apologizing, saying he's sorry, saying he was stupid. And she agrees or tells him he's right for once and that's when she laughs and he says they should give it another chance and he won't be an idiot this time and she tells him he better not and means it, but she rolls her eyes and smiles.

It plays out so perfectly in my head, but that's not real. I know that even before he turns away without a kiss or a hug or even a handshake. Before he's walking back to me with a flat face and his skateboard in hand. And she's scowling at him—or me.

Tommy just keeps going past me. I wave to her and hope she'll hang out with me when we're at school, then hurry to catch up to Tommy. We're walking as cars pass with the occasional shout of someone who knows us, but Tommy doesn't react now.

He won't tell me what they talked about. I don't ask. I have enough to think about with Tiffany.

Tommy's dad's car is still parked in front of his house so that's out, and when I ask about going to Shane's or anyone else's, he doesn't say anything. So we keep walking, past Tim's and the J n the B, past the supermarket and Sven's, whose windows are now completely filled with yellowed boxes.

We pass the Thieson twins who actually hide behind a tree until we're about to turn the corner. Down the street is Tiffany's house. My heart hurts with the hope that she's thinking about me. That she's working up the courage to change her mind.

But we pass her street and, when we round the last corner, I realize I'm taking Tommy Pescadero to my house and have no idea why. It was a mistake. It's going to be weird and he's going to think my house is lame.

We go in the side, through the garage. I never noticed how dirty it was until he was here to watch me set my bike down and we have to step over piles of clothes to get inside. Cobwebs and cracks are everywhere and the door squeaks open.

The house is quieter than his place, even though it was just the two of us there too. Also, it's more intense, which gets worse the longer he's not talking. The more he looks around the kitchen and living room and bedroom. He turns in the hallway at the sound of Daisy's nails scratching on the glass door.

"Is the dog allowed inside?"

"Yeah."

He opens the door and she rushes in, sniffing up from his feet to his crotch where she buries her head. He laughs, and the house doesn't feel so strange now. When Daisy walks over to me, Tommy goes outside and Daisy and I both follow.

"Dude," he's looking around. "Why don't we hang out here?"

"Cause your place is cooler."

"Looks like you have a TV and a couch, which is the only decent part about that shithole."

I realize his place isn't the nicest, but it always felt magical to me. The cracks in his walls, the cobwebs in his corners, the stains on his ceilings—none of it was embarrassing. None of it mattered. When we're there, we're free.

Tommy starts to act normal and is just talking about stuff: songs and bands and places he wants to go when he gets outta here. He uses the phone to call Shane, who must've called Sven and Bert and Dan to come hang out cause it's not long until I hear the beep of Shane's car alarm, slamming of doors, and all of their voices.

"Hey," Tommy says. "Thanks for today or whatever."

"Of course," I say.

He's completely back to normal when the screen door creaks open, the door handle rattles, someone pounds in rhythm and someone else shrieks until I let them inside.

"What do you have the door locked for?" Shane says.

"This place is close to the pool, right?" Bert asks.

"Yeah, that was just on the street before," Shane answers.

"We should go back there."

"I'd rather chill here," Tommy says, and I'm grateful, though I don't know if he realizes the pool house is Tiffany's house.

Shane has his guitar and starts playing. It's good to hear music in the house, like the good times with Dad. I almost disappear into it until I see Sven brought whiskey, which makes my stomach sink thinking about Mom finding out. Sven tips it, pouring a drink that he hands to me and I hold with shaking hands, not wanting to drink it and unable to set it down.

Shane's dancing around while he plays and Tommy starts singing along. Dan and Bert are sitting at the kitchen table watching. Everyone looks drunk, which feels out of place here. And it feels weird not to be part of it. Sven leans toward me from the couch, his breath like a desert breeze.

"Why the fuck aren't you drinking?" Sven asks loud enough to hear over the music.

Dan and Bert turn around in their chairs. Shane smirks but keeps playing. Tommy doesn't stop singing.

"Why do you care?"

Sven shakes his head. His eyes are heavy and dark and make me happy I'm not drinking. He stops talking and it starts not to feel so bad having everyone here when Tommy puts on the Poison the Well album that I love, *Opposite of December*. Shane plays and sings along to make it funny, everyone is laughing. The energy in the house is happy like it hasn't been in a long time. Daisy is so excited she's bouncing from person to person like an old dog mosh pit. But the gnawing in my stomach won't go away.

"How're you doin', dude?" Shane says, taking a break to get a drink and sitting next to me, his voice slipping under the music so no one else can here.

"Fine," I say, not wanting to mention the drinking cause they'll all think I'm acting like a pussy. "Just thinking about stuff."

"I was driving around earlier and I saw you talking to Christina. Tommy was hanging off to the side. I'd hate to be conducting that train wreck."

"Huh?"

"Were you the middleman for their shit?"

"No. We were just hanging out and I went to her for advice."

"Oh," he smiles. "Go on."

Tommy's leaning against the kitchen counter talking to Bert. Dan's just watching and Sven's making a drink. "I was asking her about Tiffany."

"Look, I get it. She's a fucking babe. But I think you need to move on."

"Are you still talking about Tiffany?" Sven chuckles as he walks back to the couch with his drink, and now everyone is looking. "That's so pathetic."

He says it so casually. Like he doesn't give a shit about me, and maybe he doesn't.

"What makes you think you have a chance with her?" Sven says. His voice is loud and high with delight. His eyes are shadowed. "She's so far out of your league."

I grip my glass so tight I start to shake. Little drops of whiskey spot my hand.

"What do you know, you've never kissed a girl!"

My breath is racing. I try to slow it down but can't. Sven's lips snake into a smile that I want to smack off.

"Actually, I have," he laughs, his face like Derek's stretched out.

"Yeah, right."

"He really did. You know Samantha?" Bert says.

"I don't care," I say.

"I think you do," Sven says.

"She's pretty hot," Bert says.

"Why would I care that you finally kissed a girl?"

"You and Derek always acted like you're so much cooler than me. Cause you hooked up with Sheena or you were better at video games. And I was lucky you let me hang out. But now you know that's bullshit. Now you won't have someone that you can constantly make fun of."

"What are you talking about?"

"Don't pretend you don't know."

"I always tried to *not* make fun of you."

"Let's not get too carried away, boys," Shane says.

Sven doesn't pay attention to him. I wish that I were drunk now cause I feel like I'm going to throw up anyway.

"You called *me* Sven, but now it's you. Now it's you that's trying to get with a girl who thinks you're invisible." His eyes are heavy and wild. "How does that feel? Huh? You have to deal with that. And just being quiet and hoping it will pass doesn't work. You'll get quieter and quieter until you don't have anything to say. You, who always thought he knew everything. But you fucking don't."

Sven picks up his drink and walks over to the kitchen table where Dan and Bert are hanging out. He sits down and smiles straight at me when he takes his next sip. He takes a medicine bottle out of his pocket and shakes a pill into his hand. Then he pops it in his mouth and washes it down with another drink.

I clench my fists and step forward but Shane moves between us. He starts playing music again, just staring at me with a goofy face, moving in front of me every time I try to get around until I stop and slowly everyone goes back to whatever they were doing before.

The sick feeling in my stomach won't go away, but it moves. And instead of burning because I'm angry or embarrassed, it's because I did treat Sven like he was a loser. Not as bad as Derek, but enough that I should feel like an asshole. And worse that he's noticed all this time. It made me anxious that he was so awkward. That he *was* such a loser. But, I guess that wasn't the real him. People can change. He clearly has. Maybe I could've helped.

I'm still trying not to throw up when Sven leaves with Dan and Bert. He doesn't say anything when he walks out. He doesn't even look back. I don't try to say anything either. There's too much out there.

"Well. That got tense," Shane says.

Tommy slaps my leg.

"You must've been in his head about that girl thing," Shane says.

"I guess."

"Tiffany's hotter than that chick Sam. If that helps at all."

I nod. They glance at each other. And, in the quiet after, we hear the crunch of tires in the driveway and Daisy's wagging tail thumping against the couch until she scrambles to the door.

"That's my mom," I whisper after her door closes. "You guys should go."

The house is a mess. There are empty cups all over the place. It smells like Grandpa. Luckily, not weed. Still, there's no escaping. I'm too tired to even care.

"And let you get busted alone?" Tommy says.

"What's the worst that can happen?" Shane asks.

"She kills us," I say.

"Three to one are pretty good odds," Tommy says.

"Whose side is the dog on?" Shane jokes.

Mom's feet slap the steps and her keys jingle. Shane and Tommy are smiling, holding cups up to their mouths when Mom walks in. Her shoulders are slumped, her eyes are baggy, and it looks like she might walk down the hall without noticing. I'm holding my breath, but it wheezes out like a popped balloon when she turns.

She stands in the hallway with Daisy rubbing up against her leg and closes her eyes, "What. The. Fuck."

"Hello, ma'am," Shane says.

"Nope," Mom snaps sharp and points at him.

Shane doesn't say anything. Tommy moves his drink into his lap.

Mom's eyes light up when she looks at me. "What is going on?"

"Nothing really," I say.

"After all that's happened, you're drinking here!"

"Ma'am, that's our fault," Shane says. "We thought it would be fun to try so we brought it over, but your son didn't even have a sip. He didn't even want it in here. Never-you-mind that cup he's holding."

"Cut the Eddie Haskell shit." Her voice is flat and she looks at me from the side of her eyes. "We're going to talk about this later."

"It really is our fault," Tommy says. He's serious and I'm thankful.

"I'm too tired to deal with you now. So you have two options: I call your parents and they come pick you up—I'm sure they'd be thrilled to do that at this hour—or you stay here. The choice is up to you, but either way you're dumping out those drinks *right now*."

Tommy and Shane walk straight to the kitchen and pour their drinks into the sink.

"Mom, it's not actually their fault," I say.

"It's not. This, here, is one hundred percent your responsibility," she says. "Though I'm sure you boys are perfectly capable of making your own bad decisions. Now, tell me your names."

"Shane."

"Tommy."

"So you're the new friends?"

They nod.

"And when he hangs out with you, he's stealing alcohol and getting drunk and nearly fucking dying." And she actually smiles even though she's shaking her head. "Now he's drinking again with you. Is there anything else I should know about?"

"That's about the worst of it," Shane says.

"Well that's a relief," she says sarcastically. "So, would you boys like me to call your parents now? Or are you going to be staying with us?"

"I actually wasn't drinking," I say.

She grunts and stomps into the kitchen, grabs the half-full bottle of whiskey and pours the whole thing down the drain.

"I'm not actually drunk," Shane says. "And I have a car, so I can just take Tommy and head home."

"Was that one of the options?"

For the first time I see that Shane's shocked to the point that he doesn't have anything to say.

"I hoped your friends would be smarter," Mom says. "Shane, give me your keys. You boys have your choice: sleep here tonight or I'm calling your parents now. Make your decision quick, because I'm not in the mood to wait."

"This is good. It's nice here," Shane says.

"I'll stay here, too," Tommy says with a voice that's easier than any I've heard him use before.

"Good," Mom says and walks to the hallway. "Grab them some blankets and go to your room."

"Thanks," Tommy says.

"Goodnight," Mom says and turns off the lights. "Oh, and I'll know if you sneak out tonight."

"We wouldn't dream of it, ma'am," Shane says sincerely.

The hallway creaks and when the door closes I look back to Shane and Tommy, who're staring at me with half-smiles.

"Well," Tommy says. "Looks like the party's over."

"Hurry up with those blankets," Shane adds.

I grab the extra blankets from the closet and wait for Shane and Tommy to say anything other than thanks, but they don't. I think I can hear their voices again once I'm in my room, but it's hard to tell. When I hear Mom and Daisy's steps I lie down. She opens the door and Daisy hops up and lies on my pillow. Mom sits on the edge of the bed next to me. I stare at the discolored spot on the ceiling.

It's quiet for a while, then I hear Shane's giggle. Mom doesn't say anything about it.

"What're you doing?" she asks.

"I know you think it's stupid and that they're bad people and that—"

"That's not what I said," she says and lies down, too. "The question I asked was: what are you doing?"

I stare at the ceiling and the whole summer flashes before me—a chaotic jumble of pain and elation and shame and friends and music. The hole in my hand now healed. Tiffany, smiling and kissing me then hair fluttering as she turns away from me. It's all there, but nothing makes any sense. With each scene I feel more lost, less prepared for the year ahead—for life. I want to start over but I can't. The end of summer is bearing down on me like an asteroid.

"I don't know."

18

A DOOR SHUTS and I sit straight up in bed to the clack and clatter of skateboard wheels. It's light through the blinds but it still looks early. My head feels foggy. There was music in my dreams. Dad was singing and playing guitar as Mom swayed and kicked up pine needles in the woods. There was a campfire where Derek and Tiffany sat around with their parents, but only Dad was singing and only Mom was dancing. I just watched from the other side of the fire until Dad disappeared into the darkness of the woods.

I walk out of my room and it's like walking back toward the dream. There's music and it's getting louder. The song's familiar but new. I pass the couch with the crumpled blankets and Daisy runs up, her tail wagging, and almost knocks me over. Shane's sitting at the kitchen table with his guitar, and even though I'm watching him it's hard to believe it's just him playing.

"Mornin' kiddo," Mom says from the kitchen. "Want pancakes?"

"Of course the young gentleman wants pancakes," Shane says.

Mom shakes her head but pulls down the bowls. She's dancing as she mixes the pancake batter, then puts butter in the pan. It melts and starts to bubble and the whole kitchen smells sweet. Shane's grinning at me and I realize it's just him. The skateboard I heard when I woke up was Tommy leaving.

"Where's Tommy?" I ask quietly.

His smile gets big and he nods his head at Mom. My face burns that Mom drove Tommy away.

"He had somewhere to be," Shane says.

He chuckles as he starts to sing, powerful but soft, 'This Charming Man,' and that's how I know the song. My whole body starts to tingle. That's what Dad was singing in my dream, and I can see him as the campfire flickers off his eyes. He'd sing this song all the time. It's hard not to hear Dad, but when Shane sings it's a different song and it sounds amazing.

"Ugh, I love this one," Mom says as she pours batter into the pan.

It seems unreal that he can sing like this but I've never heard him. It's like he's a different person, until he looks up between singing to make a funny face.

"How come you don't sing all the time?" I ask.

He grins and shrugs.

"No, really?"

"I just don't do it around y'all. It's not what we play," he says and stops and the only sound in the room is the hiss of the pan.

"Did you stop because I said I loved it?" Mom says.

"Cat, I would never willfully do anything that makes you unhappy," Shane says.

"Eddie freaking Haskell."

"That's twice you've mentioned him, who is that?"

"You're so young."

"You break my heart, Cat."

Mom stares at him with dead eyes then shakes her head until the ringing of the phone fills the whole house. She grabs it and wedges it between her ear and shoulder while she holds the pan and flips the pancakes.

"Hey, Amy," she says and walks out of the kitchen.

"Why did Tommy really leave?" I ask again.

"Your very concerned mother had a little chat with us this morning. And—on top of it being more than a little early for our friend, Tom—it may have been a touch overbearing, too."

I just stare.

"She was giving us a little lecture about our drinking habits. Tommy sat through it, but I'm not sure he fully appreciated it," he says,

and starts laughing while my throat is squeezed into oblivion. "Don't worry, dude. It was actually kinda cool. I mean, a total buzzkill, but your mom seems pretty badass."

And even though hearing that sends out sparks of happiness, the discomfort smothers it.

"What was she saying?"

"You know, mom stuff. That we shouldn't be drinking. That we shouldn't be getting into trouble or convincing you to do the same. That this is an important time in our lives and shit. Nothing revolutionary."

"Why didn't you leave?"

"She said she'd make us pancakes."

He starts playing and singing again. It's a song I don't know but when Mom hangs up she starts singing along. I wish she wouldn't have lectured Tommy and made him leave, but it's hard to be mad when she looks so happy right now. I think about Shane calling her a badass and then she hands us each a plate full of pancakes, and I smile.

"Thanks, Cat," Shane says in a way that makes her roll her eyes. "Oh, also, I wanted to see if you had any interest in this."

He holds out the guitar and it glimmers like magic.

"What?"

"I'm getting a new acoustic from a dude at work. Thought this would be a good one for you to learn on."

He holds it in front of me. I grab it and the twang makes us wince. But my heart is fluttering. Something about holding it makes me feel like a wizard that's finally gotten hold of a magic staff.

"How much?"

"Fifty work? I'll throw in a few lessons to get you started too."

"Yeah, yeah. That'd be amazing!"

I have the money saved up from all the days people bought us food for getting the alcohol. I'd thought about buying new clothes, but this feels so much cooler. Maybe I should feel bad, but buying something on my own, not having to ask for money for once, feels so good.

"What's this?" Mom asks.

"Cat, I'll have you know that I am not merely a man of the arts but also of commerce. Your son and I have entered into a deal for this here guitar."

I can't stop smiling.

"How much?"

"Don't be crass," Shane says, knowing that I shouldn't have the money. "You shouldn't ask the details of another person's business deals."

Mom shakes her head. "That was Amy. She wanted to make sure you were going to Derek's birthday party today."

I'd totally forgotten about his birthday, which is hard to believe cause it how I know summer's ending every year, which usually comes as a shock but this one feels like it's been forever.

"I guess he forgot to remind you."

My confusion melts and now I'm just mad. It's exactly like Derek to say that. He didn't forget. He just couldn't own up to the fact that he didn't want me there. Not that I blame him, but I hate that he's always such a baby.

"What did you tell her?"

Mom looks surprised, "I told her 'of course.' Why?"

"I don't think I'm gonna go."

"Come on, kiddo," Shane says in a fake Mom voice, "don't be such a pussy."

"None of that!" Mom's voice cuts through the room and it's a vacuum of silence. "You boys and your talk. Do you ever take a second to think about what the words you're saying mean?"

"Sorry, Cat," Shane says as he slumps into the chair.

"On top of being offensive, it's not even original." Mom's face is still serious. She points at me. "And you. Why aren't you gonna go?"

I shrug.

"Well, it's important. Amy said it's going to be his first birthday with girls. That's a big deal."

"I don't know," I say. I don't want to tell them that the most painful parts of this summer live in that house.

"Wait," Shane says. "Derek is Tiffany's brother, huh?"

Mom's serious face morphs into a smirk. My stomach twists into knots while I wait for her to say something, but she doesn't. It's quiet all around and I feel like I'm going crazy.

"It's not that," I say.

"Whatever it is, it sounds like it would mean a lot to Derek," Mom says.

"If it's so important, why doesn't he invite me?"

"Come on, man," Shane says. "Buck up."

"You don't get it," I say. "We got in a fight. He doesn't even want me there."

"That's not what it sounds like. I mean, he's got his mom calling to make sure you come."

"I'm not going." I try to make my voice tough but it comes out small.

"Dude, it's your friend—help him out."

Mom starts another round of pancakes. She won't look at us, but I can tell by the way she's not looking that she's listening.

"How come you didn't leave with Tommy this morning?"

"Me not puppy-dogging after Tommy because he was being a whiny asshole—sorry, Cat—is totally different. There have been plenty of times, hell, all the time, where Tommy and I have fought. But we're there for the real sh—stuff."

"Whatever," I say.

But now I can't help thinking of all the nights after Mom and Dad's fights, after they broke up, that I would go to Derek's. We didn't talk cause I didn't want to but Derek always acted normal, like everything was ok. And when I was there everything really was ok.

"Plus, if there are gonna be girls, maybe you can make Tiffany jealous."

"Oh my god!" Mom bursts out. She covers her mouth but she's still looking over with wide eyes. "Tiffany?" comes out muffled from behind her hand. "I always—I'm sorry. I'm sorry."

She walks out of the kitchen and down the hall with her hand over her mouth. My face feels like I was thrown headfirst into the sun.

"On that note," Shane says, "I gotta bounce. We're supposed to practice. I doubt Tommy and the boys will be in the mood, but we could use it. I'll leave this here for you."

He taps the guitar and the vibration seems to pause the heat that's overtaking me. He wiggles his eyebrows and turns around as Mom walks back into the kitchen.

"You leaving, Shane?"

"Yes, ma'am."

"I hope we see you back here, but you know the rules."

"Oh, of course, Cat. You spelled those out *very* clearly," Shane says in a laugh. "I think we will wind up here, though. The benefits definitely outweigh the detractors. And you," he says to me with a wink before he steps out the door, "go to the party."

Mom won't stop staring at me. I've barely touched my pancakes so she wraps up the stack left on the counter. She keeps glancing over. I leave my half-eaten pancakes, go to my room and put on the new Botch CD that Tommy gave me. Everything explodes away and the only thing that matters is the music that's screaming through my head. I clutch the guitar to my chest.

I can disappear into music. It's always there for me to come back when I need. I look at the little dot on my palm. That portal's gone.

Mom opens the door. She walks past the bed; her stained, unbuttoned work shirt flaps behind her. She turns the music down and folds her arms over her chest. Her mouth is tight but her eyes aren't angry. She grabs my hand and traces her finger around the dot like she knows that's what I was thinking about.

"I get that I'm just being a mom right now. Maybe I haven't always done the best job of being that and it makes these moments more annoying. But I need to make sure that you're going to go to Derek's. And, I get that you guys haven't been hanging out much—"

"How come you made Tommy leave?"

"I wasn't trying to make Tommy leave. You know that."

She looks at me like she's waiting for me to talk, but I don't have anything to say.

"I get why he left, though. I got carried away. But it's hard to see young people drinking like that—stop me if I'm making all this up, because I haven't spent a lot of time with them." She sighs and starts again, "The only things I've learned about your new friends are the worst things, I'm sure. But that's more than enough to frighten me because I've seen how this all plays out."

She sits down next to me on the bed and looks at the ground. She rubs her hands on her knees. Her eyes look tired.

"As for Derek's," she says, "I just know how hard a time I had when I was younger. Especially with the boys and girls thing. To this day, I vividly remember some of the stupid decisions I made. The times that I let friends down for what I thought were legitimate reasons, but weren't. That sucked. It sucks now. I didn't do a lot of things I should have because of that. I did a lot of things I shouldn't have, too."

"Yeah," I say, but the silence after is a weight I can't bear. "I'm sorry."

"Don't be. I'm ok," she says and turns and smiles, and the little bit of sunlight coming through the blinds makes her glow. "We're both gonna be ok, too."

"I'll go," I say, even though thinking about Tiffany and Derek and Peter makes my chest rattle.

"Thanks," she says and tousles my hair. "Ok, I gotta get to work."

Once she's gone, I turn the music back on and all the pain and pressure gets beaten back. I fall into the guitars, the screaming, the pounding drums and I feel good until it's over, and quiet, and I don't want to put anything else on.

The house is silent now. It's hard rolling out of bed, but I do. I walk into the backyard where Daisy's sitting in her hole by the wall. I sit down next to her and, as I start to pet her, I can hear the splashing of Derek's pool. My heart pounds at the walls of my chest and the fear radiates out but I breathe, just try to keep breathing long and slow and after a little while it starts to settle. The fear is there but more manageable.

My stomach's tight but I stand up, brush under the trees, and hop the fence into the Thompsons'. The splashing gets louder and I start to hear voices. I stop at the wall and listen but can't make out what anyone's saying. I grab the top of the wall, kick my foot against it and push up, peeking over, then lowering back down.

There are all kinds of people crowded around the pool but barely anyone in it. Just Derek and the Thieson twins.

Tiffany wasn't back there. Neither were Peter and Amy.

Sheena's there. And I remember how she tasted like honey and mushrooms in a good way when we kissed forever ago. How she smelled like strawberry pie. How much I cared about her and how devastated I was when she broke up with me because Katy lied to her and said I was bragging about hooking up with her. Then I think about how little I've thought about her this summer. How completely Tiffany has overtaken all my thoughts and dreams.

It's all there in my head, and I don't know what to do about it.

I hop the wall and when I jump down, Katy turns to Sheena and says something that makes her roll her eyes.

Sven sits up on the edge of one of the lounge chairs. He's not wearing a shirt and his hair's wet. He's got it slicked back and up. His shoulders are pink. When he leans forward it's hard to tell there's a dip in his chest. But it makes his ribs stick out. He looks skinnier than he ever has, and paler aside from his pink shoulders, but he sets his cup down and stands up with a grin and he looks and feels like Tommy in a way.

"About last night," he says. "It's whatever. I was just a little drunk."

I think if I didn't know Sven, I would've thought he sounded cool when he said it. Or maybe he did sound cool. Maybe I don't know Sven.

"It's ok. You were right."

"Cool," he says.

He turns around and picks up his cup and walks to the other side of the pool. Katy watches him the whole way with a scowl, but when he starts talking to her she starts smiling.

And he looks like Sven, but he's not staring at the ground. He's actually talking and smiling in front of someone, a girl. It's strange how he's the same person when he could barely look his best friends in the eye at the beginning of summer.

Out of the corner of my eye I see Derek's awkward head bobbing toward me. He swims up to the steps, while behind him the Thieson twins are giggling and splashing each other. Around the pool are all the people that are always at birthday parties even though we don't hang out with them at school. None of them are wet.

"Are you going to come in?" is all Derek says.

"I'm not wearing any trunks."

"You can borrow some of mine." He looks excited now and sounds out of breath. "Remember the yellow ones you wore that Shannon said looked good on you?"

Just hearing Shannon's name makes me mad. And it's obvious what Derek's trying to do cause he would never be this cool if he wasn't embarrassed or in trouble. Sven's shaking his head from across the pool.

"Sure," I say, thinking of what Mom said and and how much it would've meant if I were just a little nicer to Sven.

Derek's smile gets big and he blushes.

Hearing Katy's high-pitched laugh, I forget for a second why I would agree, but I still I walk toward the house. Just as I'm getting to the kitchen door I see Peter and Amy. I turn to the living room and pause, holding the handle for a second to let them get closer before I go inside. As I slide it closed, I hear the kitchen door click and slide open. I walk toward Derek's room.

I take the stairs slowly, trying to remind myself that I'm doing Derek a favor. That I want to be the bigger person, and now that I'm here all I have to do is put on some trunks to help him.

When I get to the top of the stairs I stop and look at Tiffany's room. I can't hear anything, but I can tell she's in there. I stare at the

Stay Out sign, it seems to be speaking directly to me, warning me to go no further but Tiffany has that gravitational pull that destroys me. The voices and splashing from outside barely make it up. The only other noise is my breathing and the occasional creak of the floor where I'm standing. If the floor's creaking she might know that someone's there.

I hurry into Derek's room. It's quiet and everything seems small and strange, like a scale model of where we used to hang out. It looks so different, but if I closed my eyes I'd still know where everything is. I do close my eyes, but it's not the details, just the feelings that come flooding back. It's light and warm and, even though I can remember how much we fought, it's happy and easy.

I open the drawer and hold the trunks against my shorts. They look half the size they should be but I change into them anyway. There's a big chunk of my pale leg showing. I take a deep breath and open the door, ready to get in the pool, ready to dive underwater and stay there as long as I can but I freeze at the creaking of footsteps and shadow passing along the sand-colored carpet under Tiffany's door.

Her shadow disappears and there's a puff and squeak that's her falling onto her bed, and I can imagine her tan legs lifting off the ground, golden hair spreading against the red comforter. I wish I were there. I wish I could see her and talk to her. I wish she would invite me in.

Instead, I hurry down the stairs to the sliding door. Looking out, I see Peter and Amy by the grill. Derek and the Thieson twins are still in the water. Everyone else is standing around the pool. No one's looking until I step out and then it's like I'm buried under an avalanche of eyes. My throat closes shut and my heart starts to pound, but I walk slowly. Walk like I'm supposed to be here and just keep breathing.

"Nice shorts," Katy jokes.

I walk toward the pool, the sidewalk hot on my feet and everyone staring. When it feels like the pressure is going to rip my chest open, I dive in and everything releases, everything is calm. The water bubbles and swirls around me and I can't even hear my own thoughts, just the soothing beat of my heart. I look up and see waves and blobs of color. I smile even as my chest starts to squeeze and the spots pop in my eyes.

When my lungs start to burn, I push off the bottom and burst through the surface to a swarm of sounds and color. Derek swims over.

"You put them on!"

"Yeah."

"Cool. They look cool."

"Thanks," I say and swim toward the steps.

On the other side, Sven and Katy are both laughing. Derek's swimming toward me again. Sven starts walking over, his strides are long and slow and his smile is cutting the whole way.

"Nice shorts," he says, too.

"Thanks," I say and I do actually like them despite how awkward I feel.

"You know Derek asked me to wear them too, right?"

"Shut up," Derek says.

"How come you didn't? Scared?"

"They're lame." He laughs and I swear I hear Tommy.

I shrug and he takes a sip from his drink. From the way his face twitches I can tell there's alcohol in there. Some things he can't hide. He smiles again, holding the drink by his side. The alcohol feels out of place here, especially after dealing with Peter's beers, but it makes sense that Sven would bring it.

In the deep end, the Thieson twins are still splashing and smiling, laughing in their high-pitched giggles but having fun when, around the pool, people are barely talking, unless they're pointing and laughing at me.

Sven walks back over to Katy and at some point they head toward the side of the house and Sheena's sitting alone on the brick wall of the garden. I look at her, thinking about how much it hurt the last time I saw her and how little that hurt compares to Tiffany. I wish I was upstairs in her dark room and we were listening to music and making out.

I snap out of it when I realize Sheena's waving me over, that I've been staring at her this whole time. I stand and tug down the edges of the trunks, but that doesn't do much. So I dive and swim the length of the pool underwater, popping up just below her.

"Are you trying to be Aquaman or something?" she says.

"Something," I say. "How's your summer been?"

"Good."

"That's good."

"How's yours?"

"Good," I say too, and I wonder if that's true. And if she's just saying "good," too.

"Did you do anything fun?" she asks.

I laugh. I can't help it. The wave of all the things that have happened, all the good and bad hits me.

"I guess," I say, but then it's just Tiffany in my head. I wish she'd let me in or go away.

"What does that mean?" she says through a chuckle.

"Some fun stuff, some not fun stuff. It's been an interesting summer."

I don't want to say more and luckily I don't have to cause Peter and Amy come outside to tell everyone that the pizza's ready. We get up to go inside and her hand brushes mine. I remember perfectly how soft she felt when we kissed. That hasn't changed, but it doesn't make me as sweaty now.

Sven and Katy come around the corner from the side of the house walking loosely and laughing. He grins then steps inside. Peter and Amy stare at him as he passes. They look like they're about to laugh until I walk up.

"Hey," Peter says. "Got a second?"

Sheena keeps walking.

"Ok," I say, trying not to run away.

"We're really glad that you could make it," Amy says with a smile that feels too big. "We missed you here."

"Thanks," I say.

"Ok, someone's gotta keep an eye on those kids," Amy says and walks inside.

"So," Peter says and rocks back on his heels. I didn't realize it was possible, but he looks as uncomfortable as I feel. "I've been waiting to talk to you about our run-in at the grocery store."

"I'm sorry. I'll buy you more beers."

"No! Please, don't. I'm not worried about you buying me beers. I'm worried that you're stealing them in the first place. And, also, that I freaked you out in the grocery store. I wasn't really feeling like myself there. But we all have our—Amy's gone, right?—shit to deal with."

He takes a deep breath and glances into the kitchen and then back to me.

"I guess what I mean is, we are always here when you need us. And I don't want you to worry about the beers, I just don't want you to do it again."

"I won't. I promise."

"And also," he says and his eyes get big and serious behind his glasses, "you do still owe me a Sourdough Jack."

The breath I was holding bursts out and I can't do anything but laugh. He starts laughing too. Even when the whole party in the kitchen looks out at us like we're crazy, we don't stop. For a moment it feels good to be here, like a second home again. I hope it can stay that way.

"I'll buy us both one," I say when I can finally breathe again. Paying him back feels like a good use of the last bit of money from the summer.

"Wow, big spender," he says, rocking back with his hands in his pockets. "Now go in there and get some pizza. Oh, and I never want to hear you call me Mr. Williams again, ok?"

"Ok, Pete."

I feel light when I step inside. Derek's opening presents. So I walk to stand with Sven, who's whispering to Katy, then turns to me.

"There's a party at Tim's," he says.

"Cool," I say.

"We're all gonna go," he points to Katy and Sheena, who blushes. "Bert's gonna pick us up. You in?"

"Right now? You're just gonna leave?"

"Yeah, dude. Last one before school starts, it's gonna be huge," Sven says.

"Are the guys playing music?"

"No, we're just going to fucking party," he says. It still sounds awkward when he cusses, like he's got a mouthful of peanut butter. "This is almost over, anyway. Let's go."

I glance around the party. Derek's done opening presents. A few people are talking but mostly everyone's just standing around. Amy is in the corner tapping her foot. Peter's holding a camera but not taking pictures. Sven looks at me like he doesn't care either way.

"I'm gonna stay."

"Whatever," Sven says.

"Have fun, though."

"For sure."

Sven walks out of the room without saying goodbye to Derek. Katy and Sheena follow. After that, the rest of the party trickles out until it's just Derek and me and his parents.

All I can think is that Tiffany's still in her room. It's the only place I want to be right now.

"You wanna play something two-player?" Derek asks cause we're just standing in the kitchen.

"Sure," I say.

We walk up the stairs to his room and I have to stop myself from turning toward Tiffany's. He puts on a new game that he actually seems excited about, something he just bought with his allowance. He's trying to tell me how to play but I can't focus on what he's saying.

He doesn't mention me stealing from his parents. He doesn't yell at me for hanging out with Tommy and drinking. He doesn't thank me for coming over today or wearing the trunks. His smile just widens cause he's beating me in this game. I drift away, staring at the crack under Tiffany's closed door. There's no noise and no shadow, which allows my mind to imagine an infinite amount of possibilities going on inside. All of them include me and that's how I know they're not real.

Derek beats me, badly.

"Are you even going to try?" he says, puffing up with pride.

"Gimme a second."

"What are you doing?"

I stand up and walk out, stopping in front of Tiffany's door. I knock.

"Hey."

It doesn't sound like my voice. It comes from outside of me and disappears in the silence that follows like a cry for help in outer space. My body is going to implode in that pressure vacuum.

"What?"

Even her muffled, annoyed voice gives me some relief.

"Can I come in?"

Still, my heart is beating out of my chest and I can't catch my breath no matter how hard I try. My hands shake as I wait for an answer.

"Ok," she says.

It's dark inside—there's only one lamp on but it's covered with a thin piece of red fabric. It feels different here at night. I want to know all the versions of her room. I want to be here through the changes, to be with her always.

She has her headphones on, but I can't hear anything coming out from them. She sits on the side of her bed in white shorts and dark red shirt.

"How come you weren't down there for Derek's birthday?"

"Because," she says.

The pressure builds back in my chest and throat.

"Listen," I say.

"Please, don't."

"I know, I know, I know."

"You don't. I don't want to talk about this. I don't want to think about it."

"It's all I *can* think about."

Everything is happening so fast. I can't catch my breath.

"You should stop, then."

"I love you."

"No."

"I love you. I do. And I think I always have."

"Don't."

"Do you like me?"

"It doesn't matter."

"How could it not?" "Liking you would be weird," she stares straight ahead. "No. And you're going to be a freshman so—even if I did like you—it wouldn't work. It couldn't work."

She sounds angry but when she turns toward me she looks sad. She tucks her knees up into her chest, holding them there, and on her giant bed she looks tiny.

"But…" my voice sticks in my throat. I can't catch my breath.

"And when you passed out at the party, it's all anyone would talk about. Everyone was laughing about it. And I don't want—I don't want to be *there*."

"I didn't just pass out."

"I know," she says and her eyes get misty. "I'm sorry, I am. I wanted to visit you but I couldn't."

"You should have."

She shrugs and pulls her knees tighter, covering her mouth.

"This is stupid. It's stupid because we have fun together, because we know each other, because you *do* like me."

She starts to cry. Her choked breaths are like stabs in my chest. I walk to her but she waves me away.

"No! I don't, I really don't, alright? I don't like you." Her voice is hard and her eyes are angry behind her drying tears.

It sinks in: she's not going to change her mind. She's set and stubborn, no matter how much I explain. I start to get angry that there's nothing I can do except tell myself that she's wrong and I shouldn't like her, but I can't. Even when she's cruel and unreasonable, I can't stop myself from wanting to be with her. I won't ever stop thinking about ways that I could maybe make her smile. I don't even want to leave the room because of how final it will feel to walk out of here and know that she's decided not to like me. It's all stupid. I'm being stupid and I should stop, but I can't.

It hurts to want to do something, to know what's right, but have no control.

"What can I do?" I say.

"I don't know."

"I hate that."

"Maybe when we're older, it'll be different."

But it won't be. Things don't just magically get better or easier or right because we get older.

The quiet is too heavy to take. I walk out of her room to the clicking of a controller in Derek's but can't go in.

I squeeze my hand, but there's nothing to block out this fresh pain. The hole healed over even though it almost killed me. I hope this hole in my heart will heal over without leaving the one little spot to remember it by.

Standing on the steps, I hear the puff of Tiffany's bed between Derek's game and I run down the stairs, out the back door and over the walls before the tears can take over.

I'm home. Daisy follows me into my room and I put *EndSerenading* on one last time. This is my life, the pain in my heart like a knife. I'll have to see her every day at school. I can't imagine how I can possibly make it through, but I don't really understand how I made it through this summer. Through Brad, Dad, Christina and Tommy, Sven and Derek, and Tiffany. Of course, Tiffany. But somehow I did make it through. I just kept breathing.

I take a deep breath, long and slow, and I pick up Shane's guitar—my guitar. I pluck a string and it cuts apart the music. It sounds awful. But the vibration runs up my arms and into my chest and I smile.

19

"YOU SURE YOU don't want me to walk you a little further?" Mom asks.

She knows Sven and Derek and I always rode our bikes to school together. It was my job to start. I'd swing by Derek's then get Sven and we'd all race there. But I was sitting awake this morning staring at the ceiling, fighting off waves of dread that kept me from sleeping, and decided I'd walk alone. Mom was up, though, and asked if she could join me 'til we got to the end of the neighborhood. She knows something's wrong.

"I'm ok," I say. Part of me does want her to walk me all the way into the classroom like she did my first day of preschool, holding my hand the whole way to make sure I got where I belonged. But that'd only make things worse. She understands because she still remembers Grandpa embarrassing her when he'd drop her off.

She hugs me and messes my hair, then fixes it before backing toward the house.

"You're gonna be alright," she says and smiles. "We're gonna be alright."

"Yeah," I say. I want to believe her. I know she thinks it's true, at least.

When she turns back to the house I take out the Discman she gave me and put on a new mix that Shane burned for me. It starts with American Football's "But the Regrets are Killing Me." It's funny how sad songs can make you happy just knowing someone else feels like you.

It's cold even though September just started. The fog hangs low, leaving a layer of dew on the Discman which skips when I step so I shuffle a little.

I wonder if Derek or Sven are waiting for me. Or if they'll ride together without me. I wonder if they'll talk to me. Tiffany once said that everything was different in high school. I didn't understand at the time. She won't talk to me, now. Again. At least that's the same as last year. I laugh at the thought because that's what hurts the least.

As the song is ending I hear a screaming and rip off the headphones. I turn to see Dan's green Accord with a pale, skinny butt hanging out the passenger window. Bert's laughing in the back seat. The butt disappears into the car and is replaced by Sven's grinning face. The wind barely moves his gelled hair.

I guess he's not riding bikes with Derek.

The car fades into the distance, swallowed by the fog, and I put my headphones back on and restart "Take Her to the Music Store." I dream of being back in Tim's backyard and crashing around the mosh pit. It's at the top of the million places I'd rather be. At the bottom is here, in front of the high school, which emerges from the grey and my chest and throat squeeze. A line of cars a mile long are stopped at the light, waiting to turn in. My head is screaming to run, go home, go anywhere. The crosswalk turns green and the robot voice barks, "Walk." But I can't move.

My heart is starting to pound and my eyes are blurring at the edges. I don't want to be here. I look at the small dot on my hand that the wound turned into and wish it was still fresh and I could disappear instead of having everyone stare at me like I'm an idiot.

"Hey!" I turn to see Derek huffing and puffing on his bike. "Wait up!"

He skids up next to me and hops off.

"How come you didn't stop by?" he asks.

I shrug. The stoplight turns red. Cars filled with unfamiliar faces pull away.

"This sucks, huh? I wish it could be summer forever."

"Same," I say.

Then it's quiet. What's left for us to say to each other? The light turns green again. He walks his bike. I walk too.

The school was intimidating enough when Tommy and I saw it empty. But with all the people, it looks like a war zone. Hundreds and hundreds of people circled up in their camps and talking.

We walk around the side so Derek can lock up his bike. People are streaming in through the chainlink fence. Beyond the swirl of strangers, I can see Tiffany talking to Tommy. She laughs and tucks her hair behind her ear and my body can't decide if it's going to melt or explode.

Sven's talking to a girl, too. Their faces come in and out amongst the waves of people. My stomach sinks. Breathing is hard but I keep trying to breathe. Keep breathing.

I walk toward the gate like a moth to a campfire but can't bring myself to enter. Someone knocks my shoulder, then another, shaking me out of the haze. Each knock a reminder that I'm here.

James Smalling passes. Tommy touches Tiffany's shoulder then turns away. It's a jungle. It's all colliding. Breathe.

"What's your first class?" Derek is standing next to me now. It offers small comfort.

"English," I barely squeak out.

"Thank God. Do you even know where the hell room 237B is?"

I shake my head. I don't know anything. Derek starts for the entrance and I follow until we reach the gate. The first bell rings and I remember the sound of the bb hitting the football players' bike spoke when Tommy shot at them from the river. That same fear bubbles up as the groups of people begin to break apart.

"Get in there, big dog," a voice speaks as a hand pushes me forward into the stream of backpacks and elbows and for a moment I'm back in the mosh pit, remembering how fun chaos can be. I get through the entrance and I'm smiling when I turn and see Shane, who says, "You looked lost."

"Always," I try to joke.

"So profound," he says with a laugh.

Derek sneaks up and stands at my side quietly, so I say, "Shane, this is Derek."

"You're real?" Shane jokes. "All this time I thought he was making you up."

"Obviously," Derek says. He doesn't get it yet but maybe he will soon.

"Where's 237B?" I ask.

"All the way on the other side of campus," Shane says and points to the far corner.

"Let's go, then," Derek says like he's in a hurry.

Then I realize why. Tommy's here, towering over us. He punches me playfully in the chest. Then turns to Shane and asks, "Ready?"

"Lead the way, fine scholar."

Derek chuckles. And for a second it looks like Tommy might do something. I laugh, too. He could kick the shit out of us, but that doesn't scare me as much anymore. He grins but doesn't do anything else.

"Fuckin' tough guy," Tommy says.

"See you later, Tom," I say then turn to Derek. "Let's go."

"Don't be late," Shane says with mock-concern. "I'd hate to have to inform your mother you were already in trouble on your first day."

"You and moms," Tommy says.

They walk away and Derek and I start in the opposite direction. The crowd has thinned as the second bell approaches. They're too busy trying to get where they're going to care about Derek and me. It is chaotic, but that's life.

"Your music's still playing," Derek says.

The headphones around my neck are blaring out the end of On the Might of Princes' "For Meg." I leave it on, listening to the guitar build and the drums crash, walking like I belong until we reach room 237B.

It looks about the same as any other room in our old middle school.

CPSIA information can be obtained
at www.ICGtesting.com
Printed in the USA
FSHW020957190821
84174FS